A NIGHT OF BRIGHT STARS

A NIGHT OF BRIGHT STARS
Richard Llewellyn

Robert, Andrea + Gioia
are fictional.

NEW ENGLISH LIBRARY/TIMES MIRROR

First published in Great Britain in 1979 by
Michael Joseph Ltd
Copyright © 1979 by Richard Llewellyn

First NEL Paperback Edition December 1980

NEL Books are published by
New English Library Limited,
Barnard's Inn, Holborn,
London EC1N 2JR.
Printed and bound in Great Britain by
Collins, Glasgow.

45004947 7

Chapter 1

'Monsieur Alberto Santos-Dumont, sir,' Mme Dufresne said, opening the door wide. 'The balloonist. His letter and your reply are in the blue cover.'

Alberto Santos-Dumont came in, shorter than Mme Dufresne, taking off a panama hat with a floppy brim, clipped by a black silk cord to one lapel of a dark grey suit buttoned on three. He wore polished black boots with tan uppers under little boy turn-ups, a high white collar tied with an orange grosgrain cravat, a white handker-chief flat in the pocket and another poking points from the starched left-hand cuff of the shirt. Black hair glossed in sunlight, dark eyes held silver points, and the gentlest smile I ever saw spread the razored black moustache along the length of the upper lip, showing whitest teeth.

'Sir,' I said. 'I am privileged.'

He bowed slightly, and I gestured towards my late father's red-leather armchair and sat, opening the cover, taking out his letter.

'Captain Ferber is an old friend of mine,' I said. 'I supply the Army School of Balloonists. Any word from him is a command to me. What may I do for you?'

'Well,' he said, putting the panama on the floor. 'You see. This ballooning affair is quite new. At least, the dirigible. The type that can be guided instead of travelling at the mercy of the wind. I have a simple problem. There is no theory and little practice. Nobody has studied the air. And so, of course, nobody has what I want. What I *can* get is miserably deficient. I have a list here of what I require. Captain Ferber told me that you were the man to come to. So? Here I am.'

'May I see the list?'

He took from the left-hand pocket a fold of sheets, all in his handwriting, small, even minute, the fist of a mathema-tician, and in a glance, while the pages flapped, I saw items in the price column that jolted. I made no comment and

5

turned pages, seeing more and more to outrage in the price columns – filled in by another hand – and on the end page, I rang for Mme Dufresne.

'Your problem *begins* here,' I said, looking at him, tapping the sheets. 'We shall find out where this nonsense *ends*!'

Mme Dufresne knocked and came in.

'Take this and verify the entire scale of prices,' I said. 'Ask Monsieur Vaudroux to calculate and submit a total at our prices for the same items. Meantime, a coffee and cognac might be in order, if you please?'

'Something wrong with the accounting?' he asked, agreeably enough. 'I shall plead guilty to being an amateur. But what raises doubts in your mind? By the way. I find ourselves speaking English. I prefer it. It's the language of the sea. It will be the language of the air. I intend it *shall* be so.'

'Why?'

'It is clear, precise, pragmatic, effective. I realized at Bristol, when I attended university there, that no other language could do what English does.'

'And not Portuguese?'

'No. And not French or German. I speak them, certainly, but I prefer English. It has a crystal quality. Commands are direct, and on the sea and in the air, we require what is direct, and without loss of time in explanation or argument. On the sea, there is no time. In the air, less!'

I sat back and laughed.

'I've read about you, of course, all the headlines and the articles and the photographs,' I said. 'I've seen you a couple of times from this window, over those trees. A speck. So high up. I expected to meet a god. What do I find? Somebody who goes to my own tailor and bootmaker, and so far as I see, my shirtmaker. I know by the cut. What's godlike? The fact that you get in that basket. I? I shudder. I *do*. With only the basket between me and a drop from that height? No, sir. Let us say, you are a demigod. At least you are different from ordinary men. You are in the line of Leonardo da Vinci. I am honoured to do whatever I may to further your idea!'

He crossed his knees, looked impatient, pulled the hand-

6

kerchief from the cuff and blew his nose.

'That's to remind you that I'm human,' he said. 'This demigod business is nonsense. I've been playing with balloons since I was a little boy. Montgolfiers. Fire balloons. Light a fire beneath and warm air carries them up. Well, I've grown up since then. I have other ideas. But sometimes they still fall down, just like the Montgolfiers, and you find yourself being rescued from the roof of the Trocadero Hotel like any fairground entertainer. That airship was a complete wreck, of course. And I can't get the materials. What I'm doing now is basic. I learn about the winds and the currents. What I want to do is to *defy* the winds. Make *use* of the currents. Propel. Guide. But I haven't the materials to work with. I told Captain Ferber in utter desperation. He put me on to you.'

Mme Dufresne knocked and came in to put the folded sheets on the blotter, and another on our blue paper beside it.

'Our prices are in pencil in the margin of the original,' she said, in her quiet way. 'Monsieur Vaudroux's totals are here. He is shocked. Some of these items supposedly came from us. They did not. We have no record. Will that be all, sir?'

I nodded, looked down at the price columns, glanced at ours, and handed both the blue and white to Mr Santos-Dumont. He pressed his chin toward the bottom lip, eyebrows up, nodding, folded the sheets into the right-hand pocket, and looked at me, still smiling, but in a curiously different manner, as if hurt and, in a way, defensive.

'Amateur,' he said. 'That's all. I'm grateful to Captain Ferber. He said you would help me. I think we are well-met. May I invite you to luncheon?'

'Most kind of you, but if you're going to get this order in the next couple of days, I shall have to start now. There are one hundred and fifteen items. This one, a half-kilometre of prime silk, for example? I have it in the warehouse, downstairs. Would you care to see it?'

'I have an appointment in fifteen minutes,' he said, looking at a wrist-watch, the first I had seen, a small gold square framing a white face houred in black roman numerals, with a cabochon sapphire winder, an aesthetic triumph of design entirely suitable to him. 'Will ten minutes be enough? I cannot keep my guests waiting.'

I led the way downstairs to the main floor where all the packing was done, and through to the warehouse, stacked to the roof with everything from pins to copper sheeting.

'A big place,' he said. 'I wish I had this space.'

'Very simple,' I said, a little puzzled by an apparent lack of initiative. 'A couple of hundred metres away, near the Bois, there's a large area for sale. Used to be a farm, so it's cleared, flat. What do you wish to build there?'

'A hangar large enough to house at least three of my airships,' he said, pulling out drawers of studs, screws, nails, pins, bodkins. 'Yes. I've come to the right man, thank God. You have everything here I need. Where I can be free of Aéro-Club supervision. Would you please make an appointment for me to see the place?'

'Tomorrow, eleven o'clock?'

'I have an appointment with the Minister of War. Make it three-thirty?'

'I've never heard that word before. Hangar.'

'It's a shed, workshop, office. Nothing more. I'm really most happy to have met you. I'll tell Captain Ferber.'

We shook hands just beyond the front entrance, which seemed dark, and then we were outside, and the enormous balloon was over us.

'You came here by balloon?' I gaped.

'By *dirigible*,' he said, laughing. 'It's under my hand. I guide. It does as I tell it. Until tomorrow!'

He leapt as an athlete over the rim of a woven rattan basket, and waved to four men holding a rope about twenty metres away.

'Let her go!' he shouted, and as the rope fell loose, he went into the air, not a sound, a veritable fakir, a holy man, truly a demigod, rising, rising, until, a midge in size, he was over the trees.

'My God!' Mme Dufresne said, wiping tears. 'Only think. I can tell my family he came right to the door. The man – the *man*! – who sailed right round the Eiffel Tower and back to a point I think in Saint Cloud somewhere, and he won a prize of some colossal sum, a hundred thousand francs, something like that, a complete fairy tale, but he shared it among the poor of Paris. What a way of doing things! And I *saw* him and gave him papers. *I* did. Who'll believe me?'

'You've got witnesses,' I said. 'If I hadn't seen it, I don't think I've have believed it either. Going up in the air to that height in nothing better than a hencoop? To the devil!'

'Ah, no, M'sieu Robert!' Mme Dufresne said. 'That's a curse, no? But we should bless.'

She brought the rosary from her corsage, drawing it between her fingers, whispering with closed eyes, and all the girls joined her and the beads clicked, and I heard the hummed whisper of an Ave Maria.

A beautiful sound, in honour and prayer for that vital speck, just beyond the trees.

Chapter 2

Good as his word, Santos-Dumont came out of the sky at three-thirty that afternoon, and we walked the short distance to the area. We met Mr Norbréau, the agent, on the way, and I made a price for a five-year rental with an option for five more years and Norbréau shakily made his offer for about a half more, and since obviously he wanted his commission, I said take it or leave it, and he took it. He signed on his knee, and Santos-Dumont signed on his, and the deal was done.

'I've been offered places nothing near so absolutely right as this for more than twenty times as much,' he said. 'I'm so very grateful. I have enough but I haven't an endless fortune. A lot of people seem to think so. They're wrong. People like you help me. I'm eternally grateful. It helps me towards my ideal. The dream I've had since I was a boy. Playing with balloons. But a balloon is childhood. The pretty colours. The smell of smoke. As a man, it is different. We have other dreams.'

'But surely, you've achieved it? The whole world talks of you. Open any newspaper. You're a hero. What more can you want?'

'Well,' he said, seeming to shake off a weight. 'The day after tomorrow I shall try to make another circuit of the Eiffel Tower, and back to Saint Cloud. It may be difficult but I think it possible depending upon a good breeze. You see? I am dependent on the force of the wind. *That's* my dream. To be beyond the power of the wind. From any quarter. Sailors must trim their sails. I don't want any of that. I want to fly. *Fly!*'

'But even insects and birds are blown by the wind,' I said. 'On what principle do you base your assumption? Or your wish. Or your dream. What do you mean by *flying*?'

He stood in the middle of that overgrown field, red with poppies, yellow with mustard, and laughed at white clouds in puff against a lovely blue sky.

'That's my world,' he said, and in that moment I believed him utterly, and determined to help. 'Icarus and all since then have failed. So far, so have I!'

'Ah, but sir,' I said. 'Good God, you're sailing about the skies all day. You land at my front door. Isn't that flying?'

He shook his head.

'That's floating,' he said. 'A bag of hydrogen is always lighter than air. No. I'm building this place to make a craft that will fly in the air under its own power, guided by me, with aid of a compass, and a rudder to steer, and wings to keep me up, and an engine to push me. Now, Mister Robert, what do you think of *that*?'

'Beyond me,' I said, in the air. 'Completely beyond *me*. But then, many things are beyond me. Who the devil am I? A factor in many markets worldwide. Very well. My ideas are restricted to buying and selling. Yours? You're free to indulge. And that's *it*. But have no doubt. I'll help you. Tell me what you want and I'll sweat to get it!'

'Thank God for a friend,' he said. 'May I ask an intimate question? Are you married?'

I shook my head.

'Not yet.'

'You are free at the weekend?'

'No. I go to my farm. My great-great-grandfather's place. There I breathe. I look at my garden, my fields, my horses, my cattle. There I am once more a man. Human. Respecting

10

other life and helping to sustain a pure breed. It is as much a passion with me as, I presume, flying is with you.'

'I'm enchanted,' he said, and put a hand on my shoulder. 'You remind me of my father. He loved his farm and the animals. I suppose I do, too. Horses, I love. I ride here. But a hired horse is not the same as one of your own.'

'Come down to me and I'll give you one. Let me know.'

'I shall take advantage of your generosity when this place is built and ready for work. Please find a builder for me. No nonsense. No pretty gestures. I want timber walls. A thick canvas roof. It will be a skylight. A place apart for the metal foundry. A building for hydrogen storage. A room completely apart for the women.'

'What have women to do?'

'They will sew, of course. First, the airship covers. And then the aircraft wings. Women have the hands. Why do you look so surprised?'

'I didn't think they had anything to do with the air.'

'How, dear Robert, do you think I got this one in the air?' he said, pointing over his shoulder to the airship. 'Whenever you see me floating, remember more than forty pairs of beautiful women's hands sewed, intent, dedicated, to put me up there to *stay* there. If one of them were careless, where would I be?'

'How about a coffee and a cognac?'

'Splendid idea. The blueprints will be here tomorrow morning. When will the builders be here?'

'Tomorrow morning. I'll give the job to a villager. He's bright.'

'You give the job? Without knowing?'

'I am fairly certain. Aren't you?'

He took off the panama and wiped the headband, laughing.

'We are two of a kind,' he said. 'Very well. I trust you. When will the timber and canvas be here?'

'Look along that road. Those drays are bringing in the first of the load. By tomorrow morning they will be digging the foundations, and all the materials will be here. Any complaints?'

'None. You said something about a coffee and cognac?'

'Follow me.'

11

'We need a team to cut this growth,' he said, lifting knees over flower-tops.

'We don't,' I said. 'Cut all this, and start moving about, you're in a cloud of dust. Leave it alone. Later, when the hangar is built, make a vegetable garden. Your employees will help. They'll love growing fresh vegetables. Free!'

'Pragmatist,' he said, and laughed. 'You're right. But when shall it be planted?'

'I'll talk to the Mayor. He'll find the men wanting a couple of hours' work in the evenings. You can take his advice on what to plant, where to get the seeds, and the rest of it.'

'I leave it to you,' he said. 'I have problems enough. Who is the foreman of the job?'

'Jean Thuillier. A very good workman, and a dedicated blockhead. The essence of a Midi peasant. They have learned to do things in *one* way, and that is the *only* way. A new idea is plague, a new concept is the use of tools nothing but heresy. You'll enjoy him!'

'We have some of the same sort. We call them *caboclos*. But at least they have humour and some lovely music.'

'You won't find much of that here. An accordion in a bistro, perhaps. Or the women when they sing a baby to sleep or while they do the washing. Otherwise music is something for the *conservatoire*. Nothing to do with hard work.'

He looked over my shoulder at the church. Pealing bells echoed, and a hen somewhere cackled evensong, if bad-temperedly.

'Have you met, or have you heard of, someone called Aimé?' he asked, very quietly, but with a look almost of amusement in his eyes.

'Not that I can remember, no. Why?'

'He once told me he was a good friend of yours.'

'Well, then. Let's say, somebody's mistaken. Why?'

'I feel you may get a call from him. He may introduce himself as someone to do with me. He is not. Clear?'

'Perfectly. What's he likely to talk to be about?'

He waved the cigar.

'Nothing of importance. Simply close the door.'

'And supposing I lose an excellent client?'

He bent backwards in a shout of laughter that, too, echoed in a background of cackle and pealing bells, an agreeably bucolic mixture especially then, with the milcn herd lowing out of the field and along the lane.

'In reverse, perhaps,' he said. 'But that's all I want to say about him. And who is this?'

'Aha,' I said. 'Good fortune. That's Jean Thuillier, the big one, and the Mayor, Marcel Gavroche. The north and south poles. One, a blockhead of unparalleled density, and the other a truly professional idiot. The two, with the town clerk, a long-eared donkey of purest breed, together make a circus. No need for clowns or decoration. People should pay to go to the town meetings. There isn't a theatre in Paris can put on that show. Ho, Mister Mayor, good to see you. I present Monsieur Alberto Santos-Dumont. Sir, I present Monsieur Jean Thuillier, your building contractor.'

'Help me in this,' Alberto said, aside.

'Talk to them,' I said. 'The contracts are in my office. If Thuillier is there at nine o'clock, he can sign for, and receive, first money. Talk to them. Get to know them. After all, you *are* the boss. Well, gentlemen, I must leave you. I have work to do, but I shall expect you at nine in the morning.'

Disregarding Alberto's half-amused, half-angry frown, I walked across the field and down the lane to my own place, my desk, and a pile of letters to sign, and of course a goblet of my father's champagne, direct from the stock laid down years before, and a real delight.

I heard knocking below. The staff had gone except for Mme Dufresne, Mlle Bosanquet, and Mlle Zuckermann. Monsieur Vaudroux always left as soon as his sheets were in order. He had another job in Paris. He had a son to put through university. I sympathized.

Mme Dufresne knocked – I knew her knock, one, one, and two – and opened the door.

'Monsieur Santos-Dumont, sir,' she said, patient as a saint. 'He asks for that cognac you promised him.'

'Show him in!'

His smile was a light to banish the evening's shadows.

'Madame Dufresne, another goblet of champagne, please. Sit down, Alberto. I'm sorry I forgot.'

He waved a glove.

'I came for a reason,' he said. 'I'm glad I had that talk. They're both good men. Not as sophisticated as the rest of us, perhaps, but why should they be? The fact that they have their own disciples strengthens them in what they know they should do, and how they should do it. They don't intend that others dictate what's to be done, or how. They know their *own* way. There's no other. Let us drink to them. To the strong and devoted and obstinate people of France. To them!'

We drank, and he put down the goblet with a certain deliberation.

'I made a mistake in my planning,' he said. 'The hangar will do for the milder seasons. It will never do for the end of autumn and the oncome of winter. We can't light fires in there. With hydrogen? A disaster would always be imminent. We must have a separate building a little further away to hold the sewing tables where the women can have fires to warm them. I also forgot a canteen. The Mayor tells me they've got an ex-ship's cook, by all accounts a treasure. He owns the local café.'

'Your people could use ours.'

He shook his head.

'I'm warned of deep snow in winter. Imagine walking from there to here, and then back. Impossible. They must have their own canteen. Nothing but the best. If they work for me, I insist. How else do you keep your most qualified people? Well-fed, well-paid. That's the secret. How about dinner tomorrow night? I have some interesting people. Including Captain Ferber. Eight o'clock. Fouquet's? Good. Now you may continue with your work!'

I went back to signing paper, but somewhere behind the eyes I had thoughts of marriage, a home, a woman to welcome me. I had my apartment, just off the Champs-Élysées, and my farm about sixty miles south of Paris. And no woman. No pivot. Why? Curious.

14

Chapter 3

That night I had a telegram from the skipper of my ship in Marseilles to say he was held by Customs and threatened with prison. Since there is no dirtier thief on earth than the Customs ruffian, I caught the night train, had an excellent breakfast, satisfied the thieves, saw my cargo ashore, and caught the night train back to Paris. I was never more rested. The roll of the train could have been my Mama's hand on the cradle – I still had it at the farm – and I loved the sound of its whistle before I went to sleep. I don't think I enjoy breakfast more than in a dining car. Everything seems to have a different, fresher taste, and a little way up the line the newspapers appear as a gift from those at the top.

I went down to my farm that afternoon, and had the most wonderful four days to myself, with my Percherons, Charolais, the goats, sheep, chickens, ducks, and my lovely river where I caught my luncheon three days running, and the final Sunday night dinner cooked by my peerless Marguerite, a ptarmigan in a clay pot, and tell me what is better.

I was at the station to catch the six thirty-five express, and I got to the warehouse a little before eleven, all the better for the green days. I waved Mme Dufresne down and went into the office, absolutely astonished at the pile of paper in the IN tray. I had never seen anything quite like it. Turning it over, it was not as I thought, a lot of pulp, but orders for all types of merchandize. I sorted them for the warehouse, and I was left with seven notes – all from Alberto, timed by hour and date – the last, that morning – all asking that I go to the hangar. I felt guilty, even irresponsible, but when the paper was safely with Mme Dufresne, I went downstairs and walked along the path, smelling the bounty of farmland, seeing above the spiky ears of wheat the village's red roofs and the spire of the church, hearing the larks and a lowing of cattle, stepping about the riches of cowpats, walking into a gentle waft bringing promise of rich harvest.

15

The hangar surprised me. It was built, and enormous, a timbered palace with a canvas roof, and Breton fishermen were still in the rope rigging sixty feet or more up, dabbing pitch where the roofing met the walls. It was, in fact, something to see.

But the front was open.

Thuillier, Gavroche, and a few others stood about two huge oblongs of timber lying flat in the pasture. They all seemed to see me at the same time, and all of them came running, Thuillier first, throwing out his arms as a child appealing to parental authority, and as a child, certain he was right. I had to calm him and ask what the devil was the matter. He brought the blueprints out of his pocket and traced the doorway with a thick black-rimmed fingernail. It was impossible to hang that doorway, those doors, in that place. Monsieur Santos-Dumont had insisted, persisted, over the past few days. It could not be done. That was that.

I pointed to the three steel girders I had ordered from the railway workshops. They lay coyly rusting among the poppies and mustard. The last of the Breton fishermen came down from the rigging and stood to light cigarettes. Captain Cabeluchard pushed his beret to the front of his head. I nodded him across.

I ask him if, for extra money, his lads would take on the business of heating the rivets, pulling the timbers up into place, and attaching the wheels to the girders so that they slid to open and close.

The Captain fondled his third finger, looking away, turned, and said something in his own Breton language, and all his men ran. Quickly the rope rigging was pulled up to roof height, men climbed, others bellowed the fire, a team lifted the first girder to be hauled up to the thick rafter over the doorway, red-hot rivets were thrown up to be caught in wire nets and pushed through holes made by drills, smoke sprang, and men hammered heads flat. In a little over forty minutes, girders were in place, and the Bretons lifted the doors off the grass, and hauled first one upright to fit its wheels to the right-hand girder, and that done, lifted the left-hand door to fit the wheels, and ran it in, and out.

As I expected, the shadow came across, and I looked up to see Santo setting down his balloon. Three men held the

16

rope, and he vaulted out of the basket, walking towards us, looking at the completed hangar.

He went to the closed doors.

He looked round at Thuillier and Gavroche.

With a forefinger's pressure, he rolled the right-hand door open. He held up the left-hand finger and pushed the other.

Both slid out to their furthest extent, little sound except a rumble of weight.

He walked across to the men holding the rope and took it from them, turning the airship, and walking it into the hangar as he might lead a horse into a stable.

He dropped the rope, turned to the doors, pulled one, and the other, to close, and looked about at us, all smiles.

'That's all,' he said. 'That's what I wanted. Why the arguments?'

Chapter 4

Santo – as we had begun calling him – was not a man to be argued with. Anything he said in words he would draw on a tablecloth or a menu or often a wall if it would clarify what he wanted to say. That Saturday afternoon after an excellent meal at Fouquet's, we were strolling down the Matignon with Captain Ferber and Ludovic Beres, an engineer, and the talk, as it had been through luncheon, was about the power required of a motor to push him through the air. Ferber and Beres were sure it would be impossible to put the weight of a man plus an engine plus the weight of an airframe into the air, and fly, for any distance, at any height.

Santo disagreed, calmly, without anger. He strolled with his hands in his pockets, and suddenly, he turned to his right and we stopped, and he took his famous black crayon from his inside pocket and began to draw on the white wall of a clothier's shop, a broad expanse exactly suited to what he wanted to do, and that was to show that his theory of adding one lightweight engine to another was not just the meat of argument but practicable and practical. It would work.

'You're inventing everything as you go along, for God's sake!' Captain Ferber said, laughing hugely in the quiet street. 'I've never seen anything like that. Where the devil are you going to find it?'

'I'm *making* it,' Santo said, and put the pencil in his pocket. 'Robbie here has found me half a dozen pensioner mechanics from Panhard and Daimler, and I've got a couple of foundrymen from Krupp. I have two tricyclette motors I'm building into one, and next time we meet, I hope to ram your doubts down your gullets, because I'll show you it *works*!'

'Is that an excuse for defacing other people's property?' a loud voice said behind us. 'Come with me. If the proprietor wishes to place charges, very well!'

A gendarme turned to walk, thumbs in belt, to the corner, and into the front door of the clothier.

'The proprietor,' he said to a young man, and he ran clumsily to the rear of the shop, and came out with a bearded whitehair, hands out to placate God-knows-what. But he began to smile and went out with the gendarme to look for a moment at the drawing, and came back.

'Name?' the gendarme said, wetting his pencil.

'Alberto Santos-Dumont.'

'Ahhhhhh!' the proprietor said. 'The first man in the sky?'

Santo bent his head.

'You will please allow me to take that drawing off the wall and frame it,' Whitebeard said. 'I am inexpressibly honoured. One favour. Will you sign it?'

'With greatest pleasure, Mister –?'

'Oznana. Promfet, a magnum of champagne!'

The young man hurried, and the gendarme shut his book.

'No charge?' he said. 'It's trespass and possibly more.'

'It is an honour. Stay and have a glass with us.'

'If my inspector comes along, I'm in the sewer. No thanks. Good luck, Mister Balloon. I'll drink to you to-night!'

Santo looked across the shop, drank a health, and walked to a tie rack, pointing.

'These two,' he said, and nodded again. 'And that waist-coat.'

'They will be sent immediately,' Oznana said. 'And your address?'

'The Bellevue.'

'Round the corner.'

'May I pay now?'

'Of no importance. Let us drink another glass to final and splendid success. You are the joy of our Parisian skies. My small son regards you as the hero of heroes. Long may you fly!'

We managed to get out, and in the warm sun, the champagne played the devil, at any rate with me. I wanted to sleep. Even Captain Ferber in his pale-blue uniform with all the braid frogs looked a little sluggish. Beres walked head down, hands clasped, not quite certain in his step. After all, it had been a magnum among five.

'I have to get another place to live,' Santo said, a little out-of-sorts. 'The Bellevue's all right, but it's by no means amenable. I want an anchorage. A place entirely mine.'

'I've got it,' I said, coldly awake. 'I have an apartment in a building I own. It's on the corner a few doors down from the Champs. All it wants is painting out. Let's go and see it.'

'Robbie again!' Santo shouted, startling a few in the street and waking Beres. 'What would I do without you? Let's all go and see it!'

'I'm off to the hammock,' Beres said, almost asleep. 'A wonderful afternoon. I'll get you those figures. *Cab!*'

'I'll join him,' Captain Ferber said. 'Santo, remember if you want anything, or if there's anything I can do, simply let me know. And I want to see what's happening about that engine. Keep well!'

We waved and walked on, in the russet and gold leaf-fall of Paris in autumn – always a wonder – and in the Bois, a glory, a scent of summer dying in her beauty, a fragrant reminder to remember her until she came back with spring-time to beautify and die again, an elbow in the ribs to assure that what dies, however beautiful, lives on, again and again. And how many summers had Paris, or Lutetia, seen?

We turned off the Champs at the rue Washington, and

19

went along about a hundred yards to Number 9, and I rang for the concierge, a dear old biddy, once of the Moulin de la Galette, and because of arthritis and possibly other matters best left unsaid, not so lively but well able to take charge of the building, a perfect *gamine* and a strict disciplinarian because she knew her job depended on it.

She opened the door, and swung it wide on seeing me.

'Ah, Monsieur Robert!' she crowed, music-hall style, which I suppose is between a song and a chant. 'Why did I know you'd be here today? Why did I bake madeleines? It's fate, isn't it? It's all fate. Either you know it or you don't. If you don't you're a simple damn fool. That's all there is to it!'

'We've come to see the apartments, Tanzi,' I said. 'I hope all's in order?'

'When hasn't it been? You'd think I'd allow pigeons to roost in there? Belfon waxes the floor every morning. I do the dusting. Should we put our feet up and sing to each other?'

'That's enough, Tanzi. Comport yourself. Show Monsieur Alberto Santos-Dumont the apartments. And is the kitchen in order?'

'It is in *perfect* order. I am in charge here. All it wants is one of those new gas stoves. They've put the pipes in. After all, we have to live with our time, no?'

'I agree,' Santo said, laughing. 'Madame is a modernist!'

'I was a dancer,' she said. 'Everything modern we loved. We had the ballets from Russia. What marvels. We never saw people dance like that. They were feathers in the air. We? We wrapped our skirts round our knees and twiddled a leg. I suppose they were lovely legs. But after all!'

We were in the lift called a parrot cage, and she pulled down on the rope to take us up. Santo tried to take the rope, but the look she gave him and the shove of her shoulder put him away.

'This is *my* job, 'sieu,' she said, making her meaning plain. 'While I can fit a pair of drawers and get into them, I don't need help!'

'Tanzi,' I said. 'A little respect is necessary.'

'She is correct,' Santo said. 'I don't permit anyone to interfere with what I consider to be my job. Very well. Then why should she? Another thing. We speak of her as "she" as if her world were not of ours. I find this odious. I live in the same world as Madame Tanzi, I hope. It is a world of courage, of a constancy of courage, of absolute determination in all pride to accomplish what we believe to be correct. I sound like a politician. I'm not. But she doesn't have to pull that rope every time I come in?'

'Very good for the muscles,' she said. 'I hope you take this place. I don't sleep a lot. So when you youngsters come in smelling of girls, I love it!'

We stopped at the first floor, and went in to the long, wide room with windows on the rue Washington, shining parquet, high ceilings, clean air, almost a silence except for a trotting horse below, soon gone.

'Perfect,' Santo said.

'Take Monsieur Santos-Dumont through the rest of the rooms,' I said. 'There's a loose shutter I want repaired. It's annoying.'

'I told Descargues about it,' Tanzi said, a shaken head and frail voice. 'What else can I do? Hit him?'

They went into the drawing room, almost the same size, except for a small wine store and bar, and into the bedroom, and down the circular staircase to the dining room and kitchen, and I followed their feet and voices upstairs to the other bedrooms and bath, and down, to the small arched doorway at the end of the drawing room.

'I want it!' Santo said, throwing out his arms. 'It's perfect. You've been my guardian angel since on a godly day we met. You remember? The day of All Saints. My wonderful Mama always had a tremendous party for all the children. I think I shall, also. Well, for the moment, I would like the place painted. Sky-blue ceilings, because that's where I think. In the sky. I want the walls a little off-white. Cream. A touch of pink, perhaps. I shall want to see. Then I want builders here. If you permit? I require a strong cradle in the middle of this room, I think from four points, to hold a table and chair. I want to eat in the air. If I am to fly for distances, possibly for hours, then I have to learn how to eat without discomfort. At the moment I eat with a chicken bone in one hand and a piece of bread in the other. It's uncivilized. I must learn to eat in the air, with all the strange movements

21

of the breeze. It's not easy. I must learn. You agree? You permit?'

'With all my heart. We can sign a lease at any time you please. Tanzi, call Deschamps and Melland. They should be here tomorrow. By the midweek everything should be in order.'

'Wonderful,' Santo said. 'I shall sleep here tonight. My man will bring everything over. I am in an eighth heaven. I feel I can work here. Remember the ceilings must be sky-blue. You don't object?'

'If a man wants to sleep under the skies, why should I? The costs, of course, are yours?'

Santo took off his hat and laughed, ho-ho, and the high ceiling gave it back ho-ho-ho-ho-ho, ringing, and Tanzi bent down in a he-he-he!

'The businessman, of course,' he said. 'Naturally. All extra costs are mine. Madame Tanzi, please find me a cook-housekeeper you trust, and an extra maid to help her. I am a very untidy man. *Very* untidy. You understand?'

Tanzi nodded into a corner, old eyes, shrugged shoulders.

'I believe I do,' she said. 'Untidiness is only a little thing. Moments, everything in order. Nothing. How often do you expect her in your bed?'

'Ahhhh!' Santo breathed, and held up his hands at the ceiling. 'This is furthest from the idea I have. Tanzi, we're not all the same, don't you know that?'

She turned away, pulling the shawl closer, and cackled. It really *was* a cackle, a hen's salute to an egg.

'I'll get her, first,' she said, still in a private cackle. 'Cook-housekeeper, hm? And a girl to help her? I guarantee it won't be an hour until the three of you are on the floor or the mattress. You'll be taken care of, never fear. One's a Breton, and the other's from the south. Both have the skirts of angels, and they *eat* men who roam the skies. Up there's nothing. Down here, women dance. And they eat!'

'I think I made a mistake,' Santo said, looking at me. 'Am I starting a whorehouse?'

'At least, it'll be private,' I said. 'Simply tell them what you want and don't want. Tanzi will help. Won't you, Tanzi?'

'When the two of them are naked in front of him, I'll

answer the question,' she said, all pious innocence, a dried-out nun. 'I never heard of a man who didn't love a naked woman. It does something. A woman dressed, very well, she excites. But when she's naked, it's more. You haven't found it so?'

I nodded, realizing an ancient truth, seeing Santo go to the window and look into the street, left and right.

'What a pity I have no terrace,' he said, and slapped hands at his sides.

'You have the roof,' I said. 'I'm next door. I have a roof garden. Loveliest place in Paris. I never have to buy flowers even in winter.'

'Marvellous idea!' he said, almost dancing. 'Please tell your gardener to see me. I am passionate about flowers!'

'What a waste,' Tanzi said. 'But wait till I get those two girls here. We'll see!'

'Tanzi,' I said. 'You go beyond your place, you understand?'

She nodded into shadow.

'I wish I was a fine lady with silk drawers and stockings to here,' she said, a small plaint. 'I had them once. I'd have took his mind off flowers, and quick. Let's see what Lotti and Miri can do.'

'Enough,' I said. 'Let Monsieur Santos-Dumont and his valet have complete access until I can give him his keys.'

She led the way, and we followed down the main stairway.

'You think it wise to allow this crone to choose my staff and run my life?' Santo asked, half-laughing. 'Where did you find her?'

'Not far away. Leaning against a lamp post. Too faint with hunger to walk. I brought her in. It was raining. My cook gave her some food and she slept in the pantry. I needed a concierge. In fact, she's been with me more than ten years. I vouch for her strict honesty. Loyalty. She would never introduce anyone dishonest. Never anyone incapable. You'll be getting the best. See them and judge for yourself!'

'And you'll get your gardener to see me? Wonderful. A simply glorious day. Yesterday I thought everything was going to the devil. That fellow Thuillier howled that I was putting ideas in people's heads by wanting running water

23

in the women's room. He refused. So? I paid him off, and Chéline will finish the smaller buildings and the kitchen. People must be taught to do what they are paid for. I have a further list I want. Iron sheeting for the foundry walls, wire and whatnot.'

'Send it over. It's in stock. All sizes.'

'Why would you want to stock such an amazing mass of goods?'

'Export, primarily. Our colonies deal almost exclusively with me. We've been in business for more than a hundred years. There is a question of trust. Either I've got it, or I get it. My head is with the warehouse. Yours is with the air. I've got that steam engine you asked about. It's no good. Sparks from the chimney, you'd blow up!'

'The wind would send the sparks away, mh?'

'See it and make up your mind.'

'How about dinner and a promenade tonight?'

'Excellent. Send your man when you're ready. No hurry.'

He raised his stick and walked towards the Bellevue, and Tanzi swung doors to close.

'He's a real dish of pastry, isn't he?' she said. 'A lovely man. They'll like working for him!'

'How do you know he's going to engage them?'

'Wait till he sees them. A little bet, perhaps?'

'Five francs?'

'To ten centimes? It's on!'

I heard her still cackling behind the door.

Chapter 5

The promenade was always a night out. We had a good dinner at Maxim's, though I noticed that Santo ate very little, which I put down to nerves, and I was wrong. He told me that when he worked on a problem, he had no patience with eating. A little of the taste would suffice, and with a glass of wine, he was satisfied. He had to look at his weight all the time, because the real problem was flight by a heavier-than-air vehicle. That was difficult enough without adding extra weight. Two or three pounds made a great deal of difference. Five pounds could make the odds between success and failure.

'You live the life of a saint,' I said.

'I find it enjoyable enough. At least I have a pilot light ahead. I know what I want to do. How many others have an aim in life? I want to climb into the air and travel as I wish under my own power. Flies and bees can. A bird can. Why not us?'

'Nature is against you.'

'When I find out why, then I'm free. But at this moment I'm on the wrong tack. I'm going the wrong way. And it's worrying. Hydrogen lets me float. The solution is elsewhere. I must find it!'

It was not by any means a mood for promenading, far less philandering, but anyway we got our silk hats, and called a fiacre and off we went to Montmartre, in a cool breeze and an enchantment of street lights unending.

The Empire Bar bloomed in cigar smoke and a perfume of many women and the bowls of red roses everywhere, with music from below and the loud voices and laughter of perhaps five hundred people strolling or in groups or at tables, and the waiters bawled orders across the bar and ran with full trays, a mélange, perfect picture of the wealthy at play.

Santo always enjoyed our nights out, though he never seemed a part of what went on. He looked at it, I think, as a naturalist looks at a nest of beetles, interested, even fascinated, but never with any desire to join in, certainly not to take a girl home, though he knew what the rest of us went there for. That apart, he was always ready to talk to any girl wanting a drink, for that was how they made their money beyond bed, and he was always ready with a big tip, and after a few times it made him popular, though there was, too, a genuine liking for him. The girls felt he was not one to take advantage. Only one of them, a slut from Austria, questioned his masculinity. Brows up, he looked at her, such a calm face, but the eyes showed the strange Brazilian blood that never forgives insult or permits a liberty.

'I have never bedded other men's women,' he said, in that peculiar tenor voice that cut through all the noise. 'I

25

have regard for my health. Drink up and go away. Never come near me again!'

Somebody must have told Madame Cora, because she came hurrying through the crush, all apologies that Santo tried to deprecate, but then she saw the slut, and went towards her screaming and followed her out. I never saw her again, poor girl. Beautiful, but an idiot.

We were there for an hour, we drank two bottles of champagne with sharers, of course, and because I failed to see my favourite girl, I was ready to go home, and Santo agreed.

'Don't you ever feel the desire for a girl?' I asked him, in the fiacre. 'Is it all the same to you?'

'Nnnnno,' he said, dragging it out. 'It's simply the same as being a monk and having your mind on something beyond you. Perhaps I shall meet a girl one day. I don't know. But she'll have to be patient. No domestic ties will keep me from what I want to do. I shall fly all over Europe. You'll see, the day will come. The day *must* come. I want to be first!'

I left him at the door, the keys worked, and I went to my place, strangely dissatisfied that my girl had been missing. I had no belief in Santo's theory. Every women's body is her own, and her escort is of her choice, alone. Her health is a matter for her own care. I never thought of other men with her. She gave me no reason. We simply went to her place, a delightful apartment on the top floor, small, with antique furniture she had been buying piece by piece, and she had an eye for paintings, and I suspect most of the artists had been in that enormous bed. She had all the most modern painters of that time, Picasso, Monet, Van Gogh, a beautiful Cézanne, and a Cassatt I found particularly lovely because it was painted by a woman. Why, I am not sure. Perhaps they had a liaison. Was it any business of mine?

Next morning I pulled myself out alone to catch the early train for an appointment with Captain Ferber at the Army School of Ballooning. A lonely business. I always liked taking a girl home when I had an early call, because then I could leave her in bed and let her decide for herself when she got up. A guest, after all, is a guest, and that is how she must be treated.

I got to the School in time for luncheon at the Mess, in a magnificent décor of table silver and medallions and guidons

26

of a hundred years or more, and all the uniforms in glass cases, a veritable museum of military prowess, and deeply impressive to myself, a layman. Only then, looking about, are we able to gauge the importance of the Army and its influence on the course of national history. At other times we are prone to forget them. I was, certainly, but I was pulled up short by that meal, excellent, and with splendid wines. Most of the officers came of vintner families, and they got the best. I shared it, thank God.

We came to business after luncheon, and we settled items and prices, balloon silk, rope, sandbags, and the rest, and Captain Ferber lifted his bubble of cognac.

'I speak in strictest confidence,' he said. 'I have always found you trustworthy. This does not go beyond us two. For the moment. General Gautier, whom you know, has been speaking to the President. As the Minister of War, he has the responsibility of protecting the Republic. This man Santos-Dumont has an idea which could result in a flying machine. I'm not speaking of airships or balloons. A flying *machine*. One, let us say, that could fly at speeds out of the question on roads?'

'I haven't heard of this?' I said, astounded.

'We have,' he said. 'We have an intelligence arm. It is most competent. We know that he makes experiments with engines, with frames. With lifting power. We want those details. I want to know what he orders, let's say, in the way of stores. He pays for everything himself?'

'Everything. At the moment of presentation I have his draft on the bank.'

'Are you close to him?'

'I believe as close as anyone else.'

'Then you might tell him, or simply throw out the idea, that a certain somebody in France would present him with one million francs for a flight, sustained or in pauses, to the frontier with Germany. From his present base it is a considerable distance. But he can be sure of his million francs!'

'Why do you choose me?'

'We find you an honest man, and a patriot. Our military intelligence service, you know, is as good as the next.'

'They work in his hangar?'

'From the beginning.'

27

'What do you wish me to do?'

'Simply plant an idea. When he has a hope of getting off the ground and flying a distance that can be made longer and higher, then somebody is ready with a million francs. The mapping, and all the patrol work to find flat landing grounds is already done. We have not been idle. Will you help us?'

'I must. It's my duty.'

'But no talk.'

'None.'

'Your health!'

I went back to Paris in a positive muddle, because I felt I had elected to spy on Santo. That was far from any intention of mine. I would not. But then I had a duty. Between one thought and another I was tired out, blank, and when I got home – ah, lovely word! – I told Maria to tell everybody I was out, and went to bed.

So thankfully.

Chapter 6

That morning I had a mountain of packet mail from abroad, and I knew there would be a bigger mountain at the warehouse. I put it all in a portmanteau and went downstairs to call a fiacre, but Santo was just getting into his Panhard and waved me over to get in. He said that the promenade had been a great success because the idea that eluded him for so long exploded while Madame Cora screamed, and he had it down within two hours when he got home.

'You don't need much sleep?'

'When I'm working, no. It seems a waste of time. And anyway, one can always lie down. How was Captain Ferber?'

'In excellent health. He asked me to present his compliments.'

'Good. I like him. More broadminded than the average soldier. But he's on the wrong tack, too. Balloons can be shot down. A flying machine has a hundred more chances

28

of survival. It would be difficult to hit!'

I felt a sad dog, listening, but at least I had a choice of what to report and what not. This would be one of the nots, and I decided then that I would report only a list of stores purchased but never a résumé of a conversation. For some reason, I felt relieved, even content. I wondered who the agent at the hangar might be, and if I had one or two at the warehouse. I supposed so. Nobody did more business with Government departments than myself. I had to be careful, and to try without seeming to spot whoever it was, whether in the stores or the office. It seemed ridiculous. But then, gathering intelligence was an important factor in policy, and who was I to argue in matters I knew so little about?

'You're not as brisk as the lark, this morning?' he said.

'I shall have to go away for at least a couple of months, perhaps more. I have certain cargoes coming in at various ports in France and Italy. I shall have to be there to pay dues and arrange for transport here. I do it three or four times a year. It's tiresome, of course. Next year, I'll try to find someone I trust to do it for me. But that's difficult. Finding an honest man these days?'

'Aha. We have a saying in Brazil. "The oxen grow fat only under the master's eye." You are worried about your warehouse?'

'I trust my people. Madame Dufresne and the office staff, I would go to the stake for them. It's the ancillaries. I don't know them as well. There's pilfering. I know that.'

'I have a different type of rat. They whisper. I haven't caught them, but I know that my ideas are no sooner expressed in my models, then hey presto! They appear elsewhere. How?'

'Find a pensioner Inspector of Police. He'd go into their backgrounds.'

Santo pressed the horn and braked to avoid a herd of cows, and went on slowly through a yield of manure.

'I don't want that,' he said. 'I want everything in the open. Thinking of prying into another man's life offends me. No. If someone wants to steal an idea, very well. But, remark me. They *steal*. I create. That's the difference!'

We shook hands on the corner, and I went down the lane

to the warehouse. It was a few minutes to seven, but everybody was in, and we all sorted through the pile I had brought, and when the morning delivery came just after nine, it had been reduced to files, by ship and port, and my itinerary took shape. By noon I knew exactly what was coming where and when, and Mme Dufresne started to map my railway tickets and reservations, starting that night for Toulouse, two days later for Marseilles, and then on to Genoa, Trieste, down the east coast of Italy to Bari and Brindisi, across to Naples, and back by ship to Marseilles, and home.

'Two months without a doubt,' she said in her quiet inconsequential manner that hid so much. 'You need have no worries about your business.'

'Would I let you apply for reservations if I did?'

She smiled and became quite another woman.

'We are grateful for your trust. You will write or telegraph?'

'When have I not? Keep in touch with me through the Consulates. As ever, I shall require a full report. I shall send all manifests as I check them. Please have my tickets delivered at the apartment. I shall bring back a present for all of you. By the way, Madame Dufresne. Do you suspect anybody in packaging or the stores?'

'For what reason?'

'I don't trust them. Instinct?'

'Discharge them. Take care of yourselves!'

I went out in a chorus, called the carriage from the stables, and Giraud was packing my bags at the back, and Santo came over in his long airship, waving to me from the basket, and I waved him out of sight.

Chapter 7

Travel had always been a delight to me. I loved to see foreign places, other people, and to ride in trains, and think what a miracle it was that modest men, knowing their business of course, could cook delicious meals in a cubby travelling at forty miles an hour and that waiters could stand on their feet and serve and pour wine without losing balance. I could barely walk from my car to the restaurant without lurching as a drunk, but then every trade has its tricks, and seamen learn to walk even on a ship standing on her nose.

Toulouse was a charm, Marseilles was my friend and I stayed for three days to work diligently, yes, but really to eat shellfish and dishes quite beyond the genius of Paris, and bouillabaisse, naturally, plus marvels of crab and lobster. On to Villefranche, then, outside the itinerary but holding an attraction all its own. Not quite free of its village cloak, it had no really good restaurant, but made up for it in a number of small bistros, each a gem, all serving a wonderful assortment of both French and North African specialities. Happily for me, at least, the packets that called at Marseilles and Nice from Tangier, Algiers, and Tunis lost their cooks to every coastal town, and I gorged.

I had five days in Genoa, a large cargo, and we had barely signed the forms when a second ship came in, and another two days' work. She was in bad condition after a five-day storm, but her stores were intact, which meant first-class seamanship, and I invited the Captain to dinner. He told me about the storm, but words tell only so much, the rest, the bravery, the risk, goes for little.

'But she'll need heavy repairs,' he said, 'I lost a suit of sails, to start with. I believe they'll ditch me. Put me ashore. And masters' jobs are scarce. I've got two boys and a girl to put through school. I'm worried!'

He was thin, black with sun, pale-blue eyes glowing in that face so bleak with threat, and my heart went to him. After all, he had my cargo safe ashore. We must help our friends.

'I shall write to the owners, and I shall tell them how I found your ship, and how grateful I am to you. Without your master's hand, everything aboard would be on the seabed. I have a cargo almost ready for the Côte d'Ivoire. I shall want you in Marseilles when I am ready in two or three weeks. Otherwise I shall find another ship. Will you be ready to sail?'

'Yes, sir,' he said, tears in his eyes. 'You are a prince!'

'No prince. I think of your children. And your wife. The best of good luck!'

I caught the early train, but he was there with most of his crew, and he presented a most beautiful model of a four-master, boxed, with my name on it and a strap to carry it. I gave the mate a banknote for them all to have a drink and climbed aboard with the guard's whistle. At least, I was in a few good minds, and children would go to school.

I slept to Trieste, and went across that stretch of water in a lighter carrying casks of rum and garlands of Chianti bottles, a lovely voyage in calm water with dawn in so many colours, a mug of rum in hand, not as sober as I should have liked, but then, I lost a lot of fat in hard work, and what the hell. The lightermen went alongside the ship, and I was piped aboard in royal style.

Captain Nordholm took me to my stateroom, all polished walnut and shining teak flooring. We started after coffee, and worked all day on the manifests, breaking only for a sump-tuous lunch of creamiest *seppie*, succulent turkey poult, and a lemon zabaglione. That night I fell into a bunk with a feather mattress and a down quilt. I awoke to eight bells and another day of checking, and in the evening I took the Captain to a trattoria I knew for a lobster beyond any recipe, with its secrets in a woman's heart. Mamma Yolanda cooked. There was no menu. No blackboards, nothing writ-ten. You sat down, and one of her fishermen sons asked you what you wanted, you told him, and the plates came, each a masterpiece, no fuss. By masterpiece, I mean exactly that. Even in Trieste her stove was renowned. In those three days I put on more pounds, and gratefully. My trousers were tightening, and I ate little on the way down the east coast to Fano, and the little towns round about where the girls wove silk for linings to military jackets and caps, and on down to Bari and Brindisi.

I love Italy, the people, certainly the countryside, the food, wine, music and courtesy. And there I was, lulling my fatheaded self into a sort of opium dream of heavenly food, soft beds and glorious sunny weather, and as we came into Bari station, there on the platform, parasol, flowered dress, gold reticule, all of it, Mme Dufresne.

'What's this?' I asked. 'I've had your reports?'

'I had to come. I couldn't trust the mails.'

'Let's talk over lunch.'

'You're not pleased to see me?'

'It has the scent of trouble. Let me claim my baggage.'

I bustled about for the five crates and odd packages, and had them sent to the Trionfo Hotel, and I got to the carriage in a thoroughly bad temper I made no effort to disguise. Everything had gone so well, but now there seemed an element of disaster in the air. I was almost afraid to ask.

'The warehouse was burgled last Wednesday,' Mme Dufresne said, looking away at the seafront. 'All they took were files concerning our dealings with Monsieur Santos-Dumont. Fortunately, we still have the records of the stores and packing bays. On the same night Monsieur Santos-Dumont's hangar was burgled and every piece of paper, including his new drawings and notes, was stolen. Last Saturday, a man calling himself Lessonier asked to see you, and I talked to him. He said he was from Internal Security with an office on the Quai d'Orsay. He insisted that the two men I had discharged must be reinstated.'

'You have a cold nose,' I said.

She nodded the flowers, and the straw brim made her face a dusky gold.

'A vixen's,' she said. 'I told him you were away and that I could do nothing without your directive. He wrote in a book and asked me to sign. I refused. He became very angry. He said I could be accused of being a traitress!'

'A fool with bells. What did you do?'

'I called Salles, and had him shown out.'

'Well done. And the hangar?'

'Monsieur Santos-Dumont came over. He told me he'd expected it. Many countries are interested in flight.'

'Did you telephone to the Quai d'Orsay?'

'Naturally. Nobody of that name is known. Or at the Bureau of Security. I took on three night watchmen, and Monsieur Santos-Dumont has four at the hangar, and four more to patrol the fields between us. Unfortunately, Mademoiselle Bosanquet and Mademoiselle Zuckermann are frightened. They want to leave, and so does Monsieur Vaudroux. They feel threatened.'

'Have they jobs to go to?'

'Yes. At better money.'

'Aha. Obviously a nest of snakes. Not your two outside, but our three in the office.'

The coachman stopped, and the porters came to carry the baggage. Mme Dufresne went in the restaurant to wait and I watched storage, and talked to the hall porter to find where my ship was in the port, and to have a carriage ready after luncheon.

My appetite had left me, but Mme Dufresne made up for any shortcomings, and spaghetti Bolognese was followed by a veal cutlet and spinach, and cassata, coffee and amaretti. I waited for her to end in a final crunch and a big smile in a sigh of repleteness.

'First good meal I've eaten since I left Paris,' she said. 'Now I can go back completely in order. I think of my little apartment with love, and I pray that my next-door neighbour fed my canaries, and the cat.'

'Isn't that dangerous?'

'Not a bit. He lets them perch on his back.'

'Mm. Your train's at three-forty-five? Give me your ticket and I'll have the porter check your reservation on the sleeping car, and take your luggage, and reserve a place in the restaurant.'

'Quite unnecessary, thank you. I have my ticket.'

'Let me have it, then. I'll clarify any doubts.'

She hesitated, and then opened the reticule and slowly, almost with a blush, gave me a slip of green pasteboard giving her return passage to Paris, third class.

I stuck my tongue in the back of my mouth.

'And you came here third class? How did you eat?'

'Oh. A sandwich. After all, I didn't need much.'

'But what the devil!'

'Why should I spend your money without permission?'

I got up, too angry – and grateful – to speak, and went out to the hall porter, told him to change the ticket to first class on the fast direct express, with a sleeping car parlour and a table in the restaurant, and to send the courier to accompany the lady to the train.

I went along for a coffee and cognac, and asked about replacements for the office, and she told me she had two good women from her university, and an accountant, a gold medallist of last year.

'And how is Monsieur Santos-Dumont?'

'A small minus and a large plus. He tried to fly to somewhere, and something awful happened. The machine was damaged, of course.'

'Was he hurt?'

'He went to lunch at The Cascades. He came in the next morning just as always, extremely smart, top hat, an orchid, and he laughed when I said I couldn't bear to read about it. He came to say you were right about the steam engine. He's going to use it to heat steam pipes to warm the workshop and provide hot water. He wants a dynamo and generator.'

'Send him the catalogues.'

'He took them with him. The day before I came away he tried again and he flew over a man's height. Another huge prize he gave away!'

'A marvellous man. I'm proud to be his friend. Anything new he wants?'

'Bamboo, copper ingots, and thin steel slats.'

'Beats me. He must have half a million francs worth of stuff over there. And that enormous wage bill? Did you reinstate those two?'

'On such a challenge I felt it necessary. But I couldn't find them. Their addresses were false. Funny, after these years?'

'Check everybody's address. Let's see how many more sheep in wolves' clothing we have. Or the other way about? I hate an informer. A spy. Lowest of worms. Only a thief is lower. Well, my dear? In Paris, perhaps in three weeks?'

She leaned out of the window, the sleeping-car conductor gave her the tickets, and she looked down at me.

'I think we pass through the town where I was born,' she said. 'I'm going to telegraph ahead. They'll all be there to see me in first class *and* a sleeping car. Ah, but *this* is fame. I am an empress. And I have you to thank. And I do!'

The train moved, she blew a kiss, I waved my hat, a far greater admirer of hers than I had ever thought. Who can repay loyalty, or that journey of days and nights jolting on a wooden seat? And a sandwich here and there, if you please?

At any rate, I had seen to it, between the conductor and the restaurant head waiter, that she would be well looked after on the way back.

I went out to find my carriage, and so, to the port.

Chapter 8

We crossed some of the world's loveliest country to reach Naples, that raffish wen of wonderful bandits, and found three, not two, of my ships were in. Five long days of checking, and cargoes were off-loaded from two to the far larger third, and I stayed on her, instead of at an hotel. The ship was almost new, Greek-built, and well found. Captain Constantinopoulos, a Cypriot, had his wife on board, but since she was the cook, and in a class of her own, I had no need to go ashore, and we sailed for Marseilles on the evening of the eighth day, after a lot of hard work and sweat, in a fair wind and a sea of molten glass, green as that, and only schools of porpoise to shatter.

I was able to do the donkey work with paper in my cabin, and spent the rest of the day in a hammock on the aft deck, a halcyon existence disturbed only by meals that put pounds on me and I was, in a word, careless.

We berthed at Marseilles at dawn, and I had a couple of hours with Customs and the transport people, and went ashore for breakfast in the Canebière, a favourite street of mine, and had croissants and salt butter and several sorts of jam and two of honey. On steady ground that felt soothing as a father's hand, I read all the newspapers, and Santo was on the front page of all. Some sort of a box he had built actually made a flight of many metres at over a man's height and might have gone farther except that a lumphead crowd were in the way and he came down to save lives. When did breakfast have such a taste? I felt like calling for eggs and ham and fruit, but after all enough is enough, and there was still a restaurant car on the train. But I had to drink to him, and while the waiter opened a bottle, I asked what he thought of Santo, and he raised his eyes, and shrugged as the cork came out.

'For me it's unbelievable,' he said. 'But obviously, without any nonsense, he is a son of God. No? He flies. He has wings, no? Wings. You see them in church. A mark only of angels. *Only* of angels. You see that now he doesn't even have a gasbag. No more the balloon. A man in the air. Believable? There's the picture. And I? What do I say?'

He put his palm under his chin and flapped the fingers out, open-mouthed.

I saw my luggage on the train after being sure my entire cargo was packed in the goods wagons, and had a wash in my parlour. I thought of spending a couple of days at Nice, but decided against, and sent Santo a telegram to say that his items were en route and to have at least a gang of twenty with heavy drays at the station.

We arrived at midnight to a platform crammed with people meeting whoever, and I picked out Santo's top hat because of the Baron de Rothschild, the Comte de Dion and the Prince of Monaco, all members of the Aéro Club, in evening dress, though Santo's top hat was at least a foot below theirs, the first time I realized how short he was. I waved to them, and they came behind until the train stopped, but they were held up by a company of Zouaves, going towards the goods waggons.

We shook hands through the window, and the conductor brought a bottle of champagne and we all drank on the platform.

'A complete success?' Santo asked.

'Every single item you wanted is here,' I said. 'Where's the gang?'

Santo looked at the Prince and laughed. Everybody seemed in highest good humour.

'What's the use of having the Minister of War for a friend if he can't help?' the Prince said, and nodded down the platform at the Zouaves. 'They'll off-load and take it by military transport to Neuilly. It'll be there by the morning!'

'Ah, but I know the Army,' I said, and gave my glass to the conductor. 'I must be there to check.'

'Aha,' the Prince said. 'Well done, thou good and faithful servant, what?'

'Your excellency, I am no man's servant,' I said. 'A friend

of everyman, yes. Of Santo, absolutely!'

'All right,' the Baron called after me. 'We'll be at the Folies. Do please join us!'

I went down to the wagons, but as ever, there was no need. Those lads had cleared two, into small trucks, and were emptying a third, and the young Lieutenant smiled, leaning on his sword, and tipped fingers to his képi.

'My Sergeant-Major is seeing everything into military transport,' he said. 'You may be quite sure it is safe. We have that reputation!'

'Then I shall not waste time. I wish to make a small gift to each of these men. It would have cost me a great deal more!'

He waved the cigarette, still smiling.

'We do not accept money,' he said, a father to a child. 'Of course, a few bottles of wine to the Mess, that is a different order!'

'It shall be done,' I said. 'I'm grateful.'

'Kindly tell that to the Minister of War. Good night!'

What do you say?

Chapter 9

It took weeks of work by all of us to translate the new stock, which kept on arriving at the goods sidings, into our catalogues, and have it sent out. I ordered that the Santos-Dumont items should be first, though when he came over to see me I was always out on Ministry business, and when I returned I never had time to go over and see him. But that Saturday afternoon, my desk at last was free of paper, and I walked across the fields to see him, and I heard the breathy grunts of an engine that seemed to snort twice, and stop.

I looked in complete surprise.

Santo, in a frock coat, got out of what looked to me an arrangement of clumsy box kites, took a handle from under the seat, and tried to start the motor. It wheezed, no more.

He threw the handle at it and went off hands in pockets,

shouting to somebody in the hangar. I followed, and passed the strange canvas-and-bamboo monster, and half a dozen men ran out to pass me and push whatever-it-was to face the wind.

I went into the hangar. Santo was on the stairway to his office, about twenty feet up, going toward a board covered in what appeared to be algebraic symbols.

'Santo!' I called. 'Do I trespass?'

He turned, and threw out his arms.

'Ah, Bob-a-dee-Bob,' he shouted. 'Dear lad, how I have missed you. Come on up. Lucien, bring a bottle!'

We met, clasped shoulders, and sat to talk, and the bottle came, and we drank, speaking of everything, and on the second glass I asked about the curiosity outside.

'That's exactly what it is,' he said. 'It's won me a prize but it's not what I want. It's clumsy. Unwieldy. A nonsense. But it rides the air. That's what I'm after. I don't know enough about it. The air's like a sensitive woman. You can be carried so far, and then you offend, and she drops you, pushes you aside, tips you up, neglects you, lets you fall and leaves you. You have no answer. You have nobody to address. You would like to take her by the shoulders and shake her. She cannot be found. You would like to kiss her. She eludes you. You would love to place her in a shrine and adore her. She lifts her nose. She is a mistress to be worshipped. But where is she?'

'She?'

'No man would behave in such a ridiculous manner. Of course, *she*. I caress her. I challenge her. She accepts. Sometimes she permits me *really* to fly. In that ridiculous contraption. Sometimes she tips me over. Each time I learn. A matter of trying this and that, and simplifying. Always, more simple. We have enough data now for a couple of mathematicians at the Sorbonne to indulge in theories. It's the first time it's been done. That's the kernel of the problem. Nothing in this field has been attempted. Neither theory nor practice. I know what Krebs has done in Germany. Very well. But that's an airship. It's not what I want. I want heavier-than-air *powered* flight. I go on cracking my skull against my lady. You saw what happened this afternoon? I was disgusted!'

'You're never disheartened?'

He opened his hands, eyes wide that made them wider.

'Dis*heart*ened?' he whispered. 'Why in the name of God should I be dis*heart*ened? Every time I fail, I learn a little more. It's why I believe I was put on this earth. For example. You saw what happened this afternoon? With that contraption? But so obviously my lady was telling me to simplify, simplify, *simplify*. In all those idiot boxes, those kite forms, every breeze is like Caliban. They do as they please. They blow against one wall and it turns this way. They blow against another and it turns that way. There is no way to steer. Caliban blows like a devil incarnate. And? My lady permits. She laughs. I curse? She laughs more. I must go on until I have her completely under control. It *can* be done. You got me that wonderful new engine. We're trying it out on the bench. Then? I shall build a simplified version. Wit*hout* those kite forms. They were an aberration!'

'Then why did you use it for so long? Or should I say them? I've seen you buzzing about for God-knows-how-long. I infinitely prefer your beautiful silent airship. Her shadow I feel is a blessing!'

'Thank you for that. But it's not what I want. Have you ever watched a dragonfly? The most graceful of all the things that fly? A marvel of design. Of flight. Slender. Diaphanous. A simple glory to watch. A most lovely poetry. I go out to the ponds at the back here. I watch them through binoculars. And what happens? They are on, for example, a bulrush. Then? They open their wings and they fly. Imagine! That most delicate and delightful beauty, she flies!'

'After all, they were made so. No?'

'Yes, but we may learn. I made up my mind this afternoon I shall make a dragonfly. The cargo you brought me is a selection of all I require. I can't think why I've been so dense. The air requires only simplicity in the method of flying. What's complicated is the power and steering. Steering is difficult, of course, but it *can* be dominated. Power is the very devil!'

'You don't see a way?'

He sighed, drank, and sat back, looking over my head.

'I have rather more than hope in this new engine,' he said,

nodding. 'It's far more powerful than anything I've used up till now. It might twist me around in the air. I don't know. I'm just beginning to know a little about torque.'

'Torque? What's that?'

'Twisting. The propeller creates it. It's a devil of a problem. I tell you, nobody's looked into this before. I asked those mathematicians to help me. From what I've seen, I'm not sure they can. It has to be done practically. For one small example, I've changed the design of the propeller. Now it's twisted. One blade one way, one blade the other. And it *works*!'

He laughed and poured us another glass.

'Everything by accident,' he said. 'Or, let's say, almost. They were wheeling this idiot arrangement out of the hangar and they bumped the propeller against the door. I didn't notice it and the men said nothing. But when I started the motor I knew I had more power. More thrust. I stopped the engine and looked. The prop was twisted. In one blade. I had her taken back and *both* blades were twisted, one this way and one that. It was the very devil of a job. Hammering's hard work. Anyway, that twisted prop is the secret of the new command and further speed of my flight. Can you believe that?'

'It doesn't quite put you in the class of the dragonfly?'

He pulled in a deep breath, and reached for the glass.

'Perfectly true,' he said, almost sadly. 'But I have the faith that every day I learn more. Every day I come nearer. With friends like yourself, I shall do what I wish, and dream, and desire. Health!'

That afternoon I was checking my stocklist with the ship's manifest from Toulon, and from the window I saw Frère Chevrillon short-cutting from the village across to my place and getting the skirts of his *soutane* decorated with burrs and straws, penalty of impatience. I knew that Sostre, downstairs, would take care of him with a clothes-brush, and of course he did, and the reverend man tapped and came in and fell, rather than sat, in my father's chair.

'Bwah,' he said, and breathed garlic. 'I don't know what it is. Something gets into them. The devil or simply the idiocy of their own horrible human natures.'

'Exactly what are you talking about?'

He pointed a thumb towards Santo's place.

'That lot up there,' he said. 'That's why I tramped my old knees over here. There's no time. Tomorrow is a religious day in this area. It's entirely pagan. I shan't go into it. But the seamstresses over there are waiting for Santos to come back tomorrow evening. You see?'

'No,' I said. 'What's it got to do with me?'

'I know from certain sources,' he said, and I thought of the Confessional. 'Once he arrives, they will take off their clothing and dance naked around the eight fires. They already have the wood piled. I heard the details this afternoon. That's why I'm here!'

'But what did you think *I* might do?'

'Warn them,' he said. 'They respect you. They don't respect me. I'm only – who –?'

'Representative of their Redeemer? Comforter in doubts and sorrows?'

He laughed while Mme Dufresne poured the wine, but his eyes were sad.

'I've had long enough to know,' he said. 'If you look at that little village you wonder if anything could be more peaceful, more innocent, or healthier for the people living there. In reality the place is a cess of brimstone. They stink with the Pit's own sulphur. The pagan Gaul and Roman never died. Scratch any of them and you find the barbarian. The churchgoers go to Confession and Communion. It's a façade, of course. Tomorrow, for example, there is a festival. I shan't describe it. It sullies the mind to think of it. That's why, tomorrow, I shall be at my monastery, and I shan't be back until next week. When natural airs have blown the stench away!'

'Oughtn't you to be there to fight it? Isn't it your duty?'

'A priest is a natural target for the Devil and his handmaidens,' he said. 'I have no wish to be seduced by the naked and wanton. People too often forget that we wear trousers. Well, I got *that* off my suffering chest. A helpless fellow, really. A mere gravedigger's adjunct. I enjoyed talking to you. I know you're an agnostic. That's why I can say to you what I'd never dream of hinting to others. It lets me breathe. But I shouldn't complain. And I shouldn't run away. Fortunately my Prior understands that some of us are weak. I most of all. Thank you, my dear friend Robert. You are remembered in my prayers. If a weakling's prayers are of value?'

'All prayers have value. And thank you. I shall often think of you. Amounts to about the same thing?'

He turned in the doorway, and nodded without looking back.

'Possibly,' he said, and closed the door.

I had no time to think about it, but only to feel sorry for a man caught in a vocation that could be shoved aside by rustics, mocked, derided for those few days of the year, and forced by the duties imposed by his oath to minister to them for the rest of the year. And for the rest of his life, and for all of them, until he read the prayers they had never believed over their graves. Comparing my life with his, I turned to my heap of manifests with a feeling of ineffable content. I employed more than a hundred people, and because of their wages they were able to send their children to school, pay the rent, and generally live a decent life. I had no reason to question their morals. I was a hedonist, a philistine, and a selfish brute, very well. I accepted it and enjoyed it, and had no intention of altering it, unless luck, fate, or some other idiot quality interfered, and since I was not a believer in any of them, I went my way, did the job for everybody, sailed my ships, paid my way, enjoyed my farm and the vineyard, and generally lived at the other end of the human spectrum from Frère Chevrillon and his rustics. Whether it was right or wrong held no interest. I had no time to waste on pallid philosophy, the wheres and whyfores, which always struck me as being essentially useless. Only working men getting things done held any measure of reason. The rest was theory, and nobody ever earned the price of a meal from it except the professors, and they were kept by the universities for what reason I was never able to discover except in the matter of social cosmetics. It was a university, ergo, professors and philosophy and all the other useless nonsense they crammed down our throats. I hated the entire rigmarole. I knew I was destined to take my place in my father's business. The rest was frippery, and as I thought then, and still think, a waste of time.

And yet.

43

The friendships made in those university years were a solid buttress both to social and business life. How many times I had been able to use my telephone or go to the office of a colleague, and, as it were, put things right. Whether it was fair to the body politic or not was neither here nor there. The fact was very simple that what I wanted was done because I had gone to the right place with the right people. I had to thank my father. He had to thank his. We were the right people. Who were we? I so often wondered.

But I worked on, without worry, confident.

If idiocies came up, they could be resolved across one desk or another, or through some subordinate. Nothing mattered except that the business was done and all brought to order.

I often thought that our way of operating was unfair to others, but after all, we have to work, and there is no sentiment in business, or so my father taught me.

I called in Mme Dufresne and told her about the seamstresses next door, and saw the flush rise from her throat, slowly, making her face a dullish-red mask that faded and left her pale with a strange glint in her eyes that were grey, and now seemed black.

'I'll see that woman Juplon,' she said in a firm voice. 'I've known for some time they were planning something of the sort. That type has to be dealt with very strictly or they'll turn anywhere into a charnel house. But should he be deprived of a little harmless amusement?'

'He's a bit of a puritan, from what I know.'

'I've met puritans, too. You, for example. There are so many quite lovely girls here. You've never even pinched one of them. And they complain!'

'Don't imagine I'm blind to their points of reference. But I don't employ people to pinch them. Next, I'll be pinching you!'

'I wouldn't mind in the least,' she said. 'At least it'd be a reminder that I'm rather different from a piece of furniture!'

To say I was astonished would be gross misuse of language.

This, from Mme Dufresne? Archdeaconess of propriety?

'I shall see this Juplon person,' she said, at her haughtiest, moving for the door in a rustle of skirts. 'Tomorrow is mid-

Lent. They have a carnival. They dance naked in the barns, in the streets. I often wish I could. I think we're all too goody-good for far too long for health and wits. Sometimes I could go *berserk*!'

I was, in a word, bemused.

'Come down to the farm with me this weekend,' I said, daring at least a gambit. 'Nakedness as you wish!'

'I shall be enchanted,' she said. 'I always wanted to see it. From a bedroom window!'

She went out and I sat, a loon, knowing I had made an error of a magnitude whose ripples worked to the furthest shores of crackpotamia, bringing horrors as yet unseen, and I could feel in my bladder that I would pay dearly. But I had made an offer, my word was in question, and I would not retract.

I saw the flowered hat pass under the window and turn towards the hangar, and I watched her figure, something I had rarely done before. I found her graceful, with the length of the skirt telling of long legs, and the belt emphasizing a small waist. I wondered why I had not particularly noticed any of those items before. I had, of course, but she always appeared so businesslike and withdrawn that I first hesitated and then – because I had no wish to lose an absolutely first-class office manager by a crass indiscretion – I put all such notions out of mind.

Now I was about to drown in a self-made bog.

Everything, my father had once said, comes in threes, whether accidents, tragedies, or the unexpected. The priest had been one, Mme Dufresne the second, and within fifteen minutes I heard the thudding of the Panhard's motor, and Santo arrived, running two at a time up the stairs, magnificent in top hat, frock coat, cravat, pearl pin, and white spats over patent-leather boots. We embraced, naturally, and he sat down and I went to pour the champagne, and he took a pile of documents from a black crocodile case.

'An extraordinary time,' he said, lifting the tulip. 'I find I shall need to build at least thirty craft of the Demoiselle type, somewhat larger, with a more powerful engine, and a different design of propeller. Dear Bob-a-dee-Bob, you'll be busy. Here you have the lists. I've just come from the Ministry. I'm promised all finance and official help. I never tried to make any money out of my activities, but I look like becoming a multimillionaire!'

'Good luck!'

'You'll also do well financially. I shall *see* that you will. I couldn't have done half without you. Look at these. Assess the tremendous scope of the venture. My fleet of aircraft will form the basis of the French air squadron. A new arm is being formed. Look at this map!'

I knew it to be a military map without titles, all proper names of towns in numerical code, and yet the short black lines, all of nearly equal length led northeast to the German border, though I kept my thoughts and surmises to myself, but I was sure Santo realized that I knew.

'I confide in you because I know you to be a man of honour,' he said, folding the map and tapping it. 'I have nobody else to rely upon, and I haven't found anyone else. Many have tried to worm themselves into what I am intent on doing. I sniff them. I ignore them. I look to you to help me. I'm tired. I've done a great deal of flying since the 14-bis and the Demoiselle. I've found out so much. I even flew over the hills. But, Bob-a-dee-Bob, imagine. Over the *hills*?'

'But did you have witnesses?' I asked, in a whisper, incredulous.

'Almost the entire General Staff. Mechanics. Cartographers. Everyone germane to the attempt. Conducted of course in greatest secrecy. Farmers think nothing of white birds hopping over their lands. Gigantic birds. They blame the wine. And they don't talk. The French peasant, the farmer and his people are wise men. They've been taught across the ages. The soldiers naturally are 'under oath. What we did has been in silence. If whispers arise, I shall find out where they come from. Bob, I am tired. I would like to go away and think. You once invited me to your farm. It sounded marvellous. A haven of splendrous peace. May I avail myself?'

I looked at the smile in his eyes, that reminded me in some way of the infinite trust in the eyes of my Basset at the farm, and I simply had not the heart to deny him, putting aside all thought of my duty to Mme Dufresne.

'Of course,' I said, in all faith. 'I'll give you a map of the route, and I'll telegraph my staff at the farm. Use the place as entirely your own for as long as you wish!'

He held out his hand.

'I shall never forget,' he said, and pushed the thick folders across the desk. 'Please have this material stock-piled as soon as possible. Deliver as you may to the place at Neuilly. It's beginning to take shape. Tomorrow I shall have a supper party at my place at nine o'clock. Please bring anyone you wish. Know that I am eternally grateful. I shall go to the farm the day after!'

Raps on the door brought in Sostre with an arm about Mme Dufresne. Her face was bloodied, hair hung, her dress was torn, and the hat in Sostre's hand fell in flowered rags.

We sprang to hold her and put her in a chair.

'It was that whore, Juplon,' Sostre said. 'She attacked her with all the others. Thank God I followed. I know them!'

It was time to state the fact, and Santo's face changed to the Brazilian blank I had become used to, that tells nothing except in the eyes.

'This is the excuse I needed,' he said quietly. 'I had worried what I was to do with those women. I had no wish to discharge them. Now I have no alternative. They assault and injure a defenceless woman? Very well. They are discharged from this moment. Robert, I shall first go to the hangar to see they are paid off, and I shall then come back to take Madame Dufresne to a nursing home I know. She will remain there until she is completely recovered. I tender the most abject apology that this atrocity should have been committed on my premises. I shall not be long!'

The door shut quietly. I poured Mme Dufresne a tot of brandy, but she shook her head.

'I never knew such savagery,' she whispered. 'In a moment. They were kicking and scratching. Only that man Sostre saved me. He beat them off with his fists. Or I wouldn't be here. I don't want to go to a nursing home. I want to go to the farm!'

'Nursing home first,' I said. 'We shall find out if there are other injuries. You don't breathe very well. You may have broken ribs. Nursing home, first. Farm after!'

'But you promise?'

'Have you known me break my work?' I said, a hypocrite

47

beyond hypocrisy. 'How could we go to the farm like this? It's a long journey. We'd get there late. You'll be taken care of in the nursing home, and when you're quite well, then, the farm and a few days' real convalescence.'

'Who will do the work here?'

'If your assistants are incapable after your training, they are not worth their jobs. Everything will be in order, rest assured. All you are asked to do is get well. I hate those bruises. I should have gone down there. I didn't think!'

'What can be done with such people?' she whispered, eyes shut. 'Who could imagine that sort of savagery? I shall be afraid to come here!'

'When you come back, they won't be here. Any of them.'

The big red rubber horn of the Panhard phoop-phooped.

'Off you go,' I said, putting an arm about her shoulders. 'Not too fast down the stairs. I shall be in to see you tomorrow after you've had a rest. Have no further worries.'

Halles and Sostre waited, and we helped her slowly down and out to the Panhard, and Santo put the heavy fur rug about her in the back. Mlle Lambert half-ran to get in beside her and cushioned her head.

Still with that blank face, Santo looked at me.

'I am ashamed,' he said. 'Really ashamed. I did *not* know I employed harpies. But they worked well. Does that perhaps blind us? I shall telephone from Paris when I am sure Madame Dufresne is comfortable. Mademoiselle Lambert will go by fiacre to her home. Until we meet!'

Mme Dufresne seemed asleep, but blood still ruddied her nose and cheeks and bruises began showing blue.

I felt cheap, standing there, less than a man, watching the dust.

I should have gone to that hangar.

Thoughtless, and so, cowardly without awareness.

Cheap.

Chapter 10

Mme Dufresne's room at the nursing home was a bower of roses in all colours in all sorts of vases, including two buckets covered with silver paper, but I liked most of all the small pot of wildflowers from our own fields sent by my staff. It hit me. She slept, and I tiptoed out.

I had an appointment with Captain Ferber at the Plaza-Athenée, and when I went into the foyer I was met by his aide, Lieutenant Descargues, and he took me to a private dining room on the first floor, and a soldier opened double doors.

'Monsieur Robert Williams,' the aide called, reading my card. 'A luncheon guest of Colonel Ferber!'

He saw my surprise, and smiled.

'The Colonel is now in command of the air arm,' he whispered. 'He is now a little brother of God. Bow down!'

Colonel Ferber, in a blue suit, came hand-out to meet me.

'Dear Robert!' he called. 'I'm not in my finery today. It's only just been designed. Let's have a drink. I've got some very good Scotch. Or do you prefer gin?'

'Not if I'm in my right mind. You got my report?'

'I just finished reading it. Splendid, absolutely. I'm so glad I have someone of substance to rely on. The others are such weeds. Have you any idea what that giant of a man did? And not a whisper? Anywhere? The President, of course, is delighted. He regards Santo as something in the nature of a son. Of course, in a sense, he is. At least, of France. First of all, let me say that all expenses are covered by grant. Send your accounts to me. Pick up the telephone and call this number, and my orderly will come to your office. I want nothing through the mails. Understood?'

'Perfectly. I have rather more than a million francs outstanding.'

'It shall be paid within two days. But it is clearly understood that nothing passes between us except by orderly from this office?'

'Understood, sir. I'm very glad you've said so. There've been strange visits by a certain Monsieur Lessonier pretending to be from Security at the Quai d'Orsay. On enquiry, he was a myth. If it hadn't been for the farsightedness of my office manager, Madame Dufresne, he might have had access to our records. As it was, he got nothing.'

'I would like to talk to your Madame Dufresne.'

'At the moment she is in a nursing home.'

'Let me have the address. I shall visit her, if she permits.'

'Doubtless she will. But in a couple of days.'

'Be certain I shall enquire. Come, let us have luncheon. We have so much to talk about. And to decide upon.'

From the tone of his voice I knew that other matters weighed, and certainly I was not wrong.

Throughout luncheon I was regaled with a day-by-day report of the air journey to the German border, every day, that is, except Sunday when Santo attended Mass at a local church.

'I didn't know he was a religious man,' I said.

'Essentially so,' the Colonel said. 'Without firm faith, how does a man support such an amazing series of what are no less than adventures that could cost him his life? He is a hero. No question about it. I have nobody who'd dare fly that machine. In two weeks' time he will start to teach a class of pilots. It's a most difficult assignment. As he says, he has to find out which lad is temperamentally suited to pilotage in the air. Not everybody is. And many good lads perfectly capable in other spheres could be failures. They could be killed. It's my responsibility. What do I say to the President? To their mothers and fathers?'

'Where is this to take place?'

'At our school, to begin. Later, when we've chosen the first cadre, at his place. They'll have trainer machines on the ground where they can't break their necks. Then, by degrees, into the air!'

'No balloons?'

'He's made them an anachronism except to spot for artillery or some other minor activity. No. It's all heavier than air from this time on. That's where you come in.'

50

An orderly served coffee in a silver service, and another presented a humidor of cigars.

'You will certainly have visits from German and Russian military attachés. Possibly Belgian, Swiss, British, and even American. I'm told that a couple of brothers from Dayton, a small place in the United States, have flown. I'm not sure what to think about it. Be that as it may, we have, thank God, a Santo here. He's done all we want. He will be supported by the Government, with the President as his first friend, and I have a further duty. I am worried about what may be offered him financially by others. He is a pathfinder. Very well. We are close on his heels. We don't want to lose that advantage. I shall rely upon you to tell me whatever may happen at those meetings. You are known as a prime source of supply. Obviously, interested parties will come to you. I want to know who they are. I want to know who makes enquiries, and for what reason. We understand each other?'

'Yes. Have you examined the records of my staff?'

'They are checked to the last detail. That's why I'm anxious to talk to Madame Dufresne. She had a German mother. She's the weak link. A lot of information has got out. I want to find out who and where!'

I looked away, thinking of a bloodied face and bruises.

'It's such a shabby thought that I cannot permit myself to give it one moment's examination,' I said. 'She is absolutely of the best!'

He looked at the end of his cigar.

'Y'know, Robert. Those are the people we're after. It's one of the reasons I want to talk to her. She may not be guilty. But I shall find out. I sent you the blueprints of a new propeller. It wasn't made? Very well. But how did the Germans get it?'

'I wasn't aware of it,' I said, miserably.

'I'm not merely aware of it,' he said, very much the Colonel. 'I am very worried about it. Don't you understand? There's a leak in our system. Where is it?'

'I wish I could tell you. We had the blueprints, didn't we? Could they have been stolen when the offices were burgled?'

'Perhaps. But why were you given a copy of a secret

51

document? What use was it?'

'If I remember correctly, it had four different metals and two types of wood. I had to find them, and did. That's why.'

'Why not a list of requirements? Why a working drawing? You see, we must tighten up everywhere. You'll have six pensioner sergeants guarding your place at night, and two during the day. They'll let nobody in unless they have authorization from me. That's a beginning!'

'A very uncomfortable way to work!'

'Now we come to the meat of this meeting,' he said, tapping an inch of ash from the cigar. 'At a later time, within the year, I shall ask if I can buy that side of your business. Obviously an Army supply depot must be run by the Army. As it is, we're half and half. Won't do, will it?

'I shall require a stiff price. A lot of work has gone into it. Apart from that, I don't want people to lose their jobs!'

'They may not have to. I'll accept however many wish to join the Civil Service. They'll probably earn more as specialists. I don't think you need to worry. I respect your devotion to your staff. You must believe me, I share the same feeling. I protect them. Your top-class mechanics will earn an officer's salary. With, of course, a pension. That's important.'

'Agreed. Any idea how many you'll want?'

'Everybody, because I respect your judgement. I said within the year because it gives you an opportunity to train a new staff. I have the same agreement with Santo. His entire staff is training my flight mechanics and engineers. In a year's time I'll have the best air arm in the world. We've stolen a march, my friend. We are well in front and I intend that we shall stay there!'

Chapter 11

Mme Dufresne's face was free of bruising, and she was calm, even a little distrait, although I'm not sure what I mean by that except that she was not her usual sharp self. I suspected drugs, because the doctor downstairs had told me that she was still not over shock. I was able to tell her that we missed her presence, that I was waiting to know when she would be able to go down to the farm. She seemed curiously hesitant, even at point of refusal, but I refrained from outright questioning, and left with smallest fuss.

But I was worried. I knew that Colonel Ferber had been to see her twice at least but she had said nothing. It was most unlike her. Normally, she would have told me every word of the interview. She had not. I knew something was wrong. It was not the most comfortable feeling.

Santo was still at the farm and enjoying himself from the notes I got every other day. My mares had foaled, my cows had calved, chickens, ducks and geese laid, and the peacocks were in their nests. It was a wonderful world, but I was hesitant for some reason in joining him down there. I had no notion why. Possibly because I had such respect for him that I felt he would think better by himself, without talk or any contact with the world outside. I was hungry for my farm, but I respected his quiet.

He came back without warning – as usual – dressed in tweeds, jersey, and scarf so that I knew he had been flying, and offered to take me to luncheon at The Cascades, one of my favourite restaurants, and I agreed. On the way in, I told him of the Dufresne incident's aftermath, and he nodded, I thought a little sadly.

'I had a report from the nursing home,' he said. 'They aren't entirely sure of her complete sanity. They thought that perhaps more harm had been done that could not be medically ascertained. They warned of a possible suit for damages.'

'That's nonsense. You can't be held responsible for a gang of hoydens?'

'It was on my property.'

'If you hear any more of it, let me know. I've got the best lawyer in France. He'll make mincemeat of them. Now, there's Colonel Ferber. I look like having to take his price or I'll lose a great deal of my business.'

'Dear Robert, I have already discussed the matter with him. The price will be fair to both sides, or I shall withdraw. He knows it, and he assured me that everything will be correct to the last proper gold *louis*.'

'Makes me happier. In fine point of fact, it will be far

easier for me to manage my own business again without the air material. It's extremely profitable, yes. But the work becomes a burden.'

'I'm so grateful I could pile it on to you. I tell you, I couldn't have done one half without your help. I shall see that you are properly reimbursed. If I ever got into the air, it was with your help. You found me the mechanics. We built that wonderful little engine. But it's far bigger now. More robust. I reached speeds of over sixty miles an hour. Next week I shall fly at over eighty. When the new engine's ready I'll be over a hundred!'

'Impossible!'

'She's done it on the bench. I found out one general fact. I must travel at least fifty-five miles an hour to have lift. That's been the error all along. You need speed into the wind. I've been flying at a thousand feet!'

'Never!'

'The record is there. I shall persist with the design of the engine I have. But it's impossible to see into the future. A couple of my engines burned out. Fortunately I was almost on the ground. If it happened in the air, I'd be dead!'

'You're not afraid?'

'Naturally. As often as I cross the street here. A man driving a dray can't pull up in time to save me. I must run. But I must still cross the street. The same in the air. It is my business to overcome all obstacles. Every problem has a just solution. But I am extremely worried about turbulence in the upper air. One's tossed about like a piece of paper. Really frightening. It doesn't happen in balloons.'

'Why?'

'Balloons float. Airplanes drive through currents of air. Up or down. If you're caught, you must manipulate. It's the greatest single danger to the airman. The downdraught. You have to wiggle to get out. Easily the most difficult drill to teach. And all those young men are my responsibility. It's not always easy to sleep!'

I began to understand his curiously withdrawn attitude. Always there had been a certain reservation, even a shyness in his dealings with people. Because of our friendship and our continuing business relationship his attitude had melted and we could have been brothers. But if he were plagued at thought of being held responsible for the lives of his charges I understood, I surmised rather, his apprehension of tragedies in being, or in the making.

At The Cascades, a lovely place in the Bois, we met Émile Matteotti, the mathematician, Jean-Paul Clothard and Ludovic Beres, both engineers, and they all had sheaves of paper to give him.

But something new came out of that meeting that I might have missed in the small talk. I made no comment because it was none of my business, and yet it informed me of the gathering influence, if not of the formidable power, he appeared to be generating even among his colleagues. He was offered three million gold marks for a flight across Germany to the Polish border. It was a merest throwaway remark by Beres, speaking of a talk with Colonel Ferber, and this hesitancy to allow what were virtually his aircraft to fly for the benefit of the Germans.

'It's for the benefit of everybody,' Santo said. 'Mankind will one day be free because of travel in the air. They will be able to go where their fathers never had any remote chance of going. No boundaries and no frontiers. The air will give them freedom. I am only a pioneer!'

'Only?'

'Nobody compared with what's to come. We have those two Americans. Our own Blériot. Voisin. Many Englishmen. Germans, and let us remember they are magnificent engineers. They will not be among the last. That's one reason I shall accept a German offer. As a pioneer it's my duty to provide an example, besides taking the Brazilian flag across the country.'

'Touch of Jingoism?' Beres said, but laughing.

'Any patriot should have a touch of it,' Clothard said. 'I know I have more than a touch. I want to see *us* Number One. And cement ourselves there!'

'That is my intention,' Santo said. 'France gave me all the help possible. Robert here, at root, is English. But he is a truest Frenchman at heart. He's even prepared to sell a good part of his business for Marianne's sake!'

'He'll be paid for it,' Matteotti said. 'A nice lump it'll be. He'll be able to buy a yacht!'

'Not for me,' I said. 'I'm a landsman. The nearest I get to water is in my boat!'

'I spent many an enchanting hour in it,' Santo said. 'I put out lines. I regularly caught my luncheon. Fat trout, and on two days the best perch I ever tasted. Of course, your cook down there is the equal of any up here. How she gets that crisp crackly skin on a fish is something of a royal mystery. But then, everything she does is superb. I can't think why you don't marry her!'

'Eight solid reasons,' I said. 'A husband – my field manager – and seven children!'

'Well,' Matteotti said. 'Once the sun goes down they have nothing else to do, no?'

'We understand you,' I said. 'But it's not the kindest thing to say. They are a healthy people, and virile, and they reproduce their kind, thank God!'

'Amen,' Beres said. 'France needs them. When do you begin your German saga?'

'When the contracts are signed,' Santo said. 'When the cash is in the bank!'

'A touch of the entrepreneur?' Beres said. 'It's time. They've cheated you for long enough. Relying on good nature. What would they have had to pay someone else for what you have given them? Free!'

'It's the run of the game,' Clothard said. 'Give, and ye shall receive. Are you religious, Santo?'

'In any church sense, no,' Santo said. 'I believe in the creative spirit. We call it everything. I prefer to use shorthand and say God. Otherwise where do we get our ideas? Our purpose? Why do we have faith?'

'From business to philosophy in two steep steps,' Matteotti said. 'Why is it, then, you go to church?'

'Most churches are a thousand years old and more,' Santo said, rolling a pill of bread. 'I kneel in the hallowed thought of generations. I rely upon the strength of those minds. They support me and sustain me. Whence cometh my help? Don't you think that in the turbulence over Alsace I had plenty of time to think about it? What saved me? My knowledge? I had none. I had never met those conditions. The air is a cruel mistress. She forgives no error. She is condign. You are an alien in a foreign element. Either you succumb to her laws, or suffer. I'm learning the laws. I have to find them for myself. But I worship her, and she answered my prayers!'

We listened to the silence of the Bois, the whisper of leaves in a thousand trees, birds chirping, a clop of hooves on the roadway, the gentle chatter of glass and china in the restaurant, and suddenly I knew the extraordinary human quality of my friend Santos-Dumont, practical idealist, dreamer and working engineer, mathematician and spiritual believer, contrast in terms and utterly believable, likeable, even lovable.

'I have another soirée on Saturday,' he said, outside on the steps. 'Please come around about nine. Or whenever you please. I'm entertaining the German delegation. Bob-a-dee-Bob, if you permit, I shall bring them out to look at your warehouse at three or so in the afternoon. You permit?'

'Of course. But why *my* place?'

'They must be made to realize the enormous stock they require merely to start. I had no idea what I'd need in the beginning. You solved most of my problems. I'd advise them to retain you as a procurator-general. You know where everything is. Where it can be got. That in itself is worth money. I'm going to see you get it!'

'Nothing like having a friend at Court,' Beres said, and pulled a tapestry waistcoat over a real *pot*. 'I've eaten too much. I always do. It's so good. With so many people all over the world starving, it's a shame to leave anything on the plate. Really disgraceful!'

'And your tailor has the profit,' Clothard said. 'Taking out the waist is a fat source of revenue. So many *pots*!'

'Santo'll never have one,' Matteotti said. 'He eats as a bird. After all, that's what he is!'

'A splendid day for France when he came here,' Beres said. 'Incidentally, also for us, no?'

'You will receive your cheque on Friday,' Santo said. 'When the Army takes over, you will be on the payroll. With, of course, a pension!'

'Thank God for a devoted patron,' Beres said, 'You have no idea how you have eased my life. My wife and children pray for you!'

'I think of them,' Santo said. 'Now I must go to Fauchon for some pleasantries. Saturday night at nine, and bring your *pots*!'

Chapter 12

I had forgotten to tell Santo that the bronze castings for his engines had come in that morning, and the drays were taking them over to his place.

I put on a dressing-gown and went up to the roof, across my garden to his, and down the stairs to the top floor, where candles sent long lights across the waxed parquet.

A door was open and I looked in.

She was incomparably the loveliest woman I had ever seen or so much as dreamed of, long legs, Eve's own rump and thighs, a waist I could span, and when she turned, the breasts of Hebe and the face, I suppose, of Aphrodite. But her maid saw me, and flew to slam the door.

I went back up the stairs, simply blank with wonder. Why had Tanzi not told me about a woman in the house – and such a woman! – or said a word to Lucien and obviously he would have retailed it as prime gossip, or had she been warned to say nothing? But why? It was perfectly normal for a man to have a mistress, especially when he was un-married and with an apartment discreetly central where no-body would be noticed coming or going. I assumed she had the top level which had a reception room, bedroom, bath and maid's room, though why she was up there and not in the master bedroom on the floor below made something of a puzzle. Did he like to visit her in her bedroom, or did she come to his? I realized I was thinking as an old crone tattle-tale and wiped my mind of it.

But it niggled.

At a few minutes after the half-hour, I went down to the street, and Tanzi let me in at Number 9 among a few people I have never met. Santo waited upstairs and I was intro-duced, but I have never been able to collect names and people, and so they were forgotten as soon as breath cooled. All the princes and barons were there, and more came in. A small orchestra played in the corner, and in the next room a long buffet, magnificently arranged by Fouquet's, challenged the trouser band, and a troop of waiters went about filling glasses. Yellow roses, never my favourite blossom, lit the rooms in baskets everywhere, and I thought I saw why in a sudden silence and a general turn towards the door.

Santo kissed the hand of my naked vision, now in satin the colour of the roses, with a narrow black ruffle around the corsage and a wider ruffle around the hem of the skirt. Vision is not too strong a word. A rosebud was stuck in the thick bun on top of her head, diamond earrings and a diamond necklace flashed prisms, but no rings on either hand, and no bracelets.

Beauty almost unadorned.

Gradually talk became louder as more guests crowded to be introduced, but I held back. I was in no hurry, chiefly because I feared she had seen me and I was most unanxious to be identified in front of Santo as a peeping Tom. In any event, after a couple of goblets of champagne cup, he led her over to me, and from the smile either she had forgiven me or I had been too quick up the stairs.

'Robert, I would like to make a special introduction. I present an American friend of my family, Maria Gioia Figueredo de Oliviera, but everybody calls her Gioia, and in English, that's Joy, and that's what she is, a joy!'

'I'm inclined to agree with you,' I said, thinking of her in candlelit nudity. 'Why have you been hiding such a treasure?'

'Her chaperone was taken ill. She could hardly stay in the hotel by herself, so I said come and stay with me. The entire floor is hers, she has her maid, and there's a real termagant on the door. She's happy with us, aren't you, Gioia?'

'I am in Paris, and I love every moment, and I am in love with my little man,' she said, in a voice that instantly struck me as being akin to scarlet velvet, contralto, with a crust on the edge, a blessing on the ear, beautiful. 'You are Rob-a-dee-Bob, the friend he speaks about so much. It's wonderful to have a friend to honour in trust. He tells me you have a lovely place in the country?'

'Please go down at any time. It'll be glorious for the next three months. Then we harvest the grapes. You'll have a special little house of your own. It was my mother's. Where she retired to be out of the way of us children. We were too noisy!'

'Were there many of you?'

'Eight. Her three and my uncle's five. He died, and she went shortly after. Now everybody's gone except me.'

'It's lonely for you?'

'Absolutely not. There's nothing I value more than silence. The privilege of being alone. Unless with a friend.'

'Or someone to love?'

I looked at those clear eyes, and nodded.

'But where is she to be found?' I asked her. 'One doesn't marry for five minutes. It's a matter of companionship, too. A life!'

'I believe that absolutely,' she said, or perhaps breathed, looking at Santo. 'Don't you?'

'I think it's far too serious a matter to be considered without a great deal of thought, and I mean, a great deal,' he said, down at the goblet. 'It's grossly tempting to think about, especially the hours one might enjoy along the lonely stretches. Scratching for an idea, for example. They can be very lonely hours. Somebody to talk to about anything at all can rest the mind. But then, I have to think again. I can vanish from the scene at the breaking of a strut. A small damage to the wing. I haven't the right, I think, to marry. That thought would be a burden to my wife, but I wouldn't stop flying for any reason, certainly not the sentimental. It would carry no weight with me. That would be unfair to my wife. Unjust. She'd have every reason to leave me. What sort of marriage would that be? A state of constant tension. Mental discomfort. Resentment. For me, the idea is not to be considered. I need every sense intact, without side issues to worry about, or anything really to think about except the work to be done. What's that English word? It combines work with responsibility?'

'Onerous?' I hazarded, but he shook his head.

'No, it's shorter,' he said. 'A *little* word.'

'For a little *man*,' she said, looking a him with what I thought were the very eyes of love, and of course, Santo was not the least lovable of men. 'But while so many of us pray for you, how *can* anything happen to you?'

'Mechanics and air currents, I fear, take little notice of

prayers,' Santo said. 'I often go to church because I feel I have a sort of bargain. So long as I do what I conceive to be my duty. When I default for any reason, then I believe I may expect disaster of one kind or another. The only time I approached it was when I came down in the Trocadero. I should have been killed. I wasn't, though. I ought to have taken the larger ship. Against better judgement I took the smaller. The winds were too strong for her. I knew before I started I was asking for trouble. There's an instinct in these matters. Or as some have told me, a psychic sense!'

He pointed an index at me.

'*Task!*' he trumpeted. 'That's the word I wanted. Short and sweet, as you say in English. A duty to be performed responsibly!'

'To the exclusion of all other facts and fancies, including the feelings of those nearest you?' Gioia said, picking up a black ostrich feather fan and a jet handbag. 'I've greatly enjoyed the party, among other reasons because it was so different from those we give at home. We haven't any princes and barons. Certainly not a Fouquet's. I must go and have another mousse of smoked salmon *vol-au-vent*. Wonderful. And another goblet of champagne. I shall get drunk!'

'Your maid and my two should take care of that,' Santo said. 'Don't go yet. Please. You decorate the place. Everything you touch you charm. Stay!'

She shrugged a beautiful chin-on-shoulder smile.

'Who could resist an invitation so passionately expressed?' she whispered, mouth almost at his ear. 'I notice you don't offer to accompany me?'

He smiled at her.

'As far as the staircase,' he said, smiling that blank Brazilian face, of the stone eyes, so that none knew what he thought.

I felt I was rather more than extraneous, and so I drifted behind until I could leave them without saying goodbyes, made a way through the crush towards the door, and met Colonel Ferber.

'Ah, Robert!' he said, in an embrace. 'Would you care to entertain an assortment of pickelhaubs tomorrow? My aide couldn't get you this evening. I see why, now. They're the newly-formed German air staff, and I want to be fair with them, and I thought a visit to your place to show them the rudiments of the job would be a merest courtesy. I doubt they have anything like your connection, and so there could be some good business for you. I think you deserve it, mh?'

'Very kind of you,' I said, thinking of the assault on my champagne. 'Three, four o'clock?'

'Make it four. They'll be lunching till three. Takes time to get to your place. If we're a little late, do please forgive me!'

'Take your time. I'm always there till seven, anyway.'

'What do you hear of Madame Dufresne?'

The change in tone set me back. A military interrogator?

'Last I heard she was at home and recovering. She expects to be with us on Monday week. I understand Santo gave her a lump sum to heal the injuries and she isn't likely to suffer any after-effects. Why?'

'Something rather serious from the reports I'm getting. Did you know she has three bank accounts outside France? I know the salary she earns. I know what her husband left her, and the value of the property left to her by her father. It doesn't explain the almost three hundred thousand francs in various banks thoughout France!'

'The sum Santo paid her?'

'That's an addition. Of little consequence. You have no knowledge?'

'None,' I said, feeling a little ill. 'She certainly never got anything like that all the time she's been with me.'

I was remembering a third-class ticket and a two-and-a-half day train journey on a hard seat, and sandwiches.

'It's a mystery we have to solve,' he said. 'A woman in such a sensitive position must be carefully scrutinized. She knows the supply position, the companies, prices, quantities. Let's have a drink!'

I felt a champagne cocktail would do some good, and went with him to the buffet, but it had no taste. The Dufresne threat soured my palate because, of course, I was involved. If she had done anything wrong, then I should have known and reported. I was thankful she had not visited the farm, and then cursed myself for a lout, ungrateful, stupidly thoughtless.

'If there's any trouble, I shall do my best to protect her,' I said. 'She's always been a first-class colleague. I've never had the slightest cause to distrust her. I find it impossible to consider that she could be what you suspect!'

He looked at me with a soldier's grey eye that can, indeed, strike fear.

'I have had occasion to say this to you before,' he said. 'I repeat that she is the type the other side is most likely to recruit. Very respectable, well-thought of, staunch friends, good family, and the rest. The rot can start there. We have to root it out. I hope I may count on your help?'

'Miserably, yes,' I said.

'I understand your feeling. I assure you I sympathize. But sympathy and duty are two quite different matters. They cancel. What's left is adamantine and not to be penetrated by any gentle feeling. If that woman is guilty of what is suspected, she will be put on trial. I hope that you will not interfere. It could have the most serious consequences. For *you*!'

I walked about in my place for most of the night. That talk under the brouhaha of the bar, those whispers of such horrifying substance, almost deprived me of the strength to think. I could only imagine Mme Dufresne in military custody. And, as a corollary, myself immediately behind. Certainly I could not be a useful witness. I knew nothing. I was surprised to find myself a weakling, afraid of any form of interrogation, skulking behind a barrier of ignorance. But ignorant was exactly what I had been and still was, and for all the thought I could not be less.

Mme Dufresne left her desk, so far as I knew, and went home, and came in with the church bells on the following morning while the cows were taken out to pasture and those going to Mass filed to the church postern. Every day for six days a week. What possible harm could she do?

In a fit of rage I consigned all the Colonel Ferbers to the devil, and had a hot bath, a stiff Scotch, and got into bed and slept until Lucien woke me with coffee and croissants at six o'clock, and I told him to go to hell and slept until after midday, the most sensible thing I ever did.

Chapter 13

At 3.40, a fleet of black Panhards stopped at the door and I went down to meet grey overcoats, though I could see flashing pickelhaubs, with Colonel Ferber in pale blue and gold braid leading the procession of moustaches curling over brass chinstraps, and we started through the main floor, of metals, engine parts, and all the bins of spares, out to the wings and struts, on to the bodies being assembled, and out to the wings being stretched.

'I'm a little confused,' a general said to me, in the most excellent English. 'I was told that all the assembling is done at the Santos hangar. Apparently it's done here. Any reason?'

'The best,' I said. 'All the rough work is done here. The castings, mouldings, sewing of wing material, and various smaller jobs are done here. At the other hangar, the refinements are made. You note that our struts and tubing are rough-cast. That will be rectified by his mechanics. The drays come at five every night and they take the finished material over there. It works very well.'

'It would work much better if the two places were together?'

'Obviously. But this is a private company. Mine. Santo now has Government backing. He will be able to build as he wishes. With, of course, the sanction of the Air Minister and Colonel Ferber.'

'You planned most of this?'

'All of it. I permit nobody to interfere in my business. It is more than two hundred years old.'

'Fortunate man,' the General said. 'Colonel Ferber said you might consider working for us in an advisory capacity. The terms will be agreed. Will you be accompanying him on the German tour?'

'I shall hope to be there on odd days. I have to supervise the transport of spare engines, and so on. There's a great deal of work to do. We shall require plenty of labour!'

Colonel-General von der Haltz looked up at the roof and laughed, waving white gloves.

'That's your smallest preoccupation,' he said. 'We are more than impatient to begin work. Before the fine flying weather begins we want to gather all we need, with an eye on the years to come. Have you any advice?'

'I have good friends at Krupp,' I said. 'You'll find I've told them to experiment with light, strong metals. You could press the question.'

'Excellent!'

'And please join me in a tulip of champagne?'

'May I ask, why do you call it a tulip?'

'It's shaped like one. It holds the bouquet and the liveliness better than the vulgar restaurant open shape that wastes both. For the same reason, a sherry glass is called a thistle. That's its shape and it holds the bouquet far better than any ordinary glass.'

'We have a preference for schnapps,' he said, and turned to point at Branault drilling brass rod-heads. 'What are those for?'

'It's part of an attachment for the petrol tank. They have to be strong. But it's that sort of weight that Santo is trying to scale down with lighter metals of greater tensile strength. And that's the great difficulty. Companies won't undertake costly experiments without being able to see a fair profit. Santo is only one. When there are thirty or forty machines to be made, then I predict an enormous rise in competition, and of course, quality.'

'Have you any idea how many the French are thinking of ordering, by any chance?'

Cunning old dog!

'I'm not in Colonel Ferber's confidence, unfortunately,' I said as if it were no matter. 'I am a source of supply, that's all. I've had no advance orders for any more supplies than in the past when Santo built balloons and started the Demoiselle project. He was always extremely conservative, and I never tried to dominate the market. I never had the power.'

'I think that you will,' he said. 'I would like to put at least three of my men to learn from one of yours. The essentials of the work involved. You will of course receive a generous fee for each man. I would like to think I had an efficient staff to begin our air force. Supplies are essential, and you have the monopoly. So much I have found out. I may say I have made rigorous enquiry. You are known to be honest, dependable and, in short, a man of your word. I would like to come here on Monday next with a series of contracts. May I rely upon your help and possible agreement?'

'Sir, we commerciants have a saying,' I said. 'Business is business. That is the be-all and the end-all. I shall welcome you on Monday. At what time?'

'I invite you to luncheon at the Restaurant von Klüg, which we use as our Regimental Mess. We can then discuss business upstairs. If that is satisfactory? A car will arrive before noon. I cannot give a more exact time because those damned cattle on these roads can stop traffic for ten minutes at a time. And not once. *Pazienza!*'

'An Italian expression?'

'I was Military Attaché in Rome for five years. I loved it!'

'I love Italy, too. The country, the people and the food. Always have. I think it isn't wrong to confuse people with food. Food is what people are. Their love of life is expressed in a platter. Their artistry in the taste. A sweet belly is a human gift they make for themselves!'

'I think you will not find our German cuisine any less,' he said. 'It is settled?'

'Settled!'

I told Colonel Ferber of that talk, and he listened to the end and looked away, and I saw he was far from pleased.

'You'll give me all details, of course,' he said. 'And for every three men of his, I'll have six of mine!'

'That will create a small chaos,' I said, thinking of a crowd at every workplace. 'Why not one for one?'

'It's not a military solution. Two to one is superiority. Three to one is victory. That's all!'

It was.

And so on Monday I had nine men grouped about every one of mine, three in invisible German uniforms and six in French, and I was quite pleased to see the Lieutenant of Zouaves in a plain soldier's garb. He looked at me, and I looked at him, and neither of us smiled, said a word, or blinked. But we knew. I had no doubt that the Germans were also officers. There was some further awareness about all of them, nothing of the bucolic, but that air which tells of education beyond the norm, of a family life, of a certain standard of behaviour, a social attitude, all summed in a self-awareness of superiority that, although I wanted to, I was unable to see or to give myself any rational explanation for.

The fact is that after a couple of hours of strolling from one group to the other, I had further information for Colonel Ferber. The Germans were superior, whether in taking notes and making sketches or in strict watching, in their constant questions, in their insistence on doing what was being shown, or quarrelling with their instructors when they were denied. The French were gentler, though I doubted they were less intelligent, yes, I doubted very much, as I told Colonel Ferber when he came in time for coffee.

'You guessed it?' he said, laughing. 'Naturally I picked the best. Those who'll be the first pilots. I told them to hold back. Watch the men who'll be our rivals. Let *them* ask the questions. You have the advantage of the answers without effort. Let *them* make the running. Then? *You* take first place!'

I had a small space of doubt.

The Germans, it seemed to me, were so much more dedicated, more intent, even vulpine, in their desire to learn. The French was so much gentler, but their questions, rarely made, were, I thought more intelligent. For example, when one lad asked why, if bamboo was used in the frame, a metal of the weight of bamboo was not used in its place, Grillot, the workman, looked up.

'For the same reason that raspberries are not strawberries,' he said. 'There is a difference. All you have to do is to find it!'

From that moment, that lad was called Raspberry. But he was a smart one, and I had no doubt he would make his way.

I lunched at the Von Klüg restaurant, and it was very good, with excellent sausage and veal and a table of wonderful desserts, and I saw why the officers wore corsets to hide the fat, and we began the discussion on what was wanted. In that bare upstairs room, over brandy and cigars,

I was appalled to find that Colonel-General von der Haltz wanted five times more than Colonel Ferber over one year, and ten times more in the second.

I said nothing. I agreed and signed, and I was taken back to my place, and a splendid party being given by Santo for the children of the village, not really on my place but on the broad space in front.

'We had so little time to plan it,' he said. 'Gioia wanted it, and she's going home. I thought you wouldn't mind?'

'Of course not. The place needed livening up. By all means. Have you enough food?'

'My old friend in the village, the pirate cook, he's put out the work of a lifetime. These children are going home stuffed. I'm also going to give them all a ride in a balloon!'

'Children? Great God, is that safe?'

'Perfectly. I shall be holding the rope!'

There, I realized I had the secret of the safety of Santo. Always on his public balloon voyages he had trailed a long rope that reached to the ground, and he never went above the height of its length. Somebody was always near to give it a pull and bring him down to what he thought was a proper height, and the balloon behaved as he had once called it, a gentle mare. I told him nothing of my talk with Colonel-General von der Haltz, and our contracts. I thought it better that Colonel Ferber should tell him. I was perfectly certain that the French requirement would be considerably more.

I was not wrong, and I was made aware of a real Colonel's temper, of the sort we read about but rarely see. He shouted his face red and suddenly he was pale and calm, but it was a calm of rage and I sat quiet, looking out of the window.

'You've done me a great service, *for* me, I mean, but a far greater service for France, and I shan't forget it,' he said, as if remarking on the weather. 'Now, have I permission to use this telephone? And may I, as an additional great favour, ask you to leave the office? I shall talk to the Minister!'

I was half out of the room before he finished.

'I shall be downstairs,' I said. 'Everything is sound-proof and the staff has gone for the day.'

The warehouse seemed to eat its silence, but the packing

shed held whispers and scurries of our cats after the mice. For the plates of chopped liver and scraps from the canteen, those mousers must have saved me thousands in keeping mice and rats out of the raw silk, to start with. Tushki, Miklo, Fatti, and Chunko were all big toms I had brought back from St Petersburg a couple of years before Santo started ordering from me. They were all about twelve years old, and I had to begin thinking of their replacements, which gave me no pleasure but a sense of guilt, especially when at my whistle they came in a scampering MIAOUUU! because they knew I was going to open the canteen bar to get them a strip of red steak each, and they sat while I carved, and jumped when I threw, but none tried to steal his neighbour's piece. They were so good-mannered and lovable, and they rubbed their heads against my ankles to thank me, making me feel an utter cur to think of them gone. But I had to. That was the tragedy. They had a Siamese mask and a Siberian body, big, furry, with odd markings. They were the especial pets of Mme Dufresne, and again I was brought to think of her.

Poor girl. Suspicions. No proof, I made up my mind to have the entire matter in the open, face to face, and damn everybody.

Colonel Ferber came down and I went with him to the car.

'I'll call you in the morning,' he said. 'You'll probably be wanted for an interview with the Minister, or perhaps someone rather more important. At any rate, it's realized you've rendered an important service to the country. You will be suitably rewarded, I assure you!'

'Do you advise me to continue with the German project?'

'Obviously. You are the chief source of our information. What you have are the facts. We want to know every detail. You will supply us, no?'

'To the best of my ability.'

Colonel Ferber smiled, putting on the gold-braided kepi.

'You won't suffer,' he said. 'Tomorrow you'll have an order for supplies that'll make this look like an attenuated cowshed. The Germans want five times? We require twenty. You'd better make plans!'

I saw him to the car, and went back in the company of

cats, and cut them another strip, with more MIAOUUU! and I was ruffling their heads when I heard the unmistakable sound of the Panhard, which had a certain voice that could only be Santo and his mechanics.

He came in with Gioia, superb in a reddish tailleur and a small reddish hat with a half-veil, long button boots, a reddish parasol, and a gold mesh bag, an extravagant dream of Eve, and only beautiful.

'We came out to take you to dinner,' he said, in what I thought was a curiously deflated voice, quite different from his normal boss's tenor. 'Gioia insisted because you might have the answers. But I hope it won't go any further!'

'You wish to scandalize me?' I said. 'Good God, when have I repeated anything you've ever said to me?'

'I *told* you!' Gioia said, and tapped him on the shoulder with the parasol. 'He's a *friend* of yours. Why should he be less?'

'Let's drink some champagne,' I said, leading the way upstairs. 'Is this something serious?'

'Extremely so,' Santo said. 'I am asked to refuse the German cross-country flight. Should I?'

'You'd be stupid if you did.'

'Why?'

'You have a name. A reputation. Worldwide. What would permit you to ignore a contract? Bring your name into disgrace? Imagine the papers. They're wolves only waiting to rend flesh. Is that what you want?'

'That's what I've been telling him,' Gioia said, with a hand on his knee. 'He must think of himself. Never mind France. The only reason France is on the map is because of him. And if the Russians want the flight to continue, then go. If *anyone* wants it, go. My *little* man will be a giant wherever he goes!'

'True,' I said, and gave them both a tulip. 'For absolutely no reason at all should you consider the cancellation of any contract now in being, or projected for the future. You are Santos-Dumont. You are a Brazilian. You owe no allegiance elsewhere. You are both pioneer and pathfinder. You are a magnificent part of history. I am honoured to have helped you. Am I such a fool as to give you wrong advice? Perfectly true, you have helped me in business terms. I am quite prepared to give the whole aerial side into other hands for *nothing*. I can exist without it. But you can't. You understand that? If you go back on what you have signed, what is the worth of the Brazilian word? Have others thought of that? Have you?'

Gioia looked at him in a smile, a real joy.

'You see?' she said, in that voice. 'I told you. I was certain he would support me. Of course you will make the overland flights. Who else could? Who has the experience and the Demoiselles? Who else has a Rob-a-dee-Bob?'

He smiled at her, at me, and I seemed to find a new Santo, gentler, more sure of himself, and certainly utterly and abandonedly in love with her, and I had nothing but sympathy.

I was in raging and blasting love with her, and thinking of it I found myself laughable. A rival to Santo?

What nonsense!

Chapter 14

In the weeks after Gioia went home, I had too much to do to be able to think of myself, and Santo was having the devil of a job with his German flights.

The planning was meticulous. The first time I went into the German map room to be shown where stores and supplies of petrol were to be taken, I had a sinking of the heart. The other map room, on the French side, was not anywhere near so perfect. Everything was down to the millimetre. Nothing I wanted was not to be got. Transport, labour, and even lodgings for my men were on sheets, in a, b, c style, and nothing ever went wrong. On the French side there was always a delightfully stifled confusion. Nothing went quite right, but it got done, and that was an end of it.

The flights in Germany were complicated because of the mountains, and so the route was designed to avoid them, and I admired how the Germans had zig-zagged, so that when Santo made a really long flight, he would perhaps be no further than where he had begun the flight, but he was clear of the mountains on the following day. It was an exhausting tour under conditions of absolute secrecy. Any stranger found in line of flight was bundled out, and that was probably how the newspapers never got a whisper. Few, of course, ever came to see me, and the two men I interviewed in those months got nothing from me except a mug of coffee. I had no notion of where he was until I was called by the Ministry, and I was never told where to go. I was taken there, lodged until my work was done, and taken back.

Santo was idolized. There is no other word. When he came in the Mess, all the officers stood, and they sat only when he did. I had a case of champagne taken up by train, with a small barrel of cognac, and he never drank anything else. I was proud that he always carried the silver flask given him by Gioia filled with my cognac. It was from my Grandfather's time, and incomparably the best of all.

I had problems beyond any I had ever known. My business had grown to eight times its former size and it was going to twenty times before the end of the year, as I could see, because in addition to the German demands, the French insisted on being ahead, but other nations were as demanding, and the new petrol-engine trucks helped, so much faster than the drays, although I regretted having to put my teams of Percherons to grass, even if they did a perfectly good job on the farms.

One of my problems was Mme Dufresne.

I had my interview with her, and she denied any link with a foreign government, and said, showing me the folios, that the foreign accounts had been the property of her husband, a stockbroker, and she had let them gather interest. The accounts in France had been her father's, and after the Franco-Prussian war, he had spread his money wherever he thought fit, and she had never seen any reason to change them. Aunts had left her properties, and a grandmother had given her the château owned by the family since the sixteenth century.

I was not part of an inquisition. She had the papers in perfect order, and I had nothing more to say. She was a wonderful right-hand at that time and got through as much work as I did, or more, and found the most excellent women

72

to join our staff. I was perfectly satisfied.

But the Colonel, now a General, was not, and every time he came to the office he bothered me about her but I laughed him off.

'I've been allowed to examine her affairs and I'm certain there's no hidden link anywhere,' I told him that late afternoon. 'I'm certainly not going to discharge an absolutely first-rate colleague to satisfy vague doubts.'

'Vague?' he said, elbow on desk, fingers across chin, looking at me sideways in grey glint. 'One of these days I'll send a squad here with a warrant, and you'll be in a peculiar position!'

'Tell me what you suspect!'

'I cannot, and you know it perfectly well. But I can give you some items you may find of interest. Did Santo ever take out a patent on any of his inventions?'

'Never to my knowledge. I've often advised him to do so. If only to protect his work. But he said it was for mankind and everyone could use it. I thought that flummery and said so. It didn't shift him. He's the only true idealist I've ever met. We could do with a few more, God knows!'

'And only God knows how the rest of us would get along. That woman out there is a large shareholder in an engineering company. In recent weeks they've taken out several patents on many of the inventions made by Santo himself, by handtooling. Where did they get them from?'

'I fear I can't help you.'

'You see? The drawings they submitted were an exact copy of Santo's own, replete with his notes. Every single line. How were they got?'

'Certainly not from this office. Nothing of that sort was ever done here. All that sort of work and, so far as I know, the drawings, were all done next door. His own place. The hangar. I doubt if the drawings were ever in the office!'

'Did you know that the chairman of that engineering company has been her lover for the past few years?'

'I have no knowledge of her private life.'

'Pity!'

'I have never interfered in the personal life of any member of my staff. It's not my intention to start. Had you that idea?'

'Not particularly. But you might start thinking about defending yourself. Remember that all the inventions of Santos-Dumont are the property of the French Government. We are jealous of our rights. We have quashed those patents. When we find out how those drawings and other papers were obtained, we shall prosecute. Do you see?'

'I don't think you're in a very strong position, that's to say, legally. And I shall make it clear that I believe Santo will be furious. Madame Dufresne spent more time on his affairs than on mine. Or let us say that his affairs in France were entirely mine. As they are now, in Germany. Everything he needs comes through this office. There isn't anything he does for himself except fly, and that's made possible by the work of Madame Dufresne among others. She's been a good and faithful colleague for many years, and I shall defend her to the last ditch. I hope that's clear?'

'You may regret it. I shall not be able to help you!'

'I'm grateful for your warning, and for the thought behind it. I shall have Madame Dufresne in this office, and I shall repeat your charges if so they may be called?'

'I shall be glad to hear her reply,' General Ferber said. 'I'll be in Paris tomorrow. Would you please telephone?'

'Be certain of it. Santo will be here, weather behaving itself, at about the end of the week. He should have plenty to tell you!'

'I doubt it,' he said, sour as crab-apple. 'I am well-informed!'

He left not in the best of tempers, but we were still friends and I really was grateful for his warning. It is certainly not the happiest idea that a Government can throw its legal weight at you. Not only is a great deal of money involved, but lawyers are notoriously incapable of ending a case giving them profit. The mere bloodsucker is an amateur.

Mme Dufresne had gone, but I left a note asking her to see me at noon after the morning mail had been dealt with, and I went home in the green Adams, a good solid car speeding at thirty miles an hour, and the fright of everybody along the way. How we love showing off!

The evening was brightened by a letter from Gioia, writing to tell me that she would be back by the *Lusitania* on the 27th, and she wanted to give a dinner party for 'my *little*

74

man!' and hoped I would attend, and every day away from him was a desert gap nothing could fill. And could I bring a nice girl?

I liked that word. 'Nice' was not the word to describe Solange, exactly, because she was mistress of a dozen or more of us, but in my eyes infinitely preferable to the stuffed bags so full of virtue on all sides. And I questioned the virtue. I had knowledge. I had almost married twice. Each time I caught them fiddle-diddling, and saw their fathers with naturally lamentable results, and that sort of word spreads, and presently I had no houses to visit and no friends among any of them, or at any rate very few, and they were not enthusiasts and neither was I. If I thought of marriage after that it was in terms of someone to go home to, but I had seen none except Gioia, and she was beyond reach. As well, perhaps.

I had to go to the Bank of France next morning to sign a draft from Santo, and another from the Air Ministry, the first, and for a large amount. Figures had to be checked, verified, and finally, when it was over, I took M le Directeur for a drink, and got back to my place a little after twelve.

Miss Zuccione came in with her notebook and looked at me with enormous black cherry eyes from behind thick lenses.

'Sir,' she began, hesitantly. 'The entire contents of Madame Dufresne's desk had been piled on mine this morning. Her desk is clear, and all the drawers. This envelope was left for you!'

I thought of General Ferber, used the paper-knife, took out a single page, read three lines, and put the page down.

'Because of personal reasons, Madame Dufresne has had to leave for Switzerland. In all probability she will not return. Are you capable of taking her place?'

'I'm sure I am!'

'Go to the cashier and adopt Madame Dufresne's salary and emoluments from this morning. If I find you satisfactory, very well. If not, I shall advertise for someone else. Understood?'

'Thank you, sir.'

A nice girl, but I wondered if she had the brain for the job.

I picked up the telephone to call General Ferber, and waited, thinking that Mme Dufresne must have come back to the office after I had gone, because her desk had been in order of business when I left. That was a sad thought. She must have had a second set of keys, which, unfortunately, I knew nothing about. She had no permission to copy mine. When would she have had the opportunity? I could think of none.

General Ferber seemed to know what I had to tell him.

'A very sly fish,' he said, almost with a laugh in his voice. 'You know also that two of your night guards have – shall we say – vanished? That's obviously how she got in without an alarm. Sly as a misbred cat. However, she's gone, and she dare not come back. The people you have now are superior and infinitely to be trusted.'

'But she chose them!'

'To the contrary. She was given their names by the University Agency. *I* chose them, and they've filed reports ever since. The same with the team accompanying Santo. They are *my* people. By the way, I know that Santo has a new and much more powerful engine. The supplies and parts went through you?'

'So far as I know.'

'I never had those reports. I was surprised. Perhaps you are?'

'Extremely so. Send a messenger, and you'll have them in an hour.'

'Good. And thank you. I no longer have doubts about you!'

A hell of a fine thing to say, and I was angered further by his patronage. I had no reverence for the Army. Both my Grandfather and my Father had never had any more than contempt for them after the Franco-Prussian War and the defeat of 1870. I had not been born, but I had listened to it through my boyhood and it left memories. I had a distinct feeling I wanted to resign all the air nonsense and simply go on with what was left. After all, it was plenty.

The messenger came, I insisted he produce evidence of identity, and he looked at me as if I challenged the validity of his parentage. Miss Zuccione took his name and number to telephone General Ferber, and came back to say that yes, the Sergeant was the messenger, and that I was to be complimented on exemplary caution.

To the Devil in Hell.

The day was made when I got a telegram from Santo sent from Berlin, telling me that the *Lusitania* was docking at Le Havre on the 27th and to meet her because he was in bed nursing a bronchitis caught by flying through snow and he would be with us in three or four days and to take greatest care of her, and prevent any attempt to visit him, and all compliments.

Liners can be three or four hours early or late, and I asked Miss Zuccione to make reservations for the early train, with a parlour, and to telegraph Le Havre for a suite for that day at, of course, the best hotel.

Everything went as it should, and I took a fiacre from the Le Havre depot to the docks, but the *Lusitania* was not yet in sight, and I went back to the hotel and went to sleep with a hot cognac.

The *Lusitania* came, a marvellous sight, white paintwork, scarlet funnels, pushed and pulled by tugs, and up there, in pale blue, waving long black gloves, Gioia with a chorus of officers and others, damn them. But I met her at the gangway, and we were off in the hotel coach, a venerable affair of white enamel and varnish, and she fell back in the deep cushions, and puffed to blow out the veil.

'Well, and what of my *little* man?' she demanded, taking my hand. 'Why isn't he here?'

I gave her the telgram, and she read, and the hand fell on her knee.

'Of course I must go to him!' she said angrily. 'But now. Immediately!'

'Where will you go?'

'To Berlin, naturally!'

'What good will it do? Which department would you consult? Do you suppose they'll give you information which is obviously held to be secret? He may be anywhere in Germany. Probably near the town of his last flight. Let's go to Paris, and I'll see what I can do. We'll go to the apartment, and by the time you've made everything to your liking, I'll be back with the answer. But I don't hold out much hope. Germans are notoriously secretive. Didn't you know?'

'I want to know where he is!'

'So do many others. For other reasons. Where is he? That's giving the game away. It'll be known how far he's flown and in how many days. It doesn't appeal to the military mind. They have the master hand and there's nothing anyone can do. How do you think Santo feels? Unable to meet you? I feel sorry for his nurses!'

'I hate them. Great lumbering blondes, thick legs, thick thighs, pumpkin busts, they'll go mad for him, so small and delicate, gentle, brave, a modern Siegfried, the most lovely hero. What will they leave of him for *me*?'

'If I know him, they won't get anywhere near. He'll be very rude. In his own language. Portuguese. Very funny to hear, but there's no mistaking the meaning!'

'*I want to know where he is!*'

An idea came into mind.

'You have as many influential friends as I have,' I said, in pretence of disinterest. 'In addition, you have beauty, and the attraction of the Garden and the Apple. Which of all the many Adams could deny you? Seeing you, listening to you. Who?'

I saw her teeth smiling through the veil.

'*You!*' she said, in a sigh, or that was how it sounded. 'You have listened to me, and you've seen more of me than any of them can ever hope for. Haven't you?'

The maid must have told her, and I felt the blush heating.

'An accident,' I said. 'But not an error!'

She laughed, to my desperate ears, a lovely sound.

'How did you know?' I asked. 'Were you told?'

'No. My maid said a man was standing in the corridor and she shut the door. I'd opened it to cool down after a hot bath. And when I met Santo and he introduced us, I saw it in your eyes. I so wanted to laugh. You looked like the monk caught in a guilty act. It was so funny, but I couldn't say anything in front of Santo and cause trouble between you.'

'That was thoughtful of you!'

'Listen to me. If I ask favours of my "influential" friends, I know them well enough to be more than certain they'll require particular favours, and we shan't go into it. I have never been married. I have never had a lover. Santo is my only love. My *little* man. I must go to him. Rob-a-dee-Bob, if you will find out where he is so that I may go to him, I will undress for you and you shall do as you will. I know what to expect from you. From any of the others, what? Gossip? Bragging? And my name?'

I took her hand. Any thought of doing as she suggested was a wound. I could never look Santo in the eye again. The notion was ruin.

'Trust me to find out where he is,' I said. 'As for reward, it will be enough that you offered yourself. I prize that above every other wonderful experience in my life. Here we are. Go up and have a rest. We leave for Paris in the morning. Do you wish to dine alone?'

'I want nothing to eat. You are a true friend. Until the morning. Good night!'

Chapter 15

But it was far more difficult than I had imagined, and I knew it would be difficult enough. I was passed from aide to aide but finally, by sheer persistence of Miss Zuccione, in late afternoon I reached General Ferber, and he was far from pleased.

'What the devil are you worrying for?' he shouted. 'You know perfectly well that his whereabouts is not for publication?'

'It's not for publication. A woman loves him, and she wants to go to him. Anything wrong with that?'

'Is this the woman you met at the *Lusitania*'s docking?'

'It is.'

'She is American?'

'What about it?'

'They claim they have a flight before his!'

'Well? By what he's done, he is infinitely in advance. Give this girl the opportunity of going to his bedside. He has a serious illness. She is terribly worried. Don't you know anything about a woman in love?'

'We do not deal with sentiments!'

'You may have to deal with the American Ambassador!'

'You would not dare to approach him?'

'No. But she would. And remember, her father is an enormous power in the railroad industry and everything pertaining to it. General, I do not speak without reason. She is a woman used, in a word, to being herself. She is her*self*. You understand?'

'We cannot always have our own way. This is a matter of our national interest!'

'She thinks of a man in *her* interest!'

'Decisions cannot be made for sentimental reasons, you know that?'

'Then they may be decided by the Ambassadors of the United States and of Brazil in an approach to your President? This is a matter of allowing a woman in love to go to the bedside of the man she is willing to make any sacrifice for. Do you deny her? She is not the type. I warn you. There is the press. The woman yearning after the man she loves is a beautiful story the press will gobble for days. You should think about it!'

I won.

About two hours after my call, Miss Zuccione came in, put the tip of her mid-finger on my desk, and smiled at me.

'General Ferber presents his compliments, sir, and asks that the lady is ready at ten o'clock tomorrow morning to be taken to the Gare du Nord. She will then be taken by train to a destination which will not be mentioned. You are asked to convey this to her, but nothing will be said to anyone else in her, or in your, household. Is that clear?'

'Please thank the General. The message is clear and will be adhered to. Would you please call Guillaume to take me back to the rue Washington.'

I took Tanzi by her black scarf, poor old girl, right out of her watchman's chair.

'Listen to me,' I said, close to her face. 'Mademoiselle Gioia is leaving tomorrow morning to see her Santo. You will not see her. You will not know she has gone, or when she will be back, because so far as you know she is out shopping, or staying with friends in the country, or upstairs, or minding her own business. You have nothing to say to any fool on earth. Good?'

'I will give her a little bunch of wildflowers and sweet herbs,' she whispered. 'He always loved them. I may?'

I put a hand on her cheek.

'Apart from that, silence!'

I went upstairs, and her maid admitted me.

That reception room was so deliciously feminine that I almost melted to a glob. There were such flowers, in baskets and vases, of such colour and scent that one imagined oneself in an anteroom to a boudoir. Ah yes, and why not?

She came in a beautiful peignoir of deep blue velvet and slippers of scarlet sequins, really a glory, and I kissed her hand.

'We vanquished him!' I said. 'You will be ready at ten in the morning and you will be taken to the Gare du Nord, but you will not be told where you are going, and neither will you ask. From then until you get back here you will ask no questions. You will not know where you have been, and so you won't be able to tell anybody. If anybody should ask, you have been here in Paris. That's all!'

'Ah, you are a marvellous man!' she said, a goddess. 'It isn't all. I pay my debt to someone I trust. Here!'

Her hands flipped aside the belt and the peignoir fell and she was herself, Eve in palest alabaster.

'What do you want to do?' she whispered. 'You have earned your reward. What?'

What indeed, and I had to think.

I knew what I wanted to do.

But I still had to look Santo in the eye.

'Most beautiful, you know that I love you,' I said. 'But I have a loyalty to Santo. He is a man of honour. I hope to be his equal. It would be too easy to take advantage of your generosity. And what? A few minutes? An exquisite hour? All night? A glory never to be repeated? What would he say? He would see it in our faces. He would know. What would I do with my love for you? Hide it? Impossible. And impossible for you, too. I appreciate your gesture. But there is a matter far more important. A question of honour. What I did was for Santo to have the woman he adores at his bedside. How could you look at him knowing I had deliberately committed sacrilege in his temple?'

'I intended a reward,' she said, tying the belt. 'You think differently!'

'Or else you would have a weight on your conscience. And so would I!'

'My father always said the English are ridiculous in the treatment of women and animals,' she said, turning away. 'Very well, I have been cast aside. I cannot be the prize I'd thought!'

'You are a most wonderful prize, but you belong to Santo. If I thought I had the remotest chance of winning you for a wife, I'd give anything. Anything!'

'You know that Santo doesn't *want* to marry!' she said. 'I *do*. I want a house, and a family. I know you love me. I feel it. *Know* it. But I have Santo in my blood. He is such a *little* man, and so gentle and brave. Until I know whether or not he will marry me, I can't *look* into the future!'

'What about the poor bastard with the misfortune to marry you after that? He puts you to bed. You have children? Of what worth, if your mind is on another man? What the hell sort of marriage would that be? I'll tell you. Hell on earth!'

'Enough!' she whispered. 'Don't say any more. I don't mean what I pretend. For a long time I've realized that Santo is a law unto himself. We have to cut our cloth. But the coat isn't always wearable. Very well. I shall go on this journey. I shall see what is to be done, or not. But if I come to you for your promise of marriage, I shall be nothing less than myself without any thought of another man. Is this agreeable to you?'

'Perfectly, and I accept. And what will Santo say?'

She put a hand over her mouth.

'I know,' she said, behind her fingers. 'I know so well. I know he loves me. But his first loves are the air and his Demoiselle. I shall never be in their place. I *hate* them!'

She swung around at me in a swirl of blue velvet.

'Please go,' she said. 'I want to howl my eyes out. Why can't we have what we want? Why are we so *help*less?'

'Well, we're human, and we have ambitions,' I said. 'Santo had his ambition from the time he was a child. It's grown. He can't throw it off. He's had the most extraordinary success. Why should he for any reason give it all up?

To become what? The sort of fatheads the rest of us are? My most beautiful, he's so far above us, whether in the air or on the ground, that to give in, or give up, is quite foreign to his nature. He is himself. How many of *us* are?'

'Please go!' she said, almost with spite. 'I don't wish to hear any more. I'm sorry you didn't have a drink. That was unforgiveable. But you have plenty in your place. I hope you are mad with thirst!'

I needed that drink. Several, in fact. To have a lifetime prize within grasp and then, by some extravagant flight of pseudo-gallantry, I had reasoned myself into a pose of befuddled Galahadism and lost a glorious opportunity that never could recur, well, fathead was absolutely correct. But I could look Santo in the eye, at any rate, and so, more importantly, could Gioia, though why her case should be more important than mine for that moment evaded me. I was in an alcoholic mush for the rest of that night, and awoke on the sofa when Mrs Damier came in. First thought was to look at the clock, and it was after ten. That settled that.

Goodbye. There can be more ineffable longing in that word than I suppose in any other, and I had the bitter juice of it in my craw. But there was work to be done, and I bathed and shaved and dressed, all the blithering little rituals we must enact to present ourselves as sane members of our society and bugger off to a place of work. Christ, how I hated it. I had never before realized that I hated what I was doing. Hate is a troublesome word, unChristian and really, given a rational thought, nonsensical. But it leaves a mark, and everything was jumbled in memories of Gioia, and Santo, the office of General Ferber, my own office, and in sudden crack, a brilliant idea. I had a further journey to make down to southern ports and to Italy in the next week or so, and I thought I would take Miss Zuccione with me to train her. *Train* her? I almost laughed. But, after all, there are other women, and Miss Zuccione, as I had found out, had a first-class brain and she knew her business, and there was little doubt – if the eye was a competent witness – an Eve in her own right.

The idea took some of the pain from the bruise. But I also had a notion that I was stupidly jealous of Santo, that I wanted what he most wanted, and I had given it away in a gesture of friendship that in essence was sheerest romanticism. That concept of human nature had always interested me, from the time Mr Marsden, my form master, had taught us – or had tried to teach us – the difference between romantic and realist literature. To this day I am quite unsure what literature *is*. Realist writing I think I recognize. The romantic may have begun with Daniel Defoe or Samuel Richardson or Jane Austen or any of the others in between, but none of them were realists. Hogarth drew Gin Row but none of the writers did, perhaps because publishers knew their market, a comfortable lot, able to afford the price of a book, but quite unable to stomach the ills of the poor.

But I had my business, and philosophy or whatever was quite outside my scope.

I looked through the mail and made notes, and when Miss Zuccione came in I asked her to shut the door and sit.

'Next week, I have to go on the tour of ports,' I said. 'This time, I have eight, from France into Italy. I'd like you to come with me to learn which shipping agents we deal with, the captains of ships, how the manifests are checked and the cargoes routed. Does that appeal to you? Your salary will be doubled, and all expenses will be paid. What do you think?'

She clapped her hands and took off her spectacles, and her eyes were just as large but they had that mist of near-sightedness that made her even more appealing, in need of protection or defence.

'I'd love it!' she said, in a trill. 'I was going to ask you if I couldn't help even more by taking some of the shipping off your desk. You've got that enormous pile for Monsieur Dumont and General Ferber, and I can't sometimes see how you get through it except by working past midnight. You can't do that for long!'

'I agree. Well, then, have the hotel and rail reservations prepared and let me see them. We start next Wednesday for Marseilles. The ship gets in two days later. We shall have that time to study the cargo and write the report. Are we agreed?'

'So far as I am concerned, completely. But I shall have to ask my father's permission!'

'But you're twenty-six years of age!'

'My father is still head of the family, isn't he?'

'Let me have a firm answer tomorrow. Meantime, make the reservations, will you? And see the accountant about letters of credit, and the shipping companies for appointments. I'd like to introduce you as my future representative, d'you see?'

She put on the spectacles, and turned for the door, and stood a moment.

'I must ask this,' she said. 'Nothing else will be expected of me?'

'If nothing else presents itself to your inventive mind, what else might there be?'

She half-turned, smiling over her shoulder, the dark smile that says far more than words, and shut the door quietly behind her.

I knew what to expect.

Chapter 16

A message from the Consulate told me that the ship we expected in Marseilles had anchored in a little port I had never heard of to the west, and all our reservations and tickets had to be gone over. Miss Zuccione found us rooms in the Hotel de la Ville, a well-known brothel as I discovered, and in view of the size of the place, ambitiously named, but at least the rooms had a wash basin, running water, and ewers of hot water constantly on order, and a large copper bath carried in when we wanted it. We stayed in different hotels in Marseilles, but in wherever-it-was we had next door rooms. Our days were long and after the paper shuffle, we added and totalled, and we had time only for dinner and good night. It was five o'clock on dark rainy mornings, coffee at the hotel, an enormous breakfast on board, and then the retelling of the cargo, up and down the decks, with luncheon taking a couple of hours, and then, until dark, more pulling and scribbling until it was time for the cutter to take us ashore.

Miss Zuccione was a little wonder. She knew exactly what

she was doing, and she even caught the Captain in his own figures. I never saw a man so annoyed. But I was there, and he dared not say a word. I could have lost money. I probably had lost a great deal in what are called Captain's Perquisites. He clearly thought I should take my watchdog off, but, on the contrary, I supported her, and at the end of three days found myself some thousands of francs better off, which taught me a lesson.

'You will pay that sum into my account by noon tomorrow or I shall prosecute,' I told Captain Querenne. 'You relinquish command of my ship from this moment. Do not apply to me for a certificate. I wonder how much more you have stolen?'

'I would like to kill that bitch!' he said.

'Attempt to lay a finger on her and you will assuredly end in a hospital or the graveyard,' I said. 'I'm content it should be either. Leave the ship, and you *will* remember the bank, won't you?'

I asked the first mate, Lars Hufthammer, if he was capable of command, and he smiled.

'I went through the Captain's school at Bergen long before that lubber knew how to coil a rope,' he said, in gentle singsong. 'I promise I will deliver this ship to any port in the world. But, sir, with a *real* crew aboard. Not with this collection of thieves!'

'Pay them off, and choose the crew you want to serve with. You will report to me at Marseilles in two days' time. Captain Hufthammer, command of *Daisybelle* is yours!'

In those pale-blue icy seaman's eyes I saw ecstasy forming.

He had his own ship.

'You will never regret!' he said, and turned away in a gulp.

We went ashore in the cutter and back to the Hotel de la Ville and a dinner cooked by the wife of the proprietor, a gaunt briar stick of a woman with a lovely smile and a way with shell-fish that would turn your heart. There was also a wine to turn your head, and a champagne to obliterate the spinning days when none of us would be there to enjoy anything. Except somewhere else, and I was simply not interested.

I remember being taken off to bed in that wide, white-washed room, that smelled of the garden and all its flowers in summer, and put in that enormous bed of goosedown, and a rattle of cognac to take care of the cracks.

When I woke up, Miss Zuccione lay beside me, asleep, long hair in dark flow about her shoulders and over the linen, one hand half-curled, and I leaned to kiss, and woke her, and the church bells clashed for seven o'clock, the door opened, and a girl came in with the tray of coffee and croissants.

'Don't take any notice of me!' she sang, almost as a lyric. 'I know all about it, and it's lovely, isn't it? Best part of life. I'll have the hot water up at seven-thirty, and you'll catch the train just in nice time. Would you like the barber, sir?'

'Indeed I would!'

'Down the corridor to your right, the bathroom. He'll be there in thirty minutes. Enjoy your repast. The paper's between the coffee and the milk. Till later?'

Miss Zuccione covered herself and smiled at me.

'If you'll lend me your dressing gown, I'll sprint for that bathroom!' she said. 'I don't want to run into the barber, do I?'

'He might think you needed the shave?' I asked, innocently.

She stuck the tip of her tongue at me, and I realized the idiocy of thinking of her as a Miss anything when she had a lovely Christian name, Andrea, which I had never used.

When she came back she poured us coffee and milk, and served me with a croissant and butter, and took the lids off the jams.

'You don't really think I've got too much hair, do you?' she asked, when I put the paper down. 'I know a lot of girls clip and shave and try to look like statues?'

'If you dare clip one millimetre, I shall question your sanity and talk to your father about putting you behind bars. Don't be nonsensical. You are perfectly beautiful, and that's all!'

'I'm glad you think I'm beautiful. I don't think I believe it. But didn't we have a wonderful time last night!'

'From that last glass of champagne till I woke up this

morning I remember absolutely nothing,' I said. 'What delights I must have missed!'

She leaned back, laughing.

'Now I know you speak the truth!' she said. 'We had to carry you up here, and I chased them all out and undressed you. A delight for me, certainly. I'd never seen a man before. It was so wonderful. To have a man all to myself, like a dolly. So I took my clothes off and got in with you. Do you object?'

'I'd be an imperial fool if I did, Andrea, don't you know that? And you call me Robert, or whatever you wish!'

'I don't think I liked my name until you just said it,' she said. 'I liked it, and now I like it for myself.'

'Andrea's a lovely name.'

'So is Robert!'

'A bit foreign?'

'All the better. I don't like the humdrum. That's why I'm here. Without, and I said with*out*, my father's permission. He will shout to rouse hell!'

'The damage seems to be done, doesn't it?'

'Well, not really. Not yet!'

'Marseilles may hold the answer?'

'I'm truly impatient for it. We have three days there?'

'If all goes well. More if it doesn't. You'd better check on ships' times. They're not always on the clock. And get our rooms and hotels changed. I want you with *me*!'

'I refuse to be anywhere else, didn't you know? D'you know what I'd most like?'

'What?'

'To go down to your farm. I've read so much about it in the reports from your manager. Yes, and the priest there. He takes such care, doesn't he? And the vineyards this year must be a glory. I never saw a grape harvest. I'd love to jump in a barrel barefoot and squeeze the grapes and feel the juice spurt up my legs!'

'Be sure you shall. I'm off to the barber!'

Chapter 17

Freak weather and winds in the Mediterranean were friends of ours, turning a three-week tour into seven weeks because ships had to anchor for days on end or sail for ports not on our list, and we followed happily, knowing that after hard days of twelve and fourteen hours, we had the end of August and all September in the sun of the Midi, grapes to pick, wheat to scythe, orchards to strip, wine to make, and cognac to refine.

Santo had been back for a week before we met at my place in the rue Washington, bronzed by the upper air, strong, amazingly confident after the success of long flights through Germany. Poland, too, had asked him to continue to the Russian border, and the Russians wanted him to continue the flights along the Trans-Siberian railway then under construction, at least while the summer weather lasted.

'It was a simple triumph!' he said. 'I had the larger Demoiselle and the more powerful engine. Ah, Rob-a-dee-Bob, *that's* the secret! Only power. It delights in tantalizing the winds. It drives through them. I become a god. What should destroy me I survive, I supersede. Winds are no longer my enemy. They help me. They know the secret. It's power. I have an even more powerful engine being evolved. I shall fly at even greater speeds!'

'Madmen are gone free!'

'No. It's on the bench under test. The winds in Russia are not the zephyrs of France. In the German mountains are real whistlers. But a little intelligence, a higher flight, and I got through and learned a great deal. My other Demoiselles had not enough wingspread. But I had to move slowly because things are not made at the touch of a wand. Steel struts, silk wings, they're not made overnight. It requires planning, mathematics, engineering, mechanics. All the forgotten details must come together, and then you have a machine that flies!'

'Why do you call it "Demoiselle"?' Andrea asked.

'It is a felicitous French word, meaning at once a young woman, and a dragonfly,' Santo said. 'She is a creature of grace and beauty, and the dragonfly is easily the most graceful and beautiful entity that flies. So? La Demoiselle!'

'When am I going to fly it?' Gioia asked from the chaise, shoes off, holding out a tulip for more champagne. 'After all, I've flown the balloon, haven't I?'

'Well, to a certain point. But you need a great deal more instruction even for that. If I weren't holding the rope you'd be in the devil of a mess!'

'I don't believe it!' she said, in a small temper. 'You're like all the men. You try to make things so much more difficult for us. Whereas really it's much easier than you lead us to think. I've found it so. That balloon was so easy to fly!'

'You weren't flying. You were floating. And I held the rope with half a dozen others nearby in case of a sudden squall. If I hadn't been there to shout the orders, you'd never have got round the course!'

'Pish, tush, and fiddlesticks!' she said. 'It's as simple as walking. I never heard such nonsense. I want to fly the Demoiselle. I *insist*!'

'You may insist when you've had a proper course of instruction, which I shall supervise, and not before,' Santo said quietly, and making no doubt that he meant it. 'You will not attempt a flight until I give permission. I've noticed in recent days you've tried to blandish poor old Jean to let you do this and that. You know he's putty in your fingers. One sniff of your perfume and he'd open the gates of the damned. I'll have none of it. I've told him that you are not to be allowed in the working area from this day forward. Is that understood?'

'I think you're a little horror!' she said, but obviously without meaning it. 'You dare to tell that oily scoundrel I'm not to be permitted to go where I've been for the past couple of months? I nurse you out of a terrible illness, and what? I'm barred from what I most desire? Your work? Simply because I'm a woman?'

'Simply because you don't know enough, and I'm responsible for you,' Santo said, curiously, even dangerously, quiet. 'You are not to go near those machines or the workshops.

90

If you wish to go there, I shall be with you. But you will not go into the machine or the flying area without me. Is that clear?'

She shrugged.

'I should have left you to those beefy fräuleins,' she said, sulky, 'Doe-eyed sluts. Milch cows. Drooling over you. *Little* man!'

I saw that Santo appeared less than pleased. I had been noticing a sort of irritation he tried to cover with a smile when she used what had been a joke in almost a tone of condescension to end an argument. I am not at all sure that his lack of height worried him at any time. The triumph of getting into the air had depended upon weight factors, in the first instance, and a small physical frame to get into the balloon's basket. Now that he used a machine, height and weight were not so important, but after a succession of amazing flights he was less than enchanted by other than a proper respect. In any event, they had been together long enough to have formed a mental relationship, and she should have known that a touchy Brazilian pride could be rubbed threadbare, and even the gentlest sympathy can wear thin. Of love, I had no notion where they were, friends or lovers, and neither was it my business.

What was between Andrea and me he knew in a moment, and the white-toothed smile showed that he understood without any words, and if anything he was even gentler with Andrea, and she, of course, was overcome.

'Why is she so stupid about that "little man" nonsense?' she asked, when we got home. 'She's nice, and I like her, but why does she presume in front of others? A good slapped bottom would do her some good!'

'You're an advocate of physical punishment?'

'That sort of remark should be reserved for the privacy of the home. Where you can have a joke, and laugh. But to be openly in contempt in front of friends is not only rude, it's killing to any sort of relationship. She's a sensible woman. Why doesn't she see it?'

'In all probability she doesn't mean it like that.'

'Perhaps. But it sounds more as if she goaded him. Into what? Aren't they living together?'

'I don't think so. As we are? I'm sure they're not.'

'That's one good reason, isn't it?'

'What's a good reason?'

'Perhaps she's trying to get him to do something he doesn't want. There's nothing like a good nag, nag, nag to wear down the opposition. He won't *be* worn down. And she's trying another way. Almost insulting him in front of his friends?'

'Very silly. He's not the type. He'll blow up. He's in a serious business, and he takes it and himself very seriously. She simply undermines herself. You've noticed Sem among his friends visiting more regularly?'

'Sem. Who's that?'

'The fat fellow when we got there. He's a cartoonist.'

'I didn't like him!'

'Typically Parisian. But he draws Santo to the life.'

'Wonder why he's done nothing of her?'

'If he's run true to form he's made suggestions, perhaps?'

'I know how she felt!'

'She might have asked Santo to break with him?'

Andrea shook her head slowly.

'Why is it men can't see it?' she said. 'After all, they're not unintelligent men. They're worldly, certainly. I think it's a lack of character. They're poisoned by the life they enjoy. Business, food and women. And lots of people to amuse them. And money!'

'Naturally. What enjoyment is there without it?'

She turned to look at me, taking out hairpins.

'But there's plenty!' she said, in a fine frown. 'One dinner at Fouquet's cost more than my father ever paid for a week's food for the house. But nobody enjoyed life more than we did. But he wouldn't have allowed that Sem in the house. A few more of them, too. They're nothing but bloodsuckers!'

'You're too hard. After all, they like to visit beautiful houses. And drink good wine, and see the famous people, and in general keep up with what's going on. Sem earns a lot of money from drawing Santo and his circle. Why should he throw it away? Santo likes him because he recognizes genius. Sem's publicized Santo in a different way, and he has to be grateful. There's scarcely a magazine or newspaper you can pick up without a cartoon of Santo in it.

That's worth a great deal. The foreign press copies them.
Wait until this German adventure becomes known. See
what happens!'

'When will it become known?'

'When the Germans are ready. Santo is a man of his word.
It won't come from him. Never!'

Chapter 18

I had decided to ask Andrea to marry me before we went
down to the farm that Saturday afternoon, but because Santo
and Gioia were coming with us for a couple of days, I
thought I would hold back to have a private celebration
for ourselves after the grape harvest, and a big party in
Paris when we got back.

Plans can go so wrong.

When we met the train, only Santo got off, and he told us
that he had to leave by the night train to be in Paris for an
important meeting on the following morning with the
Russian Ambassador and the Military Attaché to discuss
the flights beyond the Russo-Polish frontier. Gioia had felt
she would merely hamper him and in any case she had to
supervise the small dinner Santo would give that night at
the rue Washington for the Ambassador and the military
staff, and that was no small matter, with the flowers, the
plate, the porcelain, the glass, the linens, and the entertain-
ment.

'She's a marvellous girl,' he said, in the carriage. 'You
have no conception how she wanted to come here. But she
said my job is flying, and hers is the house. Something goes
wrong with the dinner, and how do I appear? An apparition
of ridicule? Well, that's what she said, and I left her among
a troop of servants, looking at plates for cracks. It'll be a
very good dinner. I wish you were both there. Can't I tempt
you?'

'I love this far too much for *any* dinner, even yours!'
Andrea said. 'Tomorrow is the first day of the wine press. I
wouldn't miss it for all the world. After all, dinner with

Russians is very nice, and I'll warrant Gioia will make it one to live in the memory of everybody. She's that kind of girl. She's had different training from me. Have you anyone there able to speak Russian?'

'I have interpreters from the Embassy,' Santo said. 'Why?'

'I'd like to hear Russian again,' Andrea said, leaning against my shoulder. 'It's such a beautiful language, isn't it?'

'Beautiful?' Santo said. 'How? Do you speak Russian?'

'Of course, why not? My Mama is Russian!'

Santo looked away, to the vineyards going up green on the hill, and he seemed to have a curious glint in his eyes shadowed in the panama.

'Is there anything I might offer you both to come back to Paris to attend the dinner?' he asked, in an oddly detached voice, as if he had no wish to hear himself. 'Interpreters can often be misleading, haven't you found? Especially if they are paid not to translate correctly!'

'Have you any suspicion of that?' I asked.

'Of course, and I don't like to think I am being deceived. The girl interpreting for me was removed two days ago. The man assigned to me now is a very small rat. He repeats everything to an officer, the officer tells him what to say, and he says it. That's not interpreting. I feel I'm being hood-winked for a purpose. Is it to fool the Germans? They've been very good to me. When I finished, the prize money was paid into the Bank of France. The language these Russians use is French. They speak it excellently well. But when there's something important to say, it's Russian, especially around the aircraft and the tooling shed. I don't like it. I'd like someone I can trust. That's you!'

I looked at Andrea's eyes and she looked at mine, and I saw a smile a long way away, but it was there.

'Look,' I said. 'You could press your first vat at seven in the morning. We'd have time to go back, bath, and catch the ten-eight to Paris. We'd be there in time to dress and attend the dinner, wouldn't we? And come back the day after?'

'If that's a promise, I'll go!' she said.

Santo went to his knees to kiss her hand and the panama flew off. The coachman pulled up at my shout and one of the postilions ran to wade into the lake and pull it out, and hit it against his gaiter to lose water. Santo dug into his pocket and I saw the gleam of gold when the hat was passed to him, and a bright twink in the lad's eyes.

'I'm so grateful!' Santo said. 'I'll tell you my deepest problem, or worry. I have been treated in the *most* excellent manner by the French and I have no intentions of being in *any* way a false friend. I have always reported my daily itinerary to General Ferber. The flights in Germany were always reported in detail. To the last day. But the Russian staff object. I'm not sure why. They don't want me to submit details of flight plans or direction, supplies, and the rest of it. That's a deception and I'll have nothing to do with it. If the Russians want my help, very well, but they'll do it *my* way. My bargain with General Ferber will be kept, and that's all!'

We turned into the house, and Santo was enchanted by tht grey stone, mossed over to the south, and the Chinese geese, and peacocks on the lawn, and the nenuphar flowering in the ponds with trout in swim about them.

'What a glorious place!' he said, almost sadly. 'Even more the second time. You make me wish for my own home. It's so much like this. How old is it?'

'The earliest recording is fifteen seventy-eight.'

He held up a finger.

'Ah!' he said, and laughed. 'My place is a couple of years older. You see? People don't recognize Brazil's age, or seniority. We are thought to be foundlings, upstarts. But we are more than twice as old as any other country in North or South America. Compared with us, the United States of America is a half-grown child. Brazil is more than twice its age. Why should I care about the Wright Brothers?'

Aha.

I thought I saw the reason for an outburst very unlike him. I had never heard Santo brag, had never heard him make any claim, and certainly I had never seen him strut. But the newspapers had been full of the Wright Brothers and their Kitty Hawk aircraft, that by some reports had flown a considerable distance before Santo got off the ground in the Bois. But then, Santo had flown before a committee of Aéro-Club members, stop-watches in hand, and a thousand witnesses, whereas the Wright Brothers had flown before an audience of birds and yokels.

Anyway, we had a drink and Santo went up to his room to lie down before luncheon, and we strolled out on the terrace to watch Pamplon putting in plants from the greenhouse along the window boxes.

'Santo seems nervous,' she said.

'It's probably the effect of years of strain, business problems, and general wear and tear. I can't think how he's stood up so well. But I think the gutter press are after him. He's been too popular, and some people want to cut him down. He won't tell them where he's been for the past few months. They're sticking their noses in, and it's bound to come out. He's been in Germany. It won't do him any good in this country. Even if it's thirty odd years away, it's remembered. With great bitterness.'

'What is?'

'The war before you were even thought of. When the Germans got to Paris. France had to pay a colossal sum to get German troops off their streets. Didn't you know that?'

'No. I was born and brought up in Athens.'

'Then you speak Greek?'

'Of course. And also Turkish, Arabic, Hebrew, French, German, Italian, Spanish, Portuguese. Also the Chinese of Macao. Some of the Indian languages, but not so much. Hindi. Urdu. Tamil. My father was professor of languages. He taught, and I used my ears. It was simple for me. As simple as for you to learn your business. I have so often thought how you keep it all in your head. I don't know!'

'Every man his own world,' I said. 'But I didn't know you were so gifted?'

'You never asked. After all, languages to me are like looking out of my eyes. I have no real need to learn. Once I have the structure I can build. I would like to translate Persian poetry. It is so utterly beautiful. But it needs a lyricist to put it into another language. I'm not a lyricist!'

'I'm not sure of that. I have a good mind to leave you here to translate, mh?'

She held my arm in strong grip, frowning her lovely eyes.

'Never leave me!' she said, shaking. 'I fear the day you'll find you can do without me. I can't bear the thought of it.

Promise me you won't? I can always make a living. Earn my way. But I won't have love. And I know you love me. Don't you?'

How to answer that question, and I took her in my arms, and a shout turned us about.

Santo leaned out of the window.

'Why the devil don't you people blather about love except under my window?' he called. 'She speaks fifty-nine languages? Very well. I'll give her a lesson in Portuguese and you'll have to douse her ears to put out the fire. Now go to hell out of here. I want to sleep. *Vai!* She knows what that means. Wake me for lunch!'

Chapter 19

Andrea had predicted a banquet and that, certainly was what we had that night, and everything went as Gioia had foreseen, always with the help of Fouquet's, naturally, just across the Champs, and a troop of chefs and waiters, with gendarmes holding up the traffic when the hot plates were brought across and the fiacres unloaded the wine for each course. I saw it all from the upper window, marvelling at Gioia's timing, her idea of supply from across the road, with the best restaurant in Europe at her disposal, and the use of the apartment's ridiculous kitchen, scarcely more than a henhouse, for unpacking, serving, repacking, and serving again all fifteen courses of wonderful food. The dessert came in with lighted torches and four chefs holding a huge carving in ice of La Demoiselle, with French flags on the tail side and German flags at the nose. The orchestra played the French and German national anthems, everybody cheered and drank, and the Russians passed beautiful bottles of what they called vodka, a damnable raw alcohol that some drank as water – and were carried out or left under the table – and the rest of us stuck to cognac or a sideboard of liqueurs and wines constantly served by wine waiters in seventeenth-century dress and powdered wigs.

'Well,' Santo said when the Ambassador had been carried

downstairs to his coach, and the rest had gone. 'What did you think?'

'Half pale-faced *aristo*, too idle to light their own cigarettes, one quarter Boyar, used to having their own way by cursing and the slash of the knout, and a quarter bootlickers if not worse. A curious mixture. How the devil does a mixture of that sort govern a country?'

'They don't,' Santo said. 'They pretend. Andrea, what did you hear? Anything interesting?'

'Very much so. First, Gioia must be bought over with gifts, jewellery, and so forth. When you begin your Russian tour, she will be fêted with dinner parties and bals masqués. Special escorts will be provided. Restaurants will be booked for the night, whether it's a luncheon or a dinner. Officers of the Preobozhensky, the Czar's bodyguard, will be brought here to dance her out of her head.'

'But what's all this *for*?' Santo asked, amused.

'She must be compromised,' Andrea said, looking at Gioia, staring open-mouthed. 'Put to bed if the opportunity arises!'

Gioia threw a shoe on the floor, and looked at it, and at Santo.

'I'm going to have such a lovely game!' she said, in a breath. 'I'm going to make them spend and spend, and I'll make them sorry for every sou!'

'You will do nothing of the sort!' Santo said, in quiet but not in any sense small fury. 'You will permit me to deal with this. What have the Russians ordered?'

'About five times more than the Germans,' I said. 'That's twice as much as the French. It means millions to me. But if I can help you, say the word!'

'Delay deliveries. Don't allow them into your working areas. Let the French, and then the Germans, take precedence. It's only fair to the French. General Ferber has the devil of a job convincing a lot of politicians. They're idiots. They can't imagine anyone sitting in a flying machine to do aything useful. The President and his entourage are far more imaginative, intelligent. They aren't bucolics. They can see what happens if Germany becomes powerful in the air. But you can't convince a fatherhead politico of that. He can't imagine power from the air. But he has the votes. The President has to move carefully to get any money voted on the budget. You see?'

I nodded. There was nothing much I *could* do. I most certainly had never seen anything political about the Santo adventure. That was, to my everlasting disgrace, what I had taken it to mean. Automobiles were carving a way over France, and roads were being built. It never struck me as being more than the wealthy enjoying a hobby that working people could never share. Flying machines were part of that hobby, or so it appeared to me. Beyond supply of parts, I wanted nothing to do with it. Beyond my thirty-mile-an-hour Adams to get to and from work. I wanted nothing to do with the automobile. It was noisy, smelly, but it got me door to door, and my horses were saved the sweat.

'The fact is, they have all come to you because of me,' Santo said, lighting a cigar. 'You are basis of supply. It will take them a long time to find other sources. You have a monopoly. For the moment. But it won't take long to find what they want elsewhere. Money will do it. You must protect yourself. And me. I have many rivals, and there's plenty of money behind them. I expect to start feeling the pinch fairly soon!'

Gioia held out the tulip, and Andrea poured.

We watched and listened.

'Where's the pinch coming from?' Gioia asked, as if it were the furthest thought from her mind. 'All the people I've seen so far, with the exception of a few of the French, some of the Germans, but *none* of the Russians, are cretins, show-offs, hangers-on, not in the same world. Where can they hurt you, those types of nothing?'

'They report to their governments,' Santo said. 'Their people abroad are brought in. They offer more money for the same sort of merchandise. It doesn't take long. They pile it up. Markets narrow. Prices go up. I've noticed your prices go up almost monthly. Why?'

'Because I have to pay more. Wages are more. Transport is more and so is insurance. The world is growing. Growth means more money.'

'Where does it come from?'

'Well,' Gioia said, hesitantly. 'From the banks?'

'Where do *they* get it from?' Santo pressed.

'Beyond me,' Gioia said, and turned to Andrea. 'How about you?'

'Beyond *me*,' Andrea said, her beautiful self. 'I don't think *any*body knows. We're all being *used*, and somebody else is using the money. And *us*. That's obvious. I pretend to be an accountant. It's a fact that I can control accounts. But money?'

Her shrug was perfect compliment to general ignorance. I had never thought about it before.

'There must be a source,' Gioia said. 'Where does money begin?'

'Trade,' Andrea said. 'Buy and sell. A bargaining. Give so much, get so much more. Profit!'

'But where did you get the money *from*?' Santo said, quietly. 'It's all very well to bargain. But where does the money come *from*?'

'Well, either you've got it or you haven't,' Gioia said. 'If you haven't, there's no bargaining!'

'Good!' Santo said. 'Now tell me, where did you get the money from?'

'Well, I suppose in my case from my Daddy!'

'Good,' Santo said. 'And where did he get it from?'

'A lifetime of work,' she said, putting her arms about her knees. 'Nobody worked harder!'

'Excellent!' Santo said, and stretched for the ashtray. 'He applied to the bank for a loan?'

'What do you mean? He *owned* the bank. And so many others!'

'How?'

'I don't know. Is it important?'

'In this discussion, probably not. Now, I suggest we all go to bed!'

'Now, Santo,' Andrea said. 'You're dodging. You mustn't. Why do you evade an issue? We're all interested!'

'I dodge nothing!' Santo said, and sat up. 'I have received prizes in millions from various countries. Why were they available to me and not to the poor of those countries? In other words, where is the *source* of the money? Who has the power to give me millions? Where does it come from? For what reason? What about the poor people? Are they never to have what they are entitled to?'

'But entitled, why?' Gioia asked.

'Because they live,' Santo said. 'For no other reason!'

'I don't think we'll get much further,' Andrea said. 'Let's go to bed!'

'Always the same isn't it?' Santo said, and lit the cigar. 'Talk about the poor, and conversation dies. People in what's called decent circumstances hate the poor. Hate their smell. Hate the way they must live. Whose fault is that?'

'Come on,' Gioia said. 'We're going to get the Christian church into this in shortest order. The blindness of Rome. Living off the fat. And the rest of it. We have enough trouble. And no answers. Come on. Bed. It's a lovely place. Thank God, we can dream, but we can't think!'

Chapter 20

Andrea wanted a keepsake, and so she wore the most unsuitable garment – a white muslin frock – for the grape press, and after the first couple of hours she looked like a purple nereid, with vine leaves bound in her plaits, juice sticking the dress to her body and legs, splashes dotting her face, really a delicious sight, I thought, and the village men had the same notion from the glances cast when they were sure their women were looking elsewhere.

But she had to give up. Trampling on grapes in a vat sounds easy and enjoyable, and it is – for five minutes – but then tender feet become scratched and raw, unlike the farm girls romping on feet used to fields and paths lifelong without shoes.

I put a sack down beside the vat, and lifted her out, and she leaned against me and sighed.

'They really *do* have a hard life, don't they?' she said, watching the girls jumping kneehigh while the men poured in the grapes, and the juice gushed from the taps. 'Look at me. Not even two hours of work, and I'm a rag. And my feet actually *hurt*!'

'They're used to it. In fact, this is regarded as a holiday by all of them. Tonight there'll be a fine old Bacchic revel. Lots of love-making and naked dancing and our local Frère Chevrillon will go back to his monastery if he hasn't already gone, and when he comes back there'll be an enormous queue at the confessional, a fine beating of breasts, dozens of candles, and virtue triumphant until the wheat's brought in. That's the way it goes, isn't it?'

'Sounds lovely. Could we see it?'

I hesitated just long enough while she grimaced into her sandals.

'These villagers are very friendly,' I said, waving to my foreman. 'That is, if left alone. I never tried any of the squire's rights nonsense. I've always kept to myself, as my father warned me. But with a gallon of wine in them, they *can* become nasty. I wouldn't care to pull a man off you. They'd all be on top of me, and then in all probability, on top of you. You wouldn't like that, would you?'

'Brr!' she shuddered. 'Too horrible to think about. No. I wouldn't take that risk, if only for your sake. Aren't there any police there?'

'They disappear on that kind of night. They're part of the crowd!'

'But aren't babies born of such an affair?'

'Of course. But the couple get married before the birth. Many babies are born in clusters tallying with the date of the previous festival. It's all excellent business for the Church. The good priest makes a fat living. Free wine, meat, poultry, eggs, milk, cream, bread, fruit and vegetables in season. It's a rich life!'

'But what good *is* the Church? Or the offices of your poor old priest?'

'Old possibly, but poor, no. He knows most of them from birth. They can go to his little box and get it all off their chests, the hate and suspicion, the doubts and worries, and come out singing. Then they light a candle and go home at peace with the world. And they've given that sly old dog one more piece of useful information about their neighbours, and never fear, he'll use it, I hasten to say, for the good of the Church!'

'Is he sly?'

'An old grey-muzzled fox, no less. They say he has a nibble at that housekeeper of his. I don't blame him. A fine hefty farmgirl, if she'll let him, a gift!'

'Aren't they supposed to be celibate?'

'"Supposed" is the operative word. After all, she's not in a state of sin. He's a holy man. All the unmarried men want a priest's housekeeper. They see how she keeps that lovely old house, and they know she'll make a good home. That's why housekeepers don't last long. They find another girl and change places!'

'He must have a few children?'

'Plenty. But he marries them off before the damage is done!'

'Having your cake and eating it?'

'If there's plenty of cake, why not?'

All the way back we heard men and women singing the wine choruses unseen in the vineyards, and carts passed loaded over the rims with bunches of grapes, black and shining, and giving off the delicate vinous scent that I remembered from early childhood.

I thought the time had come.

I gathered the reins and put my hand on hers, sticky with juice, and let the horse walk and as I knew he would, stop to crop the grass verge.

I looked at her, crowned with vine leaves, and she looked at me with that dark smile I had learned to love.

'Andrea, my beautiful,' I said. 'I think we've known each other long enough. We've proved we can work and travel and even live with each other. I'm not happy away from you. Would you like to share this place with me? As my wife? Will you marry me?'

She took my hand and held it between her breasts and, eyes shut, nodded, and tears ran and mixed with wine splashes. I brought her closer, and she rested the vine leaves on my shoulder.

'Ah, Robbie!' she whispered. 'Yes, yes, I'll marry you. And I promise we shall be happier than any other people in all the world. Where do you think it should be?'

'Here?'

She shook the vine leaves.

'I have a property near Geneva. On the lakeside, and near

a shrine. We could get the Mayor to marry us there, with his sash and flags and lanterns at night, and everybody *en fête*, and a party for the children. Do you like the idea? And I have a small place in Greece. It's lovely. We could honeymoon there. It's where I was born. Do you like the idea?'

'Love it. And come back to Villefranche on the *Rigneaud*. She's due in at Piraeus in about a month. Just nice time. And we'll go to Paris tonight and hey! for Geneva and the Mayoral sash tomorrow!'

'I've got nothing to wear!'

'You look better like that. You can buy everything in Geneva. But keep the one you've go on. We'll frame it. Come on, Plix, lazybones. Take madame-to-be to her bath. She's as sticky as toffee!'

Chapter 21

'The best laid schemes of mice and men gang aft agley' sang Robert Burns, my father's favourite poet – I was named after him – and the meaning was never clearer than that night when I reached home. A message marked URGENT with three underlinings waited for me in the hand of Tanzi.

'I promised I'd give it to you if it meant staying up all night,' she said. 'The young officer was terrible fierce. He said to give it to you personal. Lovely handsome boy, he was. So I says "Right, give me a kiss and I will". So he did!'

I went upstairs with a heart like a lump of lead, and opened the long envelope under the main lamp. As I had thought, the message was from General Ferber, and ordered me to report *without fail* to his Headquarters on the following day on a matter of highest importance.

Andrea had gone home and she had no telephone. I had to catch the 6.30 a.m. train. I went over to the desk, in two minds, whether to tell the dear General where to go while I went to Geneva, or to obey, for the good of my business, and accept a deferral of marriage.

I wrote a note to Andrea and enclosed the message, and asked her to burn it, and to reply to any questions that I was in Toulon to meet a ship.

I went to a sad bed, slept little, and got up at 5.15 red-eyed and wishing for Andrea. I missed her, and there are no words to make that meaning clear. You have to feel a yearning for a woman in your meat. I felt it in mine and it made me bad-tempered, though heaven knows why, and poor Lucien, roused by Tanzi, had the sharp edge of my tongue because the croissants were cold. Cold? At 5.45 a.m. Why not?

All the way up that Via Dolorosa, I wondered what Andrea might be thinking, but I had a good breakfast on the train, and there were no items in the papers to upset me. Certainly I had worries about supplies, whether from Africa, the Far East, or South America, and I thought that after our honeymoon, I would take Andrea on a protracted tour of all my agencies for the benefit of both of us, and we could do it on my flagship *Agape*, which means divine love, and it seemed to me appropriate and neatly right for what I intended. I had sailed in her only twice, once from Naples to Gaeta, and the other from Dubrovnik to Piraeus, both voyages a marvel of calm seas and wonderful smells from the galley. I doubt that any ship on earth has better food than the Greek. After all, they have known the business for longer than most.

And so I got there in a good mood, and met General Ferber in his office and went to the Mess for a wonderful luncheon. We spoke of little except the topics of the day and listened to the string band, but only when we got back to his inner office did I realize the seriousness of our meeting.

'Your figures for the German flights are wrong!' he said, waving the cigar under his nose. 'I want to know why!'

'When I get my wits back, I shall also want to know!' I said. 'You have all the figures. So far as I am concerned, that is the end of it. What makes you doubt?'

'I had an observer, let us say, among others, with a completely contradictory report,' he said, flicking ash. 'This applies to petrol, oil, and the exchange of spare parts. How do you explain it?'

105

'Let me see the report,' I said. 'I don't respond to rumour!'

'There is little rumourous about this, is there?' he said, and put an inch-thick folio in front of me. 'Look at it and tell me!'

I went through the folio sheet by sheet, and I think on the first page I detected a bias that worsened the further I read, and about halfway through I put it away in a brush of the wrist.

'I don't know what you think of your intelligence,' I said. 'But on this evidence you need a completely new department. They are nothing but dolts!'

'Explain that,' he said, standing in front of me.

'I took a close personal interest in those flights. I know that those figures for petrol consumption are not merely wrong but grossly exaggerated, and that leads me to think that somebody means to poison you. If you had asked me to bring my figures I could have refuted anything here out of hand. Remember, I have a business independent of spies. I have hard figures. What is supplied and what is paid. This is merest farrago. Who informed you?'

'Obviously I can't tell you. But I want an explanation for every item in that report!'

'You should have asked me to bring my figures. I won't rely on memory. But I can tell you without fear of contradiction that Demoiselle Three didn't cost one quarter of what is shown here and what's more, she uses a third of what Demoiselle One did. Demoiselle Four is the most frugal of all. I think you have an enemy on your staff. Does Santo know this?'

He moved from foot to foot and danced the cigar here to there.

'No,' he said, looking away. 'I thought it better not to worry him. He's had problems enough. This, it seems to me, is a staff matter. I thought you were the one to approach first!'

'I accept under protest,' I said. 'All the men with him, mechanics and engineers, were of my choice. I cannot believe there are any traitors among them. In any event, none of them is capable of writing this sort of report. You have some sort of clerk somewhere determined to drive a wedge between yourself and Santo. Who, and for what reason?'

He puffed, a long blue cone, and puffed, puffed, and looked around at me.

'Interesting!' he said, in a blue cloud. 'I hadn't thought of that. But for what reason?'

'I must remind you that he has agreements with several countries and a tentative offer from the Russians. They *could* have an interest or let's say, they could be rather more than inquisitive about what went on during the flights in France and Germany. We know how far he flew on certain days. Do others know? Is something being hatched to disprove what he did? For what reason?'

'This had occurred to me though not in those terms,' he said, 'What reasons have you?'

'Sir,' I said. 'I am a businessman. I pretend nothing about tactics or strategy. My figures of supply and payment tell me that I am correct. There are plenty of people wanting to discredit Santo for one reason or another. He's been too successful. But he hasn't appeared in public for some months. His balloons aren't seen any more. He doesn't give interviews. Where has he been? What's he been doing? All these things make a nervous press. The fatheaded public like their daily dose of headlines. Sensationalism. It can be healthy. It can also be poison. Who is attempting to poison you?'

He nodded.

'I accept what you say, and I'm grateful,' he said. 'Well, now tell me. Have you ever heard of a man called Aimé?'

My mind went back a long time.

'I remember that name, and Santo told me,' I said. 'Apparently some disagreement between them. I've never heard it since.'

'N'hn,' he said, and tapped the cigar. 'I shall be glad to see your figures. At least I shall know they are honest. What a pleasure. When?'

'I shall take the next train for Paris. I shall be there tonight, and I'll go direct to my office. Send your sergeant messenger to me at, let us say, four o'clock tomorrow afternoon. The figures will be an exact copy of my records. Is that satisfactory?'

'Perfect,' he said, and offered the box of cigars. 'Would there be some advantage, perhaps, in seeing this fellow Aimé?'

'When you have read my report and compared it with what you have, there may, I think, be some mutual advantage if you were to arrange a meeting between us in your office. There, I'd hope to cram those figures down his maw!'

'Delightful idea!' he said. 'And if I found he'd dared to try to deceive me, he'd spend some time in one of our military prisons. A little of my special liqueur, a ratafia, to induce a snooze on the way back?'

I drank and I snoozed, and I got to Paris almost human, and took a fiacre to the rue Washington, intending to change, go to the office, and work.

But waiting for me was a laid table, a bottle in a bucket, and Andrea, beautiful in a cream silk dressing gown. She had been on to General Ferber's office in Paris, knew I was on the train, and prepared even to having the Adams at the door waiting to take us to the office.

What is there to say about such a woman?

She knew my mind was not on our reunion so much as on the upshot of those reports, mine, which I knew to be correct, and the others, false. I had to protect my friend, Santo, and my name. Andrea, of course, was fiercely for us, and she dressed and came with me out to the warehouse, and how do you thank such a woman?

In any event between us we compiled a report that settled any nonsense, left the barebones to be typewritten, and got back to the rue Washington apartment, drank what was left in the bottle in the bucket, and got into bed, and never did a woman's thighbone come more sensuously under the hand. In the area of sense, what possibly can compete? Making love is one thing. But the sheer enjoyment of a woman's body is quite different. It is beauty itself. Who wants more?

Chapter 22

Thursday afternoon, when the coffee was served, Andrea came in to announce General Ferber, in plain clothes, and looking, I thought, tired.

'I've been over those figures page by page,' he said. 'They are so blatantly false that if yours are to be believed then there must be a reason. What is it?'

I offered the cigar humidor, and pushed the cedar chips and flame nearer.

'I think we must remember that when Santo came to me on your first introduction, there was no such entity as an air arm,' I said, and he nodded, lighting the cigar in the flame from the cedar chip.

'Now, for some years, there has been a growth of supplies, of training, of thought, and not least of business possibilities. They run into millions, as you know. When you began those years ago who would have thought that the air held wealth or any smallest reward? Today it becomes an industry. Others see it clearly. They may have had the advantage of seeing my figures. Very well. In this time they have found where my supplies come from. They may try to buy in the same area. These are not so much private industries as governments. Let us try to remember that governments have an enormous advantage, whether diplomatically or financially. They guide those instructed to buy, and those doing the buying. The middlemen. Nobody stands between you and me. I give you the correct price. It cannot – given my degree of profit – be less. But if your confidence in me is shaken, you may go elsewhere. So may Santo!'

'You think he would?'

'There's been ample opportunity. But he hasn't!'

'Why not?'

'I think because we trust each other. Any better reason?'

General Ferber drew in a deep breath that knocked the ash off his cigar.

'I feel confused,' he said, and I felt sorry for him. 'I

thought we had it so clearly in order!'

'You did, until the industrialists began looking into the possibilities,' I said. 'Aéro industry is bound to grow. It can become a serious political issue. Bankers see what is to be picked from the carcass. Governments need loans? But so do private companies. There are air frames to be built. Aéro engines to be made. Instruments. All the many items I am making at the moment, others would like the opportunity of making and selling. Germany, England, Russia, and all the rest, they have the brains. It's not only Santo who can fly. Here, you have him, and how many others? In all the other countries you have young men wanting to fly. Of course they will. And there's capital behind them. Why shouldn't a few – let's say – well-paid accountants try to falsify those lean figures of Santo's daily flights? You have nothing to compare them with. Except mine. Why should you trust me? Because on those figures I am paid. Do all the other people know that? Of course not. They accept other figures, and on them the trial flights will be made, and the profit will be all the more. Do you see?'

'I thought it so simple,' General Ferber said. 'I find I'm in a bog. Sinking. I must explain to the Minister. Even to the President. We have lost our hold where we had a simply tremendous advantage. Why?'

'You didn't give Santo the financial power he required,' I said. 'You should have created an aéro industry around him. I could have helped. Even now I can block most others from sources of supply. But that needs Government support. Have I got it? Can you get it? Financial, diplomatic? Have you got it? I've got most of the engineers and mechanics. I've got Santo. Have you the will?'

'Difficult to talk to the Minister in those terms,' he said. 'He's worried about the budget, among other things!'

I despaired.

If the Chief of Staff of the Air Arm had doubts, then who the devil was I? It occurred to me that since the moment I had met Santo, long before he made a flight – that is to say, in Demoiselle – I had been at the heart. Everything he wanted I had supplied. All his figures until the latest had been with my help. That latest flight had been a tri-

umph, as much mine as his, because I had supplied everything, to the last tooling, and all the engineers from Chapin
down had been of my choice.

'Have you thought of putting his team, mechanics and
engineers, under contract? And his constructors? They can
be enticed away, you know? More money, better terms,
pensions? It's a temptation.'

'What's the difference between an engineer and a mechanic?'

'An engineer makes the engine. The mechanic keeps it
in order. Constructors are responsible for the air frames
and wings. Not many have that experience. They should
be taken into the service. Garnered against recruitment by
someone else, not so jealous of France's needs?'

'It deserves thought.'

'More than that. It requires immediate decision!'

He put the cigar on the ashtray and sat back, folding
his hands.

'I want you to do something for me,' he said. 'I can't
trust anyone else. Fatuous thing to say, but nobody else
has your experience. I'd like you to go to where Santo is
now, and take note of what's happening. Have a quiet talk
with him. Ask him to fly for three or four days laterally
along the frontier. Not, of course, to cross it. Take note
of mileage, consumption of petrol, oil, spares and payments
to the team. As importantly, ask him how he feels about
the entire idea. And specifically, what the Germans are most
anxious to know. I must have a cast-iron case. No gossip or
nonsense. Hard facts. Will you do that? Your fee will be
commensurate!'

'I have no wish to sound sententious,' I said. 'I shall do
this for France. I believe she is losing a golden opportunity
in more ways than one. Golden in the sense that an entire
industry can blossom in profit. Golden in the sense that
such an opportunity will never repeat. Others will take
advantage. Others will profit. I'm not speaking in terms of
money, necessarily. But in terms of advantage, ah, yes!'

'Advantage?' he said, sideways to me.

'Of course,' I said. 'You're at least ten years ahead of
everybody. Aren't you? Are you going to give that away?'

He stood, and pulled down the waistcoat. It, in a word,

111

bulged, and I thought of that palatial Mess.

I could see the Regimental silver, and I heard the string band. A fattening on privilege.

'How many will you be?'

'Eight, including myself. I shall require two secretaries and a woman to look after them. My senior accountant and his assistant. And a valet. I shall insist upon first-class accommodation. If I find the slightest nonsense, I shall return immediately and without report!'

'What would you call nonsense?'

'I think you underestimate your competition. You had it all your own way for long enough. Now you give it away? I reported to you long ago that the German flights should have been made under franchise. No notice was taken. Do you suppose that your enemies will allow me to stick a cold nose into what they are doing without any defence? I would also like a small squad for guard duty. Preferably of the Foreign Legion in plain clothes, of course. Them, yes, I'd trust!'

'You amaze me!'

'Let me amaze you. But also, let me wake you up!'

He turned and put his fists on the desk.

'You insult me?' he said.

'I bring you to your place. You have none!'

He turned away from me and walked to the door.

I saw those sloping shoulders and the slack hands.

I knew that Santo had no champion, and neither had I.

The fellow was a careerist concerned only with himself. He used Santo, me, or anybody else to push himself up the ladder. Had it not been for thought of Santo, that magnificent striver for an ideal, I would have told that fat lout to find someone else to give him his facts. But in silence I accepted, and he went out and down the stairs, hoofbeats I hated because he had so little regard for my friend and his only claim to public regard, his lodestone, Alberto Santos-Dumont.

Andrea came in and looked at me. She must have seen in my face what I felt, and she came around the desk to take my head in her hands. I needed it.

'Pack a little bag for both of us,' I said. 'We shall be in Germany in the next few hours. Warn both the girls, and the accountants. Take a maid and a valet. It's cold there. Remember clothing. And remember Santo. He is under surveillance here. Every detail must be made apparent. Obviously, others are trying to falsify figures. Ours must be correct. Understood?'

'Naturally!'

'Warn the others. Detail by detail, we must be correct. Nothing else will do. For our sakes, and for the sake of Santo!'

She pulled my head into the warm space under her breasts, and I stayed there. It was the nicest place to be.

Chapter 23

We had gone through Germany without any notion where we were but we stopped at a little before ten o'clock next day in the loveliest village I had ever seen, and we got into coaches and were taken to an inn, again, a simply lovely place, with hanging hams and sausages and pewter pots, and the smells of a thousand years of good cooking. The beds were two feet deep in goose down and copper baths were filled with hot water scented with a woman's secret herbal, and who can tell it?

I saw Santo that afternoon at about five o'clock in the privacy of the noisy bar. I could barely hear what he said. He put a hand over his ear. I told him why I was there. He seemed to have no interest.

'Listen to me!' he shouted behind his hand. 'To hell with all of them. I am doing what I want to do. I have done far more than I ever thought. I am completely happy. The figures have no interest for me. I am doing exactly what I wanted to do. The other nonsense has no concern for me. I have paid my way. I owe nobody anything. Everything I have said I would do, I have done. What more's to be said?'

A difficult question to answer, given my position and his.

'All right,' I said. 'But why the hell don't you think of your friends? Don't they mean anything? God damn it,

Santo, we've been going for you for many years. From the small apprentice of a few weeks ago to your top men. The men who put you in the air. Are they really worth nothing?'

'Ahhh, now you catch a raw nerve!' he said. 'Let's take a bottle up to my room, and talk out of this damned noise!'

Andrea had gone to Berlin that afternoon to look at finery with Gioia and we were expecting them back on the late night mail. I still did not know where we were, though I could guess, and I am morally certain that Santo cared not a damn. He waited only to get back to Paris, and the building of the gigantic Demoiselle 8. I found it almost impossible to think about. A wing span of eighty feet, an engine of unimaginable power, to carry five passengers and their baggage, was quite beyond my scale of thinking. But the draughtsmen had it on their boards, the mathematicians had signed approval, and the engineers were building it in Paris. I was glad of that. At least General Ferber and his crew could never accuse Santo of intention to deceive.

'Anything can happen to me and at any time,' he said, when we had sat and poured. 'I've had near-misses in the past few weeks. Two machines burned out. It's not funny. From one moment to the next, one never knows. It comes from every side. We have no art or science yet. Idiot premises, yes. They are banished from one moment to the next. In that moment, you die. I've been lucky. I'm still here. I shouldn't be!'

'While you're playing in the luck, that's it!' I said. 'I think you've always been lucky. I often think of you going out on that bar over the Champs. You must have been two or three hundred feet up. Your engine was burning. You walked along that pole or whatever it was, and you slapped the flames out with your panama. I could hardly bear to watch it. Then you went back and got in the basket, and came down, as usual, for lunch. Isn't that luck?'

He shrugged.

'It's what you do if you must,' he said. 'This business of pensions is worrying me. I'm grateful you've brought it up. Could you possibly summarize for me a pensions plan for all my people? How much I would need to set aside?'

114

'If you play the right cards, what you are doing now will give you more than adequate provision. They offer you a prize for flying from here to there? There should also be a sum to provide for accidents and pensions. If anything happened to you, all those men would be out of a job. They might get other employment. Where's the guarantee?'

'What do you suggest?' he said. 'How much, and under what terms?'

'I'll see my insurance people and the actuaries. I'll let you know. Are you committed to France?'

He hesitated.

'I've had the most extraordinary offers here,' he said. 'They seem to care far more than the French. They have far more drive. Money is of no importance. Have you any advice?'

'Be loyal to France,' I said. 'A blockhead here and there shouldn't discourage you. Marianne is a fond woman. She has her arms about you. Stay!'

'I know you're right,' he said. 'When do you think I should start packing?'

'After you've done the three or four days I need for the figures I want. Then we can all go back to Paris and a splendrous dinner. I want to present General Ferber with a massive report which will expose the people working against him and his Government. I don't think he knows what goes on. Worse, I don't think *you* do!'

'I?'

'I don't think you take enough notice!'

He turned away, nodding.

'Perhaps you are right,' he said. 'I've never taken much interest in detail. I was always interested in flying. Nothing else mattered. Now, I see that it does. Very well, I'll fly up and down. I've got the new Demoiselle Seven. Lovely ship. I think the Eight will be a marvel. I have an engine that does really almost frighten me. What a wonderful time to live!'

'And isn't it almost a wonderful time to go and collect our girls?'

At that moment, there were knocks on the door, and I went to open it.

The concierge looked at me through pebble glass mounted in thick gold frames.

'Sir, I have received a message from the station,' he said, bending at the waist. 'The two ladies cannot be here tonight because the line is blocked by derailment. They will stay in Berlin until the line is clear. Will that be satisfactory?'

'I suppose it'll have to be,' Santo said, behind me. 'But I hope to know a little more. Two girls on the town?'

'They can take care of themselves,' I said.

'I don't trust those Berliners,' Santo said. 'They have a way!'

'Not with *my* girl,' I said. 'And even Jesus Christ wouldn't get to Gioia!'

'That's a horrible thing to say!'

'Why? Who the hell is Jesus Christ?'

'The founder of a religion that's lasted for almost two thousand years!'

'Very well, and God love him. And what?'

'And what?'

'Yes. And *what*?'

Santo looked at me with those large, almost protuberant eyes, and I thought of the cartoons of Sem.

'If you have so little regard for grace, I think I must consider whether I want you for a friend!'

'So far as I am concerned, you and your fatheaded considerations may go to the devil in hell. You're stupid!'

'You dare say that to me?' he shouted.

'I've said it. The record shows it. The men you have relied upon for years can be taken away from you with a little more money. Doesn't that tell you something?'

He took the bottle off the table and threw it against the wall, covering his face with his arms.

'Too much to drink,' he said, in a fall of glass. 'We shall talk in the morning!'

'Good,' I said. 'But I still think you're stupid!'

Chapter 24

I was awake only because the clock had called me a moment before, and Santo slammed back the door and came in, smelling of soap, and sat on my bed. He was dressed in grey and he wore the panama.

'I think you were right to call me stupid,' he said. 'I acknowledge that I have allowed others to deal for me. That was stupid. They took advantage? Very well. I wish to know nothing about it. My business is exclusively in the air.'

'All very well,' I said. 'But in putting your nose so high, you evade the smell of the herd. This may be extremely *aristo*. You can afford it. Others can't. I, among them. My accounts with you are in perfect order. But compared with the accounts of others over the same period, they show a lamentable discrepancy. You permitted it? You concurred? You allowed dishonesty to persist? Which is worst? One knowing dishonesty goes on, one who knows and promotes, or one who is patron to dishonesty for his own benefit?'

'Where am I patron to dishonesty?'

'You knew about it!'

'I deny that!'

'How can you deny what's in front of your nose? Look at those account sheets!'

'Account sheets don't interest me!'

'They interest others. They line their pockets with your tacit permission. You know of it. You do nothing about it. You allow the rats to eat the corn. Too high and mighty to acknowledge you harbour criminals?'

'I?'

'You!'

He stood and took off the panama.

'Who are they and where are they?' he shouted, in a finer rage than I had ever seen him. 'I will not condone any misconduct. Bring me their names and the proof. I challenge you!'

117

'A small business,' I said, and threw off the bedclothes. 'Here are the operational sheets of yesterday as compiled by the people with you. This is the compilation of my team. They had the same information. As you see, almost seventy per cent *less*. This has been going on with your permission or assent for some years. How much have you lost? It doesn't matter whether you can afford it or not. It *does* matter that you promote criminals and permit them to flourish!'

He stamped about the room, trying to speak.

'Deus Christos!' he whispered, and that was the first time I had ever heard him blaspheme. 'Why didn't you tell me before?'

'Everything you gave to others was not a part of my business and therefore I had no figures. Without figures, there is no proof. You allowed others to supply you with petrol and oil. Hydrogen for your balloons. I said nothing. I am a tradesman and others have a trade and a family to take care of. I don't deny them their business or their profit. I didn't even think about it. After all, I had enough.'

'But who *is* it?' he whispered, from the window. 'You make it sound like a conspiracy!'

'But dear Santo, for Christ's sake what *else* is it? This is a matter of thousands of francs a *day*. It's been going on for how long?'

He nodded, looking down at the panama.

'You're right,' he said, almost without sound. 'I didn't think about it. I made criminals? Very well. Who are they?'

'You have no need to look further than the people you asked to supply you. How many years ago was that? I never questioned it.'

'I shall have to think,' he said.

'But surely to God you knew the people supplying you with petrol and oil? Up until this moment? I've never interfered. The supplies came and it never occurred to me to question either them or the suppliers. But I can't help thinking that I've been unjust to General Ferber!'

He turned to me, raising his hands.

'Why?' he said. 'Unjust in what way?'

I folded the blanket about me, and sat more in comfort. 'I seem to see now that he had further intelligence,' I said.

'I'd thought that he was simply a careerist making a name on your work and to a lesser degree on mine. I believe now that he had other information. Let us say, that you were paying far more for your fuel supplies than necessary. And that I was a collaborator!'

He turned away in anguish that could be seen.

'Impossible!' he said.

'Very well, impossible. But it's been going on for a long time. Long enough to become a habit?'

'Tell me who!'

'Well, tell me who supplied you. Who supplied the hydrogen? Who sent up the barrels? Who's supplying you here?'

He looked at me as though he were haunted.

'I don't know,' he said. 'Surely it's the German Army?'

I lost patience.

'Santo,' I said, flat. 'You mean to tell me you don't know who supplies you with fuel? You can tell me who cuts your suits and shirts and makes your shoes, but you don't know who takes you into the air?'

'I quite thought it was you!' he said.

I stood and threw the blanket on the bed.

'I'm going to bath and shave!' I said. 'Get out and start thinking. I want to know who's supplied you all this time. I thought you had a business agreement. I never questioned it. But now I know why General Ferber has a distrust of me and the way I work. I don't even know myself. Isn't that a damned joke?'

'But Bob-a-dee-Bob,' he pleaded. 'I'm not sure what you mean!'

'God damn it!' I said. 'Are you really such a child? The information has been mounting for some time, hasn't it? The information from my office, and what comes from yours. They don't agree. What is the General to think? Obviously I have something to hide!'

'I refuse to let that happen!'

'Then let me know. *Who* is your supplier?'

He held out his arms and his hands slapped.

'I have no idea!' he said. 'You must think me an idiot!'

'No, dear lad,' I said. 'We've been operating at different levels. From now on, you permit me to take charge?'

He threw out his hands.

'All yours,' he said. 'But I still can't tell you the name of my suppliers!'

'Don't worry,' I said. 'I'll have them within the hour. And in the Courts of Justice within minutes more!'

'You think it criminal?'

'What else?'

He stared up at the ceiling, and again I thought of the cartoonist and the way he drew those bulging eyes.

'I cannot bear to think that my Demoiselle has anything of the criminal anywhere near her,' he said, more whisper than voice. 'She will go into the air, as I have always intended, and nothing to do with the earth except as product of its best minds and hands. So far, it has been true. Except for this!'

'Then let nothing interfere with your thinking,' I said. 'Every activity leaves its trail of – let's call it – humus, or rubbish. Nothing is done without a negative spill. Even you have to take down your trousers and sit on a pot. Why not? You couldn't do anything unless you did. So? Go on down and order breakfast while I get dressed. We have to meet the girls!'

He put his arms around me.

'Ah, Bob-a-dee!' he whispered. 'God sent you!'

Chapter 25

I shall never be sure why it is that when I get off a train after a few hours I feel grimy as a sweep's neckcloth, yet those girls were handed down by the guard looking as if they came direct from the bandbox via the bath.

They were, in fact, a pair of beauties, each entirely different in her own style, Andrea in a dark-blue caped coat and a small hat of blue feathers, and Gioia in red with a hat of red flowers. They were followed by porters carrying half Berlin, in packages, boxes, crates, and a couple of huge laundry baskets filled with smaller parcels.

'Great Moloch!' Santo said, hands in the air. 'Is anything left in that place?'

120

'Don't worry,' Gioia said. 'You won't have to pay for anything. Berlin's a lovely place. We had two lovely life-guardsmen as our dinner escorts and the Opera afterwards. And don't worry, there must have been at least half a dozen men who looked to us like policemen in plain clothes always on the hover so that even hand-holding – if we'd wanted to – was quite out of the question!'

'That's what they were there for!' Santo said, and certainly surprised me. 'You don't think I'd let you go off to Berlin without precaution, do you? It's a notorious city. I wanted you safeguarded the entire time, and weren't you?'

Gioia looked at me and at Andrea in that funny, slit-eyed stare that made her seem orientally menacing.

'No element of jealousy in this, of course?' she said. 'I suppose I ought to feel flattered. It makes me feel like an infant sent out on a secret picnic with a dozen grooms. No fun at all!'

'You're safe, and that's what matters,' Santo said, in a grand air of indifference. 'Supposing something had happened to you?'

'What for example?'

Santo turned up a palm.

'In a place like that anything is possible. And if something *had* happened – a footpad, a skulker, any devious animal – what would I have said to myself? I relieved myself of the stupidity of repining and regret. I took action!'

Gioia towered over him, and so softly, her smile came back, and he looked up at her as to a goddess, and in those moments, she was.

'My little man!' she whispered. 'My *little* man!'

'All the porters are waiting,' Andrea said, the practical one. 'And I'm simply ravenous. I didn't have breakfast and there was no time for luncheon. I think they ought to time trains better!'

'Yes, but then we couldn't give you the very special meal *we've* ordered,' I said. 'A tray of sandwiches and a glass of hock. Santo has a flight in ten minutes. Business first. We'll have an early dinner!'

'If I'm to starve until then?' Andrea said, in a bit of a pet. 'At least I expected a meal!'

'You haven't seen the sandwiches!' I said.

Santo laughed. We had seen the buffet before we left the hotel. It was a mound of plate on silver plate to feed an army all among the flowers and fruits. Germans do everything with exceptional skill, and nobody can teach them about food, even the simplest. When the girls saw the buffet, they gave their coats to the chambermaid and sat down to eat. The hotel was small, taken over by General von Meischel and run by soldiers as an Officers' Mess.

Every dish I had ever thought about was on display and the Mess orderlies in starched tunics served us in a manner that loosened my buttons and made the girls regret they wore corsets.

But at four minutes to one, Major Klemmach came in with his stopwatch, and Santo drank from Gioia's glass and followed.

We went out to see him fly overhead at a height, it appeared to me, almost above the mountains, and Gioia looked and wrung her hands to see that buzzing bird, and Andrea put an arm about her, and we stood there until he had flown across the forest.

'Marvellous man, wonderful machine,' Major Klemmach said. 'Always on the second. Amazing!'

He rubbed a white-gloved thumb over the stopwatch dial.

'This is a new sort of history,' he said. 'That man proves to us that there is a third dimension! War has gone into the air.'

Gioia turned to him, a wildcat.

'Don't let him hear you say that!' she said.

'He's already recorded as saying that underwater craft can be detected from the air,' Major Klemmach said, giving her not a glance. 'What's the difference? What's down below can be seen and bombed. It's an extension of the artillery, is it not?'

'Never let *him* hear you say it!' Gioia spat in a whisper of white eyes so unlike her. 'His prayer is for peace. Free frontiers. All lands one. And never any war!'

Major Klemmach closed the watch in a snap, clicked his heels, and nodded his head in a bow.

'Herr Santos-Dumont has landed at his field, and he will fly back at ten minutes past three,' he said, as if nobody were there. 'I shall be at the Officers' Mess until he is due to arrive. You are invited to join me or not, as you wish!'

I must say I felt helpless. I felt we were being treated as retarded infants, allowed to see a show but only as a special treat. I know the girls felt the same way and Gioia could barely stay inside ther skin, whereas Andrea saw the matter on the pragmatic side, and spoke of the advantage in the air.

'After all, he's a soldier, isn't he?' she said. 'I suppose they see everything in terms of war. Santo's just the opposite. He hates any idea of fighting or killing. So do I. But there's a lot of it going on everywhere. We need the Army. Never feel safe without the soldiers. And sailors, of course. Now there'll be the airmen. I feel proud to have seen the first flights. I can tell my grandchildren I *knew* Santos-Dumont. Sat at table with him. Not many can say *that*!'

'I know how Santo feels about using aircraft in war,' Gioia said. 'He's heard whispers, of course. He sees the interest of the soldiers. He knows the prizes are his for their eventual benefit. But he won't allow that matter to be discussed in front of him. He detests the idea!'

'Detestation will stop nothing,' I said. 'He knows too well it's a tool made for the age and whether he likes it or not, it'll be used for good or bad, and that is that. There's *nothing* he can do to stop it. It's caught fire in too many countries. Too many good brains are at work on it. As a realist, he knows it. That's all!'

'Hark at ol' Gran'pa Bob-a-dee!' Gioia said. 'But I suppose you're right. I hadn't quite thought about it like that. What could Santo do?'

'Do?' I said. 'Precious little. If he cleared out altogether, somebody else would simply carry on. They've got drawings of everything. There aren't any secrets except those of piloting and even there, as he says, some of his French pupils are almost as good as he is. It's been a matter of trying and failing and starting again. Theory and practice were non-existent when he began. But there's no mystique about it. Simply put your mind to it, and if you live, you may be successful!'

'May be?' Gioia said. 'Why *may* be?'

'Well. One slip, and you've lost your life!'

'But he makes it look so *easy*, doesn't he?'

'That's practice. It's becoming an art, perhaps. A genius is born, and he can amplify and pass it on, whatever his knowledge, and his pupils will suck the juice. What's happening at this moment? At least two large schools, in France and here for air pilotage. They're in being. A couple of hundred a year, let's say, will survive and fly the sort of machine he's built. All they have to do is little by little make them better, or bigger or more powerful. Consider what he's done. Engines to give power in the air. Who thought of it? Wings for lift, and air frames strong enough to carry an engine and a man. Who thought of it? Who worked for it? Who paid for it? Who found the fuel and the way to make it work? Santo. Who else? The rest copied!'

'What about these Americans, the Wright brothers?' Andrea asked. 'They seem to have had a remarkable success?'

'Why not?' I said. 'How many people have copied me? All they've got to do is follow my ideas. But they need my ideas *first*. Then they can go. So with Santo!'

'I'd murder the lot!' Gioia said, from her teeth. 'He gives everything away. Why hasn't he got a business manager?'

'A matter of temperament. And of upbringing. Let's not forget that any talk of money, even when I was a boy, was absolutely forbidden. Talk about acreage or cattle or sheep in any number, very well. But money? Never!'

'What changed it?' Gioia asked, following Major Klemmach's broad back through the inn door and a clicking of heels from the orderlies. 'What makes things change so soon?'

'Possibly the arrival of wealthy Americans? You never had any trouble talking in terms of money. You had it and used it. You taught the Europeans that money was a commodity to be used wisely to buy and conserve. It was not something to be put into sovereign cases and stuck in a waistcoat pocket, or tinkle in a bank vault. It had to be *used*. American daughters married into the *aristo* families. They brought in wealth. Money became fashionable. After all, look what you could do with it!'

'And Santo?' Gioia asked, head up.

'He still has the old idea. Money is to be used for the good of all. Money is what is left after bargains have been made. The profit. Everybody should feel the sprinkle of it because everybody's helped. If they weren't alive, there wouldn't be the mouths to feed or the hands to help!'

'Doesn't sound like Santo!' Gioia said. 'He spends it and that's that. It's for what he wants and what he thinks should be done with it!'

'But wasn't he very lucky to get it in the first place?' Andrea said, giving her coat to a maid. 'After all, we're what we *are* by circumstance. I could be one of the girls here. But I'm not. I'm *me*. Therefore I have a different condition in life. Who decides it? Who decides that Santo has a genius, and Major Klemmach has a stopwatch? How does it happen? But it does and we are witnesses. And?'

'And I'm going to have a bath and go to bed, and I don't want to see any living thing until at least noon tomorrow!' Gioia said. 'But I'm terribly hungry and what have they got?'

We heard Santo coming over very low, and the noise of the engine shook the glassware and then was gone.

'I'll wait for him,' she said. 'Why must he be so noisy?'

'Probably he's flying under the weather because he wants to get back safely,' Andrea said. 'What d'you want him to do? Sail in with his arms out?'

'No,' Gioia said. 'I'd just like somebody to show me a wonderful underdone steak. Santo can come in any time after and open a bottle. So far as I'm concerned, under the weather is a lovely place to be, especially in bed!'

Chapter 26

Sitting cross-legged on my bed in the rue Washington – Andrea had gone home – opening the pile of telegrams Tanzi had given me, I was amazed, even dumbfounded, by the size of ordnance requirements by the French and German Governments, with lesser orders from others, and so many from companies I rarely dealt with, but all wanting the same type of item. One telegram I set aside, from General Ferber, wanting to see me without fail, at eleven o'clock on the following morning. It annoyed me that I should be addressed as some raw recruit. It made me steam, except to turn off the light and roll over, certain I would say all I had to next morning.

General Ferber came in on the dot of eleven o'clock, in plain clothes, making him altogether more human and in a certain way far more approachable.

'It was idiocy of an aide,' he said. 'Really of small importance. It shall not happen again. I congratulate you on your report. It exactly coincides with mine. But neither of them has anything to do with the report from the company supplying oil and petrol. Have you seen it?'

'I have nothing to do with it, as I've told you.'

'Look at these figures. He's being charged all this extra money. Why does he permit it?'

'He doesn't care about money!'

'I do. Will you talk to him, or shall I?'

'Knowing him, I think I'd better!'

'Very well. It's the only region where we disagree, and I don't like it. Is he making extra money? It's a considerable sum taken over the year, don't you think?'

I looked at the figures and wondered if Santo even knew what was going on.

'Let me explain to you that when Santo came to me, it was with a letter from you,' I said. 'On your recommendation I supplied everything he required. Petrol and oil were not mentioned. Who owns this company?'

General Ferber turned his head to me, eyes down, sideways, a sharp grey challenge.

'I thought you did!' he said.

'You're quite wrong,' I said. 'Completely and eternally wrong. I never had anything to do with it. I never ordered and I never supplied. Who are these people?'

'I think it such a shame that we should have to engage in an argument in this manner,' the General said, and it endeared him. 'The company is known to us. Obviously? For a long time. Santo has consistently used it. He's never made an attempt to challenge the figures.'

'If I know Santo, he never even looked at them!'

'Why not? They are more than seventy per cent of the market price. D'you call that responsible?'

'If Santo can get what he wants, price is not in question!'

'Look, sir,' the General said, 'I appeal to your sense of responsibility. The Army, which I represent, simply will not accept that criminality!'

He butted his fist on the desk and I knew I had to be careful.

'Who owns the company?' I asked.

'I regret to have to tell you that Monsieur Santos-Dumont is on the board of directors!' he said. 'What does that mean?'

'I regret to have to tell *you* that I don't believe it!' I said. 'He's not the type to attend a board meeting, and he's not the sort to apply a price to the fuel he uses. I think the whole business is a hoax in his name. I'll derive the most inordinate pleasure in proving to you that he never had the smallest, the remotest, interest in making money out of anything he did. Is that plain?'

The General turned to the window and nodded.

'Whether he did or not, God knows, a lot of money was made by somebody out of the body politic. The taxpayers. The people who live to pay!'

'Simply tell me the name of the fellow in charge, and I'll set about him. Why don't you?'

'It might well be Santo himself. After all, he uses the fuel. That's the greatest cost. Can you suggest another?'

'The man purportedly heading that company, Central Petrol and Oil. What's his name?'

'Aimé. D'you know him?'

'I've heard of him. From Santo himself. It seemed to me, then, a warning not to deal with him. I never did. Have there been any enquiries from your side?'

'Naturally. A full intelligence report. He lives in style, I may say, off the Avenue Matignon, not exactly a pauper's domicile. It is shared by a woman, Pauline Dufresne, once of this office!'

'Impossible!'

'Then you understand the source of my suspicion?'

'More than that. I wish you'd told me. What makes people do things like that?'

'Find out who the people are they're working for.'

'Any idea?'

127

'Find out for yourself!'

'Very well. I have no wish to go any further. I shall tell Santo to deal with someone else.'

'Yourself, preferably!'

'If he agrees. In any event I shall see this Aimé and I'll put him in place. You wish me to supply Santo in future?'

'And all the flying schools. That's what I came here to say. Any objection?'

'You invite me to create another department?'

'Whatever you create will eventually be taken in control by the Army. You cannot lose. Incidentally, you might look into the system of supply. Petrol and oil are not indigenous. Where does it come from? Who supplies it? How? This would be useful information. Remember, we shall want unlimited quantities and you could provide a solid basis, with profit over the years to you!'

He had an appointment for luncheon, and so I was left to myself, and I went to an Alsatian place where Mama stood at a stove and we all sat at rough tables around her, and she cooked what we had chosen from her buffet in the entrance. She had everything on show, and all you did was pick out what you wanted. A girl would take it to her, and she would wave a hand, and a little later you would have a wonderful dish. I am sure that Europe or anywhere else can never offer more than a woman's kitchen love. Men may cook in knowledge or an idea of profit, but women cook in love, and I'll take the women every time. When I took Andrea to the Auberge de Mimimi, she never stopped laughing, because of course, Mimi stuttered, but not in cooking. The girls helping her ran, and ran and ran. They were darlings. Half the joy of going there was in those girls. One imagined the sweat between their legs, underarm, under their breasts, and why not? So far as I am concerned, a girl's sweat has never been a problem. A probing tongue finds rarer caviar.

But to find General von Meischel and five of his staff waiting for me outside the door of the rue Washington apartment was almost too much. I wanted so much to sleep. They did not. I could almost see the pickelhaubs they'd left behind glitter in lamplight. General von Meischel explained that certain matters had come to attention, and he would like the opportunity of talking to me. I used my key, and led them past Tanzi and upstairs, where Lucien helped them off with their wet overcoats, and then brought in the tray of drinks and hot water.

General von Meischel seemed in a stamp, as if he had some problem to get out of himself.

'I have a most serious matter to confide,' he said. 'I have reason to believe you are supplying the figures of our purchases to the French Government. Are you also supplying the British?'

I thought I caught a glimpse of General Ferber's grey eyes in smiling glint.

'You may be quite sure I am not supplying the British Government with anything unless it is ordered in the normal way,' I said. 'As to the French Government, I have dealt with various Departments over the years. Why would my figures be of any significance?'

'I have no intention of going into that,' he said. 'What I wish to do is to prevent any access to the French of what is being supplied to us!'

'But, General,' I said, in soothe. 'The people supplying me could tell them. So many tons of steel, so many of this and that, all they have to do is look at the order books, and that tells the story!'

He tugged at the ends of his moustache, really a work of art, and turned to take a cognac from Lucien's tray, drink at a gulp, and take another.

'It's obvious that we must take command of all aspects of this flying business,' he said. 'I've never liked the idea, but now it's approved policy. My men training with your own are capable of staffing an establishment. Do you agree?'

'Entirely. They're very good men, in fact. When do you intend to start?'

'Midnight tonight,' he said, matter-of-factly. 'I came here to say that all our dealings are at an end. From tonight we shall require nothing more from you. Is that understood?'

'Perfectly. And do you realize that I have more than three years of a five-year contract to be paid for?'

He waved a hand.

'It is understood, and of course we shall comply with all requirements!'

'It will be a matter of some millions, may I say?'

Again the wave of the hand.

'Of no consequence. Submit your account and rely upon payment. You may deliver the residue of the order as and when the cargoes arrive. Is that satisfactory?'

'Completely. Two of my ships will discharge at Hamburg and another is due in Bremen, all three in the next month. You will make your own plan for transport?'

'Let me know time and date!'

'The man to tell you is the Harbourmaster. He'll know better than myself. Far sooner. The fact is, that I was going to tell Santo I wanted no more of this aéro business. I've been working far too hard. I'd like a little more time on my farm.'

'But that man made your fortune!' the General said with another tug at the moustache. 'Well, didn't he?'

'Sir,' I said, in a tone not to be misunderstood. 'My fortune was made by my great-grandfather more than a century ago. May I accompany you to the door?'

Chapter 27

We got back from Germany without a notion of where we had been, and there was still an enormous pile of work, and I rebelled. I went to see Dr Mesnard, told him I felt drab, and he ran the stethoscope, pumped my arm, looked down my throat, and this and that, and put the pince-nez on and ordered me to the sea for at least a couple of weeks with no work or any thought of it. I went back and took Andrea's lovely hand and told her, and she sat me down, gave me a tulip of champagne, and came back to say we had tickets for the night train to Villefranche, and she had cabled the inn to get us the little house along the beach a couple of miles off, with a girl to look after us, but that she insisted upon doing the cooking.

We got there the morning after, and the Mayor drove us to that lovely place, a small pink-washed house, and a white beach about a couple of hundred yards long, a hundred yards to the sea, and with every sort of tree hiding us. I undressed and lay on a towel, and Andrea came and rubbed me with olive oil, and cooked a luncheon of vegetables and cheese, with farmhouse bread and butter, and the days went by, and we swam and splashed, and then I knew we had to go back. It was a moment of regret, real regret. Clothilde, the girl, wept, Andrea put her arms around her and wept and I could have wept. But the Mayor was there with the trap and pair, and off we went, with tears everywhere, and we caught the train back to Paris and the normal life. But what is normal? In the restaurant car we spoke of buckling down to hard work. Neither of us spoke of marriage though that was in the forefront of our minds. We spoke instead of two tremendous weeks of work, and then of a lakeside couple of days, and that Grecian island. I, brown with sun-blent olive oil, could think of nothing more wonderful. Andrea, coppery, simply lovely, smoothed one hand over another to the wrist, and looked at me and that was enough. She loved me. What more could be enough?

We got back to the office, and exactly what we thought, there it was, an enormous pile of mail. I pulled out a letter from Santo and sat back to read it. He had doubts about the mathematics of the Demoiselle Nine. It was a machine to carry two engines and two men. He thought a mistake had been made in weight. That machine had been built over at his place, and he wanted me to go over and have a look at it.

I?

What the devil did I know?

Andrea put a hand at my nape and said, go over, see what there is and write back. He and Gioia were at my farm for another week or more, as they wished, and the floating idea was that they would get married with us on the same day in the blaze of the Mayoral sash.

But I was worried about his doubts of the new machine. I was even more worried about my ignorance of anything to do with it. But first of all. I put on my hat and took my stick and went to find that fellow Aimé. He had an address, and I went there, but nobody had ever heard of him.

That was a facer.

I asked next door, both sides, and up on the first floors.

Nobody I talked to knew anything or had ever heard of Central Oil and Petrol, or whatever it was.

I ran a thumb over my mouth.

How could a company supplying Santo all the way through Europe have no address? I looked up the Champs into the sunlight, leaning on my stick, and I could see General Ferber, and harmonize his doubts. Who the devil was this fellow Aimé? And without an address, where was he to be found? I had no trouble in finding a solution. I walked around to the police station, and I saw my friend Inspector Redefier and told him in full.

He looked at the sheets in front of him, and put the pen behind his ear, nodding.

'Simple,' he said. 'He supplies from another place, no? And so we find it, and then what?'

'A prosecution, naturally!'

'On what grounds?'

'Overcharging!'

He shook his head.

'The receiver made no complaint?'

'So far, no.'

'Then?'

'Well, that's as far as we go, isn't it?'

I had to acknowledge that he was in the right, and I had to go back to the sunny street, and wonder about that dear soul, Aimé, making a fortune without an address.

But after all, that simply made Santo a patron, and that apparently was what he had always been, and for many years. It puzzled me. Santo was nobody's idiot. I thought of going to General Ferber's office on the Quai where a couple of officers kept him in touch, but poor louts, they could tell me nothing. Well, there must have been something going the other way, because when I got back to the office, M Aimé had been, and would be back at five o'clock.

I was quietly surprised. Andrea was not coming back until Monday, Santo and Gioia were still at the farm, and the office went very well beneath the strict eye of Cécile Lambert, and she, of course, had been trained by Andrea.

She came in to announce M Aimé.

I nodded.

He came in, a frock coat obviously never his and a

starched shirt made for someone else, in general, false.

False. How did you know? There are no words. There is only the evidence of the eyes, and experience. And what is experience?

In those seconds it takes to think so many odd thoughts, I wondered why a man making a pretty good living off the Santos-Dumont oil and petrol account would not be better dressed or appear certainly more affluent.

'Sir,' he said. 'This is a matter of some urgency. I hear you are supplying the Santos-Dumont complex with a variety of materials?'

'That is correct!'

'Then I am entitled to a commission. I had an understanding with Santos-Dumont some years ago that I would have at least fifteen per cent of everything bought or made in his name. May I have the figures?'

'It's taken you a long time, hasn't it? Show me the agreement!'

He stood, straightening the cravat.

'It was a gentleman's agreement in words. Nothing more than a handshake is necessary. At least, when two think with the same mind. Isn't it so?'

'I was not a party to that agreement. How do you convince me?'

'I rely upon your knowledge of Santos-Dumont and myself!'

I looked at him.

'So far as I am concerned, you are a rascal,' I said. 'Now shove off to Monsieur Santos-Dumont, and bring me evidence that you are anything more!'

'You'll regret this!' he shouted. 'So will he. I intend to prosecute. I want my money!'

'You've been a long time claiming it. Get out of my office. Never come back!'

I thought he was about to faint. He tore at his collar, and his hat rolled away, the cravat pulled out of his waistcoat, and the frock coat almost fell off his arms.

Miss Lambert came in, at her iciest, most beautiful.

'This way, sir!' and held open the door.

He really did stagger from the doorway, and down the stairs.

'Never let him in again!' I said. 'I don't know what he's after, but I don't think he's up to any good. Any idea?'

'He may be working for somebody. The French, the Germans, the Russians? I don't think he's got the brains to work for anybody, even himself. You should have heard him downstairs. I thought he was mad!'

'Why?'

'The way he was talking. He was going to buy a pistol and kill anybody in his way. We were in a bit of a fright down there!'

'Did you get his address?'

'No, sir. He was nearly frothing at the mouth!'

I wondered why he had taken so many years to find me, and why he would threaten instead of seeing an attorney and putting the matter on a judicial basis. But then, obviously, he had no papers, nothing to prove his claims. I saw that Santo was just the sort of Quixote to allow the claim and order him paid. I was determined to stop it, because not only did fifteen per cent run into millions, but General Ferber's air arm and Santo would have to foot the bill between them. I thought I could hear the General's reply.

But I was worried, because Santo could be put in a rogue's place, and so I went back to the police station, but Inspector Redefier was off duty – I had forgotten that policemen go off duty – and I told a sergeant, and he turned down his mouth.

'The Inspector's going round there,' he said. 'It's a warehouse near the Gare de l'Est. They sell everything in the oil and coal line. He's gone to scratch up a few names. We can't find anything on this fellow, Aimé. But don't worry. We'll keep an eye on him!'

I knew then, that if the Police could find out, then General Ferber and his staff must certainly know, and I decided to do nothing more until Santo got back.

But not an hour later I had a telephone call from the Inspector.

'This is a cautious affair,' he said, in his best gendarmerie dry-as-the-notepad voice. 'I've been trying to sort it out. Apparently, when Monsieur Santos-Dumont first came here, there was some difficulty with money. He had a Brazilian account with the Bank of France and it took time to arrange.

In that time he borrowed money through Aimé, then on the staff of the Sorbonne and a member of the Aéro-Club. Mathematics. He's also a gambler. He also keeps three women. It's a sad case. As I said, there was some sort of bargain with Monsieur Santos-Dumont, and he agreed to a price for hydrogen and prime balloon silk, rope, and whatnot. Now.'

He seemed to be turning a page.

'When he started with engines, the prices went on to oil and the other stuff, so that Aimé got more or less the same cut. Well, not long ago, the Army started looking into things, and the owner of the business told Aimé that the arrangement was coming to an end. Aimé went a bit mad. He made all sorts of threats. The present owner of the business never liked the monthly payment. He knew Monsieur Santos-Dumont was paying out a lot of money. But the monthly payment from the Santos-Dumont office came in. There was never any complaint. Aimé got his share and that was all. That sound strange to you?'

'Very strange indeed!'

'Well, I got on to the Army, and they said it was all going to stop because they were going to supply, and their quartermaster would take charge. That's from Sunday midnight next. So I'm posting a couple of men on your house just in case he makes any trouble. All right?'

It wasn't the happiest thought, but with a madman, what do you do? I felt like going down to the farm to talk to Santo, but he was having a much-wanted rest with Gioia, and why spoil it?

But that Sunday night, there he was, jumping with farm health, and Gioia with him, marvellously beautiful, a sort of roseate beauty under the coppery tint of her face and shoulders.

'What did you do?' I asked him. 'Go out on the lake?'

'Where else?' he said. 'I supplied the entire village with trout and perch. Gioia caught the champion. I've never tasted such a fish!'

'I baked it on hot stones,' she said. 'It's the only way to cook a fish and keep all the fishy juices. What's for dinner?'

'Let's go across to Fouquet's and find out. First, Santo, a word with you, if you please?'

We went into my study, and in a few words I told him of

135

the Aimé business, and he wrinkled his nose in distaste and drew a breath and blew.

'That fellow's been an albatross ever since I've been here!' he said. 'He did, in fact, borrow some money for me. The original lender made it three per cent. Aimé multiplied by five. It took a long time to find out. When I did, I told him we were no longer friends. I didn't want him or his girl near me. But I'd given my word, and I kept up the payment. Now it comes to an end? Very good!'

'And if he sues?'

'Let him!'

'All those payments over so many years?'

'Charity!'

'A lawyer may not see it like that. A gentlemen's agreement?'

'He broke in the beginning. The interest rate was three per cent. He charged fifteen. I have the original document!'

'Let me have it. I'll stultify him!'

Chapter 28

The oysters had just been served on a bed of seaweed, and Schillot, the headwaiter, came across to give me a note. Tanzi was downstairs in a state of emotion. I showed Santo, and we left it with the girls and excused ourselves, and went down to find Tanzi, in her Grandma's bonnet, shawl wrapped tightly in her folded arms, standing in the corner behind the orchids.

'There's a dreadful man over there!' she said. 'He wants to kill you!'

Santo looked at me and nodded.

'Come on!' he said. 'I'll break the bastard's back.'

I took Tanzi's hand, and we trotted through the traffic, over to the rue Washington, but all we got was one policeman, with a cape over his shoulder, at the entrance to Number 9, all quiet, no trouble.

'Anything wrong, officer?' I asked.

'No, sir. There was a bloke here kicking up a row, so my

mate took him in. Probably be an enquiry in the morning, that's all. Must say you've got yourself a marvellous concierge. She went at him like a wildcat. We had to pull her off him!'

Santo took her hand and kissed.

'Have you eaten supper?' he asked.

'Not yet,' she said. 'That man upset me!'

'Come with us and have supper!'

'Oh, I couldn't do that, sir,' she said. 'I got my job to do!'

Santo looked at me and shrugged.

'I understand the French,' he said. 'Tanzi, your supper will be sent across, and you, Officer, will share the meal. Which wine do you prefer, Tanzi?'

'Beaujolais, where I was born!' she said. 'But you shouldn't take such trouble!'

'You took far more,' Santo said. 'Tomorrow we shall have a little talk. Bob-a-dee, the girls!'

We walked, Santo hands behind his back, across the Champs.

'I'm worried, Bob-a-dee,' he said. 'Very worried. Aimé has good friends. In the University, in the casinos. He's spent tens of thousands. My money, of course. I've never thought of stopping it. But I spoke to General Ferber. He won't think of the possibility of giving Aimé a margin of profit from the supplies they'll require. Think of it. I was always only one. There will be an air arm. Hundreds of aircraft. But how do I extricate myself from giving my word?'

'Giving your word for what?'

'Supplies of hydrogen, oil, and petrol. I was so grateful for those early – well, really – months long services. I could never have got into the air without that help. Or it would have been far longer. But I was eager. I took the bargain. I've paid ever since!'

'You're a fathead!'

'I know. D'you think it makes me more comfortable to talk to General Ferber? He is a very fine man. But he is in charge of public funds. You know the Army? Hit that wall with your cranium!'

He made me laugh. He meant head. He mistranslated, one

of the few times I ever caught him out. He had a superb command of the language and that's why a small lapse amused me. But he was angry. Because of the worry of Aimé, and my laughter, and the cursing of drivers pulling up to let us pass, Santo threw them a fistful of notes and they shouted and jumped down to collect.

'The scourge of poverty,' he said. 'They leap to filch!'

'Why not? You threw!'

'They are human beings. They aren't ducks to be fed bread. We don't use our brains. We are, at best, stupid!'

'It's a peculiar position. I think you'll have some trouble. But legally, I'll do all I may. If that document mentions three per cent for a certain period, and he's been taking fifteen, I don't know what it might be in law, but to me it's cheating, and also I think it's contrary to the law of money-lending. I'm not sure. My attorney will straighten it!'

We went in the foyer and there, in front of us, were General Ferber and two officers and three lovely women, and what else do you expect?

'Talk of the devil!' General Ferber said, and came to us hands out. 'A short word, no more. An Inspector of Police called to my office this afternoon. Something about a person wanting a commission on whatever supplies we require. The whole thing's absurd, of course. I sent my Adjutant to warn the man that if he persists, he will go into one of our own "Bastilles" for a period of refrigeration!'

'Do him a lot of good,' Santo said. 'You'll clear my store and Bob's within twenty-four hours?'

'That's my intention,' the General said. 'In other words, I shall be in complete command of all supplies of any kind on Monday midday. It appeals to you?'

'It certainly appeals to me,' I said. 'Let us introduce our guests!'

We stood about and heard names and kissed hands and all the static nonsense of introduction, when nobody recalls anyone's name except his own, and the aides went to their table in the corner, and the General stayed for a final word.

'I shall expect to meet you at St Cyr on Monday week,' he told Santo. 'We begin at six in the morning, you remember?'

'Perfectly satisfactory, or even earlier,' Santo said. 'The winds are fresh and angry. They have lift. We are very

138

heavy. Demoiselle Nine requires extra support from Mother Nature. She can so often tip up upside down!'

'Why?' Gioia asked, a delicate question that came as a bomb.

Santo scratched his head and looked at the General, smiling almost pathetically.

'Women have the most extraordinary questions that haven't any answers,' he said. 'It comes to them, I hope, as a sex. We have to confront those problems with our mechanics and engineers, and, dear General, with us. That's why I don't want to push cadet instruction beyond certain limits. We don't know enough. What remains for them?'

'Honour,' he said.

'It's not enough!' Santo said, at his sharpest. 'I concede honour in a certain sense. But should you consider the travail of knowledge? I have no second-in-command. I am only myself. I cannot shift responsibility. I must teach. Others must learn. But I must learn *first*!'

'But you don't know *now*?'

'No, I do not!' Santo said. 'Air currents, and the rest? Of course I don't know. I'm learning? Very well, but my pupils are behind me. Why should I be responsible for a life? Who could be such an idiot?'

'I wish we could go back to the balloons!' Gioia said. 'They were so beautiful. Gentle. That marvellous float at night-time. Utter silence. Everything beneath you. The trees, the streets of the city, beautifully in darkness. Lean over the basket, and look up. I let my hair flow. It wanted to. It blew dearly with the breeze. Blue, blue, blue, everywhere. And a night of bright stars. Why do you need that noisy monster?'

'She isn't a noisy monster!' Santo said. 'She's the issue of what came from Demoiselle Number One, a marvellous product of the engineering shops and the girls in the sewing tables establishment. Without them, all of them, I could never have got into the air. I remember the women as well as the men. Without those girls, I would still be on the floor!'

'Always the women!' the General said, and bowed. 'I must join my own. Please let us have coffee together!'

'A delightful man,' Andrea said, hands linked under her chin. 'But I wouldn't like to get in his way!'

139

'He's a General,' Santo said. 'In my country, we don't doubt they supersede Christ. More or less the same here!'

'I still don't understand why you persist with those noisy and smelly Demoiselles, and leave those lovely quiet balloons in the hangar!' Gioia said, in a bite of caviar toast. 'It seems to me so unnecessary!'

'If we believed people like you, we'd still be crossing seas in sailing ships,' Santo said. 'We must get on. We have the means and the ability. Let's use them!'

'I remember my darling balloon,' Gioia said, eyes up. 'The most joyous moments of my life!'

'You were the first woman pilot,' Santo said. 'You piloted a dirigible from my place and in strong winds to the Bois. A Miss Thompson was a passenger piloted by a certain Mister Livingston in eighteen-seventeen. Probably the first woman in the air. British, of course. But you were the first pilot. None can take that from you!'

Gioia raised her glass.

'Here's to me!' she toasted. 'And I'm going to pilot that noisy Demoiselle. It's a two-seater, isn't it? So Andrea can come with me. We'll be the first two women in the air. Andrea, what do you say?'

'I'd love it!' Andrea said, looking at me. 'When do I have lessons?'

'When time allows,' Santo said. 'You'll both have to train as cadets. It'll be hard, you know that?'

'I think I can manage,' Gioia said. 'After all, I know most of the drills, don't I? A lot most of them don't know?'

'That's true,' Santo said. 'But you need experience in the air. There are problems not yet solved. We haven't the instruments. We must rely on instinct. It's not enough!'

'You can teach us!' Gioia said. 'If you can teach those fatheaded cadets, you can find the time to teach us, and we're *not* fatheads!'

'I'm aware of it,' Santo said, spooning into the soup. 'But I'd like to keep you both alive. That's why the training must be strict. In the air, you are at mercy. I intend the mercy shall be extended!'

Chapter 29

It was the devil of a shock to go to my stores warehouse at midday on Sunday and find the place two-thirds empty. It was ten times the size it had once been, and the echo reminded me of a ruined cathedral.

But as I stood there, I realized that I had no jobs for men and women looking to me for their wages, about thirty of them, all good friends of many years. How to fill that space was my greatest problem, and I went back to Paris with it, a little depressed until I opened the paper.

There on the front page was my answer. It seemed to blaze in my mind. It reviewed the career of Marconi since he had sent the first wireless signal across the Atlantic, and now there were plans to set up a factory in France, near Paris, to make smaller, lightweight sets. Instantly I saw what that would do for Santo and his brethren in the air. I could barely finish a coffee at Fouquet's and I trotted across the Champs to Bouhelle's garage for a car because I knew Santo was at St Cyr. It was a lovely day and I, certainly, had not felt so uplifted for a long time, because for once I was sure I was on the right tack. That journey often took a long time by horse and trap, but it was nothing by car. I found Santo in the canteen with his engineering team, drinking to the first successful flight of his latest Demoiselle, seen through the far doors, really a monster, but delicate as her tiny sister, all white wings, black struts, and polished bolts.

He gave me a tulip and I gave him the paper, folded at the story.

'Read that, and tell me,' I said. 'I thought of you!'

He read, and looked up from the paper, staring, and I have never forgotten his eyes bulbous, black, with a smile firing behind them.

'I shall go to the British Embassy to find out where he is,' I said. 'I shall offer to buy a franchise to build them only for use in the air. It solves communication air to ground, and I'll keep my staff in employment!'

'This is the very jewel of an idea!' Santo said. 'I'll get hold of Ferber. He's got to know about this. If we can send messages from the air to land, ninety per cent of our difficulties dissolve. Meet at my place tonight?'

'If I find Marconi's in London, I'll take the afternoon train and the packet for Dover tonight,' I said. 'I want that franchise. Preferably for the whole of Europe, and I'll pay cash!'

'If you need financial help, I'm here!' Santo said. 'The sun of good luck shine upon you!'

It did, in fact, shine upon me, because at the British Embassy I went through the small postern, talked to a guard, and was led to an office, and the duty officer, hearing the names of Santo and General Ferber, went away and came back with another officer. They were both in morning dress, and the other officer – obviously a senior – took notes, snapped the book shut, and stood, smiling.

'I believe I shall be able to give you an answer in fifteen minutes or less, sir!' he said. 'We use the same system!'

My coffee was served in the private reception room in exquisite Georgian silver and Coalport china, a lovely return to my country, and then the senior officer came in, still smiling, and gave me a sheet of paper.

'Mr Marconi for the moment is in Geneva,' he said. 'But Mr Arturo Fuselli, one of his deputies, is at the Ritz, here, with his staff. He will be most happy to meet you this afternoon, and he suggests three o'clock?'

'Excellent, and thank you!'

I went out to the car, grateful, even proud, that I had roots in a country so elegant, efficient, courteous and got in the car almost in bloom.

The Ritz was what it always had been, a quiet joy, and the restaurant orchestra still played for late ones at luncheon, a waft of, I think, Floradora, or something like that. The hall porter looked at my piece of paper, and called a page, and asked me to sit in the lounge if I pleased, and I did. Before I could order a drink, Mr Fuselli was on top of me, cadaverously tall, of that sort of face telling of long hours, heavy responsibility, and desire to please which can destroy health.

We went up to the suite, and I made my purpose known,

142

and gave him my three-page plan. He looked at it, and turned the pages, and nodded.

'This is precisely what we're looking for,' he said. 'You'd manufacture in France?'

'To begin,' I said. 'I have the workpeople.'

'That's an advantage,' he said. 'Our problem is space and hands. It will be an entirely new industry. In fact, the whole idea will have to be re-planned. That is Mister Marconi's intention. Is it yours?'

'I shall have to think about it. It may be the best solution for us to meet and discuss. I have the capital. I am ready. Is *he*?'

Fuselli nodded his frowns and wrinkles.

'We haven't been idle,' he said. 'We have a team of draughtsmen working on the tooling prints. Our chief worry is for mechanics and people to put the parts together.'

'I've got them, and they and the requisite buildings are ready for work. I think our attorneys should meet, don't you? Lunch with me tomorrow and meet Monsieur Santos-Dumont and General Ferber. One o'clock, Fouquet's?'

'But I must talk to Mister Marconi first, of course!'

'Send him a telegram. We can sign contracts before the week's out. That's what you want, isn't it?'

He bowed and for the first time, in the most amazing manner, smiled, and all the wrinkles had gone.

'Sir,' he said. 'You are exigent. But I prefer that to poets and dreamers. You have references I may use?'

I gave him the file of bankers and attorneys, and the names of General Ferber's aides.

'That should quash all doubts,' I said. 'You may have a call from the General during the day. Kindly tell him we met. Good day!'

From that moment, it seemed, there was a devil's own gallimaufry of worry and hurry, of getting the material in stock, supervising the training of my people, bringing in the engineers to build the machines, setting out the areas of the factory, and generally putting the plant to work. I suppose about the hardest job I ever had to do. To crown matters, four of my ships came in, and I had to send Andrea, Miss Lambert, and M Moriset, my new accountant's deputy, down to the ports to discharge the cargoes and pay dues, which I knew must take her away from me for nearly a month, though because she promised to write to me almost every day, I could just put up with it.

Without Fuselli I could never really have approached what we did in the next month. Our progress amazed me as much as the new Marconi wireless set itself. A small box of wires and odd bits it appeared to me, and I shall never forget the faces of all my people in a crowd about one of Fuselli's men, and another man across the field with the same set, and then the sound came through, the dashes and dots of the Morse code which the operator wrote down, a greeting to us that incidentally nobody believed. Our man sent a message out to the field, tapping the key to give the same strange sounds, but because I had written the message nobody dared argue or deny. Several ran out to meet the man with the box, but then the cheers and handclapping were all the heartier when he showed them my message, exact, as it had been sent.

Simple, startled bemusement settled and many crossed themselves, certain they were in the presence of Satanas, with a lot of breath-blowing and rattling of beads. I realized I had known little of what I had chosen to call my people. But for all their superstitious hankering for the old pagan rituals, they were still devout and solid Christians, young and older. I was touched, I must say, and I saw why Frère Chevrillon would go back to his monastery for a couple of days now and again to escape what he considered a blight, and come back to cleanse and revive his flock.

They worked with a will. They helped with the off-loading of material, men and women, and they attended the training classes without a single absence. That was the difficult part. Those needlewomen had to be trained to use wire and the soldering iron, and place all those small parts in the proper place, but the days went by, and their progress was extraordinary to such an extent that Fuselli and the new chief engineer were able to say that when all the machines were in place, and the die-makers had finished the first batch, we could go into production.

During this time, Marconi was somewhere in Europe, some said Russia, but the contracts had been signed to my satisfaction by our team of attorneys, Fuselli was happy, and I waited for the return of Andrea with a tightening of the gullet whenever I thought of her. Reports had come from the consulates and details of the manifests came through the mail to show that all was in order.

I wanted to go down to the farm, but I decided to wait for Andrea. I could enjoy nothing without her. Curious, I stopped going out to dinner. First, I suppose, because Santo was away somewhere, possibly in Germany or beyond. The last time I had seen him had been at Fouquet's with General Ferber, with a demonstration at the Ritz afterwards of what Santo called the Magic Box. One set was across the space of the Place Vendôme and the other was in the room. Santo wrote a message, and it was sent by our operator, and the General wrote the return message, run across by a pageboy, and the operator wrote it word by word as the buzzes came in.

General Ferber sat back, astounded, and said he thought he saw the beginning of a new era with air machines and wireless, and thanked God, and drank another cognac and went to catch his train. Santo sat a little longer, but he was restless and said Gioia waited for him, which explained it. I stayed to talk details with Fuselli, and there were plenty, but then I went, deciding to stroll home, through the Vendôme, up to the Rivoli, and right, to the Champs.

No city has lovelier skies than Paris, especially when evening comes with the caress of a woman's hand. Suddenly all the street lights go on, and you seem to be walking in poetry. I crossed to the Marignan for a coffee and cognac, and bought a paper, but there was nothing in it except for two lines in the jobs wanted column. A female graduate required a place with a modern company, four languages, steno-dactyl, anywhere. Write *chiffre*.

I had no idea what a steno-dactyl was. Pterodactyls I knew. This was something different. I decided to find out what it was. A graduate steno-dactyl? Well, all right, I would have a look. At least there was a certain spirit there that I liked.

I cut the advertisement out, and when I got home, gave it to Tanzi to be sent to the office first thing in the morning to make an appointment.

But that morning began with bedlam at a little after six,

with the arrival of Andrea, train-weary, bringing in a foot of documents, Moriset with another two feet, and Miss Lambert with an armful of manifests that all had to be checked and delivered to the Inspector-General's office before the end of the week. I sent all three home for a rest and a fresh wardrobe. Andrea said she would invite herself for dinner at seven o'clock and she wanted it at the Ritz to assure herself she at last was in Paris, and we kissed, but she held off, saying she wanted a bath more than salvation and I let her go. Miss Lambert with a straight face gave me a tip of her hips, saying everything and nothing, and Moriset said he would be in later to start a statement of accounts, all well and good, but I could not – with every thought of loyalty to Andrea – forget the tip of those hips. In my state I had to be careful. A man always has a traitor lurking midships. I suspect women do, too, but they, possibly, are not such easy gives.

I got to the Paris office late, a far bigger place than my father had bought. I had extended it in the past couple of months and men were still working on the new décor, and I walked through a long room full of carpenters and plasterers, and down the corridor to my office, and into the anteroom, and I was stopped as if with a punch on the nose.

In the small whitewashed room, with the canvas still wrinkled on the floor, and a ladder against the far wall, a young woman in a grey tailleur sat in a hard cane chair reading *Le Figaro*, and I knew I must order more comfortable chairs for people having to wait. I suspected she was shoed by Bunting, and the hat, slightly tipped down, of huge pink roses was covered with a thrown-back veil, and her look up at me, of greyish-blue eyes with the smallest smile of hope – perhaps, yes, perhaps – almost brought me to halt, but I knew that could have been silly.

Instead I went on into the main office and through to my own, and once there with the door shut I breathed in.

The face could have been by Gainsborough or any man who ever painted beauty in a woman. I was in no temper to talk to her, and instead I called Mme Tombrouillet, the manager, and asked her to give the girl her fares to and from her home, and fare for tomorrow to the warehouse, with enough for luncheon and dinner today, and I would see her

146

tomorrow at eleven and to bring her references.

Mme Tombrouillet looked at me in a strange manner, I thought, but I said no more, and she nodded and went out.

How is it that when we meet someone, we seem to know immediately there is danger?

I had Andrea to think of.

To my shame, she had receded in some odd manner. But why *is* that?

Chapter 30

Gweniver Lutros Basilev was a mixture of Egyptian, Russian, Tunisian, and Scots, and none the worse for it. That morning she was in black, I suspected by Worth, and she wore a toque of russet flowers a shade lighter than her hair, and she took off her gloves as autumn strips the forest of leaves, gently, and her look at me was a meld of amusement and curiosity, and if not apprehension, then something a little less. From her papers she was a Bachelor of Arts from the Sorbonne, a licenciée of the business course at Saint Cloud, a something or other from somewhere else, and a sheaf of other paper and testimonials to prove that a minor genius sat in front of me, and I shall say it, in all her ravishing beauty.

This is a sad situation, because loyalty argues with that nudge in the trouser where the traitor lives, and ridiculous as it seems, he is not to be denied. There are all sorts of arguments, from the moral to the blah-blah, but through it all, the nudge persists. A standing prick knows no argument.

I think perhaps she felt as I did. I never got a good look at her eyes. She kept them down. I knew I could never put her in the Paris office. Andrea was far too intelligent, too much a woman, not to see gross competition.

Instead, I put her behind the accountant's office at the warehouse so that foreman on the various jobs could make their reports, not laboriously in writing that took hours, but talking to her so that she could take down in shorthand and

147

then type the report ready for me next morning, a saving of time and effort that proved itself over the weeks.

But when I saw the typed pages I still got the nudge, though I made no effort to see her. I had the French Air Arm to deal with, and the German demand, and my own business that went on growing, and Andrea came to dine and stay with me when she wished, though curiously there was less talk of our marriage. Very well, because there was far too much work to be done day by day to think of going off for any reason. It required a period of what Santo called Summer Fever, when everything stayed as it was, and time off could be taken without damage to what went on. I can never remember discussing it.

But I had a severe shock that Saturday noon. Tanzi had just taken her chair when I came down. It was a large chair of scarlet leather with a hood that made her look tinier than she really was, in her little bonnet and black shawl.

'Sir,' she said. 'Do you have an address in the Boulevard Haussmann of a Captain Tepperet?'

'Not that I know!'

'My loyalty is entirely to you. You send messages to Mam'selle Andrea to her home. Often they are sent on to the Boulevard Haussmann to the apartment of the Captain Tepperet. I say this because I think you should know!'

A great deal became clear. Andrea's pull-away from staying at weekends because her parents wanted her at home, her periods that were painful and went on for a couple of weeks, and her non-desire to go to dinner anywhere because she had no time to change became blindingly clear. I said and did nothing, because I have always been sure that a rotten relationship must always become apparent as the day. There is no way of keeping the curtains shut.

General Ferber came in that Thursday afternoon and, ridiculously or heartbreakingly, it all became stupidly apparent.

'You have a woman here called Basilev,' he said. 'Get rid of her immediately. Or do you wish her to be arrested on your premises?'

To say that I was tipped over would be a monstrous misuse of language.

'General, you are quite wrong,' I said, as quietly as I might. 'I found her through an advertisement. She did not apply. How could she be anything except as I find her, and the rest of us, an exceptional employee?'

'Anglers throw a hook with bait in unknown waters, don't they? Sometimes they catch a fish. You were a very big fish. She is in a most sensitive area of your business. Daily reports from your senior foremen. What could be more important? Get rid of her, *now*. Or she can be arrested at any moment, you understand?'

'But arrested for what?' I said.

'As a foreign agent. I have copies of her reports. This is intimate knowledge where we would prefer complete silence. I cannot permit such a leakage, but obviously. Because of you, I permit to a degree. But not longer. You will now discharge her, and she will be arrested as she leaves. My men are out there now. Have you anything to say?'

I looked at him, swinging a foot, arms wide on the chair arms.

'It implies that you have agents here?'

'Naturally. Why not?'

'It's not the most healthy idea. Whom may I trust?'

'Yourself, primarily. The rest can be suborned. Paid. Come on, you're grown up. You know girls. The men are ready at any time. She's bait!'

'I don't understand you,' I said. 'She's doing a perfectly good job. Does advertising in a newspaper make her some sort of spy?'

He leaned down to open a despatch case, and took out a handful of papers I saw were mine, a real jolt.

'These are your reports, which could have been of enormous importance to, let us say, our rivals?' he said. 'It's a matter of some satisfaction that they were intercepted. Have you anything further to say?'

'Nothing!'

'Good. Then she will remain in your employment until we have the next report, and then she will be arrested, but I hope not on these premises!'

'I'm sorry for her. I don't think she's the sort of girl to make fools of people employing her without pressure from somewhere. A mere catspaw?'

General Ferber leaned back, laughing without sound.

'Catspaw?' he said. 'Of course. A beautiful cat sticking her claws into anything useful to her masters? She's paid for it. The bitch!'

'But what evidence have you?'

'All we need. She'll do fifteen to twenty years. We are too soft on that type of strumpet!'

But I had a further idea. I simply could not tolerate the idea of that beautiful girl in prison. I went to lunch in the canteen, and then went out to the warehouse, into the main office, to the accountant's office, and beyond, where she took shorthand dictation from Jules Fromentin, a foreman in the steel small-parts section. I waved him outside and sat down in a warm chair, which I detest. If it had been a girl, very well, but the warmth of a man's arse annoys me. A girl's is a comfort.

We looked at each other.

'I'd like you to have dinner with me,' I said. 'Drouant at eight o'clock?'

'I'd expected you before,' she said, beautiful as ever, stroking hair over an ear. 'And supposing I have an appointment tonight?'

'That would be unfortunate,' I said, and got up. 'Drouant at eight We understand each other?'

Without looking at me, she nodded.

'I shall be there,' she said, down at the paper.

All that afternoon, looking over account sheets and stock lists, I could see her and I yearned, and perhaps there is no more sorrowful word, but there was nothing to be done except what I had decided. I left fairly late, and had time for only one drink and a wash and comb at the apartment, and went to the Place Gaillon to find her in the foyer, beautiful in green velvet – again, I thought, by Worth – and that meant funds far beyond what she earned with me. We had a champagne cocktail and went to Lussac and our table, and we both ordered a contrefilet, new potatoes, and peas, and I asked the *sommelier* for a Cheval Blanc. We spoke about this and that, and I found she had an extraordinary knowledge of horses and race courses, jockeys and trainers, on both sides of the Channel.

'But how do you know so much?'

'My father owns racehorses,' she said. 'Not here. He has several in training in England. Many more in Russia. Do you like horses?'

'Very much. Now, listen to me. When you've finished that steak, you will go to the boudoir. You will then leave and get yourself a cab and go to the Gare du Nord. You will take a ticket beyond the frontier. It's just after eleven o'clock that the train leaves. Finish your dinner and go. I shall stay here to fend off any possible enquiries!'

She nodded, put her knife and fork together, and raised her glass to me.

'To your very good health!' she said. 'I'm most disappointed we've had such little time together. But perhaps that may be remedied?'

I drank to her.

'Go!'

She put the handbag in the crook of her arm and smiled at me, a delicious smile, not an ordinary smile, but one meant for the bedroom, and I had to look up at her and curse in secret. Some gifts are beyond us.

I saw her go with a feeling of utter sadness, and Lussac, coming over to fill the glasses, must have sensed a pall of despondency.

'Something has affected you, sir?' he said. 'The dinner was not good?'

'On the contrary. It was simply delicious. My compliments to the chef. Simply that I've had bad news. It always affects the appetite, doesn't it?'

'Ah, but certainly! Certainly. Of course. Dessert, sir?'

'Coffee, please, for two. And one double brandy, I think of the House special, if you still have any?'

'For you, sir, we have everything!'

I sat there for all that time, until I was certain she was aboard the train and off. Just as I was about to call for the bill, two men came in, filled bellies and thick moustaches, and came to the table with their hats on.

'You lost your companion?' one of them said. 'Where did she go?'

'You might look in the boudoir,' I said. 'I don't know what girls do in there, but it often takes them a little time. Haven't you noticed?'

'It might interest you to know she isn't there,' the older said. 'Where's she gone?'

I waved to Lussac, and he came over.

'Who are these two?'

'You are not permitted to address the guests!' he told them, with rare dignity. 'Remove yourselves or I'll call the Police!'

'We *are* the Police!' the younger said. 'Now let's have this right. Where's the woman who sat at this table?'

'In France, everybody is free to come and go,' I said. 'Perhaps she has gone. Do I know? Do you? Is any crime committed? Have you the right to interrogate me? I shall call my attorney and find out!'

'No, sir!' the older officer said. 'We are merely enquiring, and we are satisfied that the woman is not on the premises. At all events, she is not with *you*. I think that's all?'

'I think so. Anything else?'

The older took off his hat and bowed.

'That's all, sir,' he said. 'Sorry we bothered you. I think we got the wrong information. They seem to like making fools of us!'

'Who?'

'Certain people, let us say, not of the Police Department?' the shorter man said. 'You mean she simply *left* you here?'

'We had a small quarrel, that's all. You know what women are. She wanted to go to the Opéra, and I wanted to go to the Comédie next Wednesday, that's all.'

'Ah!' he said raising eyebrows reminding me of a stoat's. 'She'll still be here on Wednesday, then?'

'So far as I know!'

'Good. Sorry to have inconvenienced you, sir. A very good night!'

I left at a quarter past midnight. There were no messages. Tanzi was cleaning the hallway. I took the smell of wax upstairs with me, and sat down with a final drink to think about things. Mme Dufresne came into mind and I wondered what could have happened to her. She had been such a beautiful and intelligent woman and I had thought her fond of me, because certainly I had been getting fonder of her. I seemed to act as an adolescent, fooled by any face and figure. But I thought of that long train ride from Paris.

152

It had touched me, whether the sense of duty or devotion to my interests, or the cheap ticket and a willingness to go back the same way without a word to me, though fortunately I had asked. Why did she leave without a word then or since? It beat me. And this latest fiasco flattened me. I saw that I had to be considerably more careful about the staff I employed.

And in it all, I hungered for a wife.

I thought of going down to the farm for a month or so and looking about the countryside families to find some good girl of blood and breed. It sounded like a cattle fair, but really it was not. The families were all of yeomen stock, the finest in France and therefore in all Europe. I would be lucky to find one, and I asked myself why the hell the thought had never occurred to me before.

I had to go down to the farm, but not for two days because I had an appointment with General Ferber.

I had to be patient, but damn it, I wanted a wife.

Andrea? Very well, but a nest on the Boulevard Haussmann was not my conception of pre-marital exercise.

Chapter 31

But then General Ferber gave me an entirely other picture. Captain Tepperet's wife, a cousin of Andrea's, had been ill for months, and there were two children to take care of, and all the little things that healthy women do without thinking were denied her. On a Captain's pay there was no room for any extravagance such as a nurse or governess or even for a housekeeper, and Andrea supplied the margin, because doctor's and chemist's bills had to be paid, and the Captain had his own expenses, plus of course, the schooling of the children. I thought with great pride of Andrea. She had said nothing. I had put another meaning in that tired face on many a morning. Things are often not what they seem, and I understood why she did not wish to come down to the farm. She had better things to do, and that was quiet proof of her lovely heart.

There was a certain distance in the General's manner.

'I understand you lost an employee?' he said, at his coldest. 'She dined with you and disappeared?'

'She did. If we speak of the same person?'

'You know we do. I gave you warning, and she went. Why?'

'Possibly she was smarter than your people?'

He shook his head, eyes down.

'I believe you warned her,' he said. 'That brings to an end any relationship between us. I'm sorry for it. You have been a good friend. You prove yourself unreliable. I can have nothing more to do with you. I leave you with greatest regret. Good night, sir!'

I let him go, asked for another coffee, and poured a brandy, and sat there, dumb in the sense that I had nothing to say. Me, unreliable? It hurt. I knew the report would have impact in other quarters. I knew without any doubt it would get back to Santo. He would be warned against talking to me, dealing with me, or employing the people I wanted him to put on his lines. There were many. He had the big Demoiselle with the twin engines and the two seats for pilot and co-pilot, something new in the air, and a close secret so far. But he needed engineers and mechanics, and I had been supplying them and the machinery.

I could see an end to it.

It hurt.

I had been part of the air programme since after his first flights by balloon. I had supplied silk, ropes, and hydrogen. I had employed the seamstresses to sew the envelopes. I had been an alter ego. His brother, in fact. In thinking, I began to realize that the General had made an extraordinary mistake. Gweniver's reports had nothing to do with the work for Santo. Fromentin had nothing to do with the work of Santo. None of the foremen had anything to do with the work of Santo. Why had I panicked?

I tried to telephone the General. I got no reply. I wrote, but with no reply. I thought I knew the answer. The show was new and the General was determined to run it by himself without help from the outside, including me.

But Santo was out in the blue and not to be found. His apartment was equally helpful. Tanzi had seen nothing for more than a month.

Where was *I*?

It seemed an excellent time to tell everybody to go to the devil and take a slow drive down to the farm with stops for luncheon and dinner at favourite places and arrive a little before eleven o'clock. The more I thought of it the better it seemed, and anyway I needed a rest. I had written what I wanted done while I was away. But, as ever, Santo kept me in Paris by coming in that afternoon with *his* knock on the door – a rap of the knuckles, *brrm brrm brm*! – and we embraced as brothers, and while I poured the tulips, he told me of flights through Germany and into Poland, and a start on the plan for Russia.

'General Ferber isn't overfond of the idea,' I said. 'He wants it all to himself. Haven't you found it so?'

'He is a blockhead,' Santo said. 'The same as the rest of them. All from the same block. They don't believe what they are told. They don't believe in flight. General Ferber is given the figures of flights. How long and how fast. But the figures are wrong. Deliberately. He knows that a cavalry squadron would cover the same ground in half the time. These items blunt his judgement. He isn't properly informed. He pretends he nurtures an infant unable to walk. I have proved him wrong. And what? He has cut back in his requirement. He is a shortsighted fool!'

'Why?'

Santo lifted his hands.

'The authorities on the other side are doubling and redoubling their requirements,' he said, in a shrug. 'When the time comes, they'll be ready. And the French, under a simple blockhead, will not!'

'Which time are you talking about?'

'When they go to war, of course?'

'Who speaks of war?'

'Travel about. This continent, or at least Germany, speaks of nothing else. Pickelhaubs, sabres, spurs, parades, bands and flags, what else? They train for war. Their minds are fixed on it. How long do we have? A couple of years? A little more? What does it matter? People will suffer. I don't want to go on with Demoiselle. She's enormous. She flies as a bird. But to think of her as a war machine is blasphemy. I hate the idea that she could be used as means of killing. Of destruction.'

155

'Then? What will you do?'

He walked to the window, hands in trouser pockets, and turned to look at me.

'I shall go back to Brazil,' he said. 'I do not wish to see civilization as I have known it destroy itself for the sake of military fools. Over the past months I've had all I can stand of them. They are fools, and they can never be reclaimed. They grow in their uniforms. A womb of idiots!'

'Where's Gioia?'

'I hope, in the apartment.'

'What do you mean, *hope*?'

'What I say. She's become intractable. She wants to fly the Demoiselle. She has the ability and the knowledge, but not the requisite experience of the vagaries of the air, and you know, none of us have any real acquaintance with it. So we argue. And I hate it. I wish to God she'd go away!'

This, from Santo?

I thought of her as I had first seen her in a sweet of candlelit Eve, pale gold, utterly a marvel of a woman, never, so far as I was concerned, to be forgotten, or even pushed to the sidelines, wherever *they* were, and I was unaware of them. How he could dream of letting her go was beyond, far beyond me. Then why Andrea? Well, if you can't get the best, get the next. Which seems a ridiculous way of looking at it. But then, Andrea had her own beauty, and I had never seen her by candlelight. That was a pity. But you can hardly say to a girl, light two dozen candles and get undressed, and call me.

She might tell you where to go.

I felt in fact that I was not always fair or just to Andrea, and then by accident I heard her speaking to some fathead in her office. The door was ajar, and plainly she was in a temper.

'You will buy me nothing!' she said, almost in a whisper, rasped in her throat. 'Get out. Never come here again!'

'Listen,' he said. 'I never saw anybody more beautiful. I'll buy them and you can put them on. Then we'll go to dinner, and I'll take them off. How's that?'

'Like this,' I said, and went in and cracked him across the skull with my heavy cherrywood stick. 'Get out. Your company will never again receive an order!'

He bled from a cut. Slowly he fell to his knees. Andrea ran to call for the porter, and I stood there watching him mop the cut with a handkerchief. The wound spouted. It was long and deep. I had meant it to be.

Lorsquier ran the stairs and came in, thudding, and took him under the arms, dragging him out backwards.

'Fling him in the street!' I said. 'Never permit the son-of-a-whore to enter this building again!'

'He won't, sir. He tries it with all the girls!'

I called Andrea and asked her, and she turned her back.

'Of course!' she said. 'They are salesmen. They try, and why not? If they can get what they want, very well. Every girl has the same problem. They've got a fist clutching one cheek or squeezing a breast or rubbing the crotch. What can a girl do? Complain, and she's instantly a willing partner. Who believes her? She's damned because she's a woman!'

'Take down a note. To all women employees. It has come to the notice of the Chairman that women of this company are being molested by visiting salesmen. This will stop. Any infraction will be reported immediately to the main office. A copy of this notice will be sent to all those companies dealing with us. Any divergence from this rule of conduct and the company need expect no further order. I think that ought to do it!'

'It's a little loosely worded, isn't it?' Andrea said, so gently, so like herself. 'Shouldn't an attorney make it iron-clad?'

'Anybody who reads that and misunderstands the meaning is an idiot and shouldn't be where he is. Let it go out. See that every girl gets a copy. Miss Lambert is a fly-by-night. Does she set the tone?'

'She may well do!'

'Get rid of her!'

'Very well, sir!'

That 'sir' between us, the two of the Mayoral sash, stuck a barb between what we had been and what we had become. I had an instant failing of the heart. I wanted to put my arms about her. But that, in the office, would never do. Then what the devil *could* I do? I looked at her, in grey skirts touching button boots, tightly-corsetted, breasts a-brim, a beauty, nothing less than delicious, and I had sympathy for those salesmen. After all, if a pinch or a squeeze could get you what you wanted, why not try? Salesmen are salesmen, most of them raw brutes trying to make a sale for commission, and if they could take a girl en route, so much the better.

I had no notion what to say to Andrea.

'Has this been your experience over your business life?' I asked her, in that quiet office. 'Do men try to impose themselves?'

'But why not?' she said. 'If a girl feels like it, wonderful. If she doesn't, well, all right, next time. It's a part of the risk of working. My father, my brothers, would cut their throats!'

'Why don't they?'

'They aren't told. We need our places. A girl without a job is helpless. Hopeless. What can she do? The rub of of a crotch, the squeeze of a cheek, is a small price to pay for permanency. You say nothing. There can always be a next time. When you feel you can go a little further!'

'Have you ever felt like that?'

'Often!'

'Then why didn't you?'

'Because I am not a sow to be filled by any pig. I am myself. And I thought I was going to marry you!'

'What's changed it?'

'*You* seem to have changed. You haven't invited me to the farm. We haven't been to dinner. Even to the apartment. I used to do the flowers there. I used to talk to your staff. I loved that. Why have I been kept away?'

There was the question, and it had no answer. None.

'You seem to have been busy with someone else,' I said, lame-duck.

'Tell me who?'

Her startling grey eyes pulled me short. She had the right. It is the hell of a moment when a man knows he is wrong.

Wrong!

When he has to go back and re-cast what he thought was correct.

'All right,' I said. 'I agree. What do *you* think?'

She squashed her eyes tight shut and began to cry, and I had to put my arms about her, press her beauty to me,

158

but I was wondering why we have to crush people, human beings, men or women, and especially women, to emotional limits before we do anything to help. I began to believe that we are all torturers at heart because torture is still so much a part of us. We seem to thrive on tales of torture from the old legends – from Foxe's *Book of Martyrs*, and others along the way – to the Russian pogroms in Poland and elsewhere, to Bulgarian and Turkish atrocities. But they seemed to affect none of us except to slap a newspaper and what? And *what*? Nobody seemed to give a damn. The churches even less. All this while I had my arms about Andrea.

What do we think about while we live? What is living and what is thinking? And there are times when questions seem fatuous.

'Let's agree that as soon as Santo is taken over by the Air Arm, and he and Gioia are free, we'll go to Geneva,' I said. 'Is that agreeable to you?'

She tightened her arms and stood tiptoe.

'Perfectly and wonderfully!' she whispered. 'All I could ever want. *Except!*'

'Except?'

'Gioia's having flying lessons. I'd like to learn too. Why not?'

'When we are married you won't have much time for flying. You'll have a fairly big place to look after. More than forty women and their families. Where will you find time to fly?'

'Oh, well. If Gioia can take lessons, I think I ought. After all, I've been as close to this air business as anyone else. Closer than most, except for you. I could tell our grandchildren that I was among the first women in the world to fly. Wouldn't that sound wonderful?'

'I never had the smallest inclination. It's not something that interests me. I'll sell the parts, the metals, the tools, and I'll find the engineers. But as to going up there, absolutely not. It's simply not my place. I have a business, a warehouse, an apartment, and a farm, and my own wine, champagne and cognac. It's enough. Why should I wish to fiddle in the clouds, when I can get into a boat and fish for a Sunday trout?'

'But if Gioia can, why can't I?'

'Two reasons. The first, she's been with Santo all this time and she's picked up what would take you the same time. A couple of years? Second. It's experience, not only lessons, Santo taught her. He loves her. So far as I see, she and flight have become one idea. She and Demoiselle have become part of a marvellous dream. The woman and the machine. She is a beautiful woman, and the air to him is a goddess. The two become one in his mind. Don't you see?'

'How long have you thought like this?'

'Since I saw them together that day at The Cascades, where we had luncheon. Don't you remember? She wore something in apricot, I think?'

'You don't remember what I wore?'

'Quite wrong. You wore pale blue and a straw hat with a plum, or something like that, ribbon, and a Japanese parasol, and Gioia was jealous. She wanted one, and you had to order it by one of our ships. Isn't it so?'

'You have a memory. But it wasn't a straw hat. It was a panama and it had a maroon ribbon, and Santo said he loved it, and I gave it to him, and Gioia was furious. Don't you remember?'

'I remember her fury. I don't remember what it was for.'

'That was girls' talk. We talked what we wanted, and it really was a relief after all that social chatter. You get the dead rats out of yourself!'

'What sort of dead rats did you have?'

'Well, she can do as she pleases. She has money. I have a little, but I have to work. I can't afford her sort of wardrobe. I don't worry about it. She wants me to go to places with her. I can't afford it, and she offers to pay for me. That grates on the nerves. Goodhearted and all that. But I don't need that sort of charity!'

'So you unsheathed the talons?'

'I did. And she laughed it off. She's a darling, really, under all that high-nose nonsense. She told me she puts it on to keep the men off. You'd be surprised what they'll try. Santo's fought two duels about it. He won both, did you know?'

'Not a word. Things are kept very quiet, aren't they?'

'When you have the Army in charge? And by the way, that large card on your desk was delivered by special messenger from the German Embassy this afternoon. If you wish to go to Berlin for the dinner to mark the flight of the first Demoiselle to be taken over by the German Army, your expenses are paid with a suite at the Adlon Hotel. You're allowed to take a companion!'

I looked at her smiling, quite beautiful, grey eyes.

'Well, now,' I said. 'The Teutons seem to be growing up. A companion, eh?'

'If you dare take some other bitch, you'll never see me again!'

I put my arms about that waist with no resistance but an instant yield.

'I've got the only bitch I'll ever want,' I said. 'Send a confirmatory telegram that we'll be there. I said *we*. That's *us*. Go to Worth or wherever you please and buy a dress and cloak and send the account to me as your husband. This time your friend Gioia will have real competition!'

Chapter 32

Anything the Germans do, I have found, is always magnificently well done. I began to find the truth of that from the moment we boarded the special train out of Paris. There was an excellent dinner with orchids on the table, wines and cognac in the sleeping compartment, an excellent breakfast next morning, and an escort of cavalry with the coach that took us to the Adlon. Our suite was palatial, flowers everywhere, a maid for Andrea and a valet for me, in addition to Lucien. We were taken to the museum and the picture gallery on the first day, and to a private cabaret after dinner that night, and I suppose Andrea saw her first nude women on the stage. They were beautiful and shameless, and she was shocked. But then, everybody has to grow, and on the way back, she told me into my shoulder she had learned a thing or two, which delighted me – though I was unbelieving – because although two young men had been on stage, and the usual happened, I was sure she had known it all before. Any sentient human has passions and temptations, and the rest is moralistic nonsense. Or perhaps not, and that may be debated by those interested. I was brought up in a narrow Calvinistic-cum-Catholic tradition because of my father and his father. My mother had little to say. I broke away from all that when I was at University. I refused to attend the family service on Sunday, and there was the hell to pay. My grandfather took to his enormous fourposter and swore he would eat no food until I attended Sunday service. I told him, in his bedcap, that he could starve, but I would not go near any church or chapel. He ate an enormous dinner that night, and the doctor told me I had saved a life by an ounce of honesty. My dear old grandfather had never believed in any of it, either. Neither, certainly, did my father, when I put it to him. He lived a curious life between agnostic and strict churchman that tore him in two spiritually and mentally, poor old lad. Nothing of the sort ever bothered me. I told the entire parcel to go to hell, and that was all. I would live as well as I might, and I would die as I must, and the rest was old wives' tales. Well, of course, my uncles and aunts were scandalized and dropped me, and nothing ever suited me better. I was free to think, and far better, free of *them*, and the stench of camphor in their houses, and mouse traps, and the odd smell of girls unused to bathing.

Anyway, before noon the following day we went to a splendid parade of the Life Guard Hussars, with the Kaiser in a coach, and a luncheon at Potsdam, and a sleep at the hotel – which we both needed – and I awoke draggy to bath and dress, to give Andrea at least two hours in the bathroom.

It was well worth it.

She wore periwinkle blue, and she was marvellous.

We met Santo and Gioia down in the foyer to have a drink, and I thought them disarrayed. I am not sure what I mean by that, but the word comes into mind, whatever it means. Gioia was not at her most beautiful, and Santo was certainly into the black of one of his black moods. He often had them when his plans did not go as he wished. I took no notice. The girls spoke little. Obviously, something had happened. I had no intention of asking the question.

'Something's gone radically wrong,' I said to Andrea,

when Gioia took Santo's arm and they walked away to take their seats upstairs. 'She's not at her best, and he's at his worst. Worse still, no officer has come over to toast or even to welcome us. That's a bad sign!'

'I believe from what Gioia said that Santo was given a copy of the speech to be made tonight by the German Minister, or whoever he is, in charge. He's threatened to walk out. I mean, of the banquet. Gioia's trying to persuade him not to. But you know what Santo is?'

'I imagine a sad situation?'

'Not *sad*. Calamitous!'

'Why?'

'She's quarrelled with him very badly. She wanted to fly the new Demoiselle to the airfield, and take a bouquet from the Kaiser. Santo said the weather was unpropitious and she was not strong enough. She burst into that snarly-screamy cat drama I don't think you've seen – it has no effect on Santo but it's simply awful – she screams, she kneels, prays, curses, all for nothing. He says no. So she won't dress up for the evening, doesn't go to the hairdresser, probably didn't bath, and merely got into her rags – as she calls them – and came here to be an apathetic, yes, but very dangerous member of the guest list!'

'How, dangerous?'

'She might say something in public. Something about women not being allowed to do their share in what men can do. After all, she knows almost as much about the machine as Santo, doesn't she?'

'But if he thinks she hasn't the strength to handle it?'

'She thinks that's nonsense. That's how the quarrel goes. It's unending. It's breaking them both. Can you bear it?'

'It's still between *them*. Given their personalities, what can we do?'

The trumpets sounded, a startlement, but it brought the force of the military into our heads and it made me weak. There was no power to withstand them. It was the sound of the Kaiser and his soldiers. I understood Santo. He was against a wall. His ideal was ruined in the map room, by the heavy crunch of marching jackboots, by the creak of saddle leather and the jingle of the sabretache. Nobody believed in the age of the air. It was not yet. Santo and his

163

kind had no importance. *But how he must have raged,* that clear-sighted one!

We went upstairs, and took our places on the right of the long horseshoe table, with the silver and the flowers, and everybody else down in the great hall, sitting at long tables, with the orchestra at the end, almost a wall of crimson jackets. Santo and Gioia were near the middle among people I had never seen, though their decorations promised distinction, and plumes in their women's hair and a dazzle of diamonds spoke of wealth. The dinner went on and on, how many courses I really am not sure. Andrea sat one seat away from me, with, as she told me later, a sauerkraut on one side and a wurst on the other, and they both wanted her to go home with them – to an hotel, of course – but she told him she was being taken home by the General making the speech, and that cured it.

But the General's speech, after three sharp clacks of the gavel, sent the air to thin height. His voice seemed to me skinny. It was not even a hem on a dress, but simply a small frill, and thinking of him on a parade ground, I was reminded of sergeant-majors posted to echo his commands.

Though my German is not of the best, I understood him to say that a certain point in human civilization had been reached where the air joined land and sea by the genius of Santos-Dumont, a magnificent Brazilian, from another continent, whose inspiration had extended the range of artillery in the science of war.

A lot of clapping from everybody, but I saw that black head of Santo's get up, and he pushed back his chair and nodded to Gioia not in the most polite manner to follow him, and he walked out, without waiting for her, and I nodded to Andrea, and pushed out my chair and hers, and followed, and in the loud, instant *bzz-bzz* of comment we went downstairs, and met them while we got our coats in the cloakrooms.

Santo was unable to speak. He trembled with rage or what, God knows. Gioia tried to put her arm about him, but he shook her off.

A bad sign, and I saw it in her eyes, black, so heavy, unlike the normal light we had grown to love. Love is a curious word. It can be used for almost any purpose except the real one we want. I loved Gioia. I loved the candlelit body of

164

the Eve I had seen. I loved her mind, I loved her womanliness, the beauty that secretly was mine.

When I had got my coat, and Andrea had her cloak, they had gone, but I had asked him to come with us for a drink.

Something, I knew, was very wrong. It was not in him to be discourteous, but an invitation flouted was the essence of discourtesy. When I telephoned, Gioia answered and said he had no wish to speak to anybody, that they were taking the night train back to Paris, and possibly would go to Monaco, and she cared nothing if they did or not, and blp! the telephone cut.

We heard no more before we left, and nothing when we returned to the rue Washington.

What to do? Going out to the hangar next morning would have been an invasion of privacy. To go next door would have been silly because Andrea was with me. We decided over a sleep-time tulip to do nothing, and Andrea went to her bed, and I to mine. Ah, such a virtuous couple for the sake of the servants, had we not in those two hours fucked ourselves into a coma on the couch. She was marvellous. I ran rod-firm and easy into her and her eyes went into her head and all the world turned to gold. More reason for the Mayoral sash, and before we kissed good night, we thought next Wednesday would be a good day.

I tried to find Santo on the telephone day after day, but I was told that he was unavailable. At his apartment, he was not at home. Gioia apparently was not in Paris. What to make of this? Had they gone off together? Had they split? I had no wish to intrude on his private life. I had no reason to visit him in any professional matter. I could go only as a friend, but what for, when I lived next door to him? But his telephone was blank, there and at the hangar. Ask a question and what is the answer? You cannot get a voice.

Andrea tried to find Gioia, and she could not. I sent Lucien to the hangar to find Santo, and he came back to say that everybody was working, but nobody knew where Santo was. The days passed. Nights passed. Telephones, messengers, nothing. Tanzi had seen nothing. Neither Santo nor Gioia had been back to the apartment, none of the garages held his car, none had rented, and his secretary, Mme Juneau, was as demented as we were. He had piles of paper to sign, and there was a payroll two weeks late. I told Andrea to call the Bank of France and say that I would guarantee the total and to pay out. Within the hour, Chapin called Andrea from the hangar to thank me and to say that Santo was expected on the following Friday, after a series of flights from Cologne. She asked about Gioia and he said that, yes, she would be with him in the second seat, and they expected a party for the entire village as a welcome home.

'What second seat?' Andrea asked.

'It's the enormous machine Gioia mentioned,' I said. 'It has two seats side by side, and she's obviously in one of them. They seem to have patched up, thank God. Let's arrange a table at Fouquet's and a little party before. Let's ask the Baron and a few others, and make it an event of some importance. Get a little colour into life!'

'Haven't you enough colour now?'

'Plenty, with you. But there's always room for more. Bright sparks make a flaming fire even more picturesque, don't you think? Commerce is a dull business, day after day. Let's put some life in it. For us!'

Against all the rules she put her arms around me.

'You don't think I'm dull, do you?' she whispered.

I held her close, thinking of her lustrously white body and the marvel of her beautiful bones in bed, the shape, the sweet of her.

'The only colour I've ever had in my life is you, and it's the only one I want,' I said. 'The sooner we get to Geneva, and on to the island, and back to the farm, the better I'll like it. I want to see you take charge. I want to see the entire place under your fist. I'll deal with the animals and the fields and vines, as I've told you. Your reign is in the house, and I shan't be satisfied until I see you there with all the keys. Is that, once for all, clear?'

'Clear,' she said and turned. 'I think it's all wonderful and I pray away my days to be there. Who is this Miss Blevasil or Basilev or whatever-her-name-is?'

'You know she was employed here. She was discharged. Why?'

'There are two letters here, one from Lille and another from Frankfurt. I'd call them love-letters!'

'Send them with my compliments to General Ferber and

say they may assist him. If there are any more, return to sender!'

She tiptoed to kiss my cheek.

'I'll do that with pleasure. The *bitch*!'

I was amused at the silage of passionate hate in her voice, and I knew I had a wife well able to take care of me and what was hers to manage and make her own.

There is no better feeling.

Chapter 33

The demand from the Germans horrified me. I felt I must tell General Ferber but he was obstinately unreachable. I tried to talk to his aides but they were fatheads of the same type. I had to try to think what to do, and it seemed to me that I must get closer to the Government. I had never had many political friends. But that afternoon I thought of the Baron de Rothschild, of the impeccable manner and the long white beard. He could enter the presence of any in France and more especially the President.

Andrea made it possible for me to see him, and I took a dossier of German purchases in the past six months and presented it, with a statement of accounts, and he as a banker was appalled.

'But these are millions!' he said. 'What are we doing?'

'Nothing at all or very little. That's why I'm here!'

He dug a little finger in his ear.

'What has Santos-Dumont to say to this?' he asked. 'Is he developing into an enemy of France?'

'To the contrary,' I said. 'He has consistently made it clear that France had domination and should continue. It is the military and the politicians holding back. They are the dolts in control!'

He bit into the cigar.

'What do you advise?' he asked.

'Please ask the President that any order of the Germans should be countermanded by a French order for at least fifty per cent more. In that way you are at parity plus. But you also need airmen. A programme for recruitment. The

167

air force in Germany *is* recruiting. Why not France?'

He shook his head, and the long white beard brushed the desk of cigar ash. I have never understood why men wear beards to take the place of a kitchen brush.

'There'll be the devil to pay,' he said. 'Nobody knows much about this. How is it to be publicized? The politicians are not even decent farmers. They are the most disgusting self-seeking bawlers. When were they ever less? To spend money on the air? What more idiot scheme could be devised? Who is to be responsible? Which party? For what reason?'

'War!'

He looked away, and I was sorry for him, thinking of that part of the Bible that told of grey hairs coming down to the grave.

'No chance of that for the moment,' he said.

'Moments pass. You should go to Berlin and find out what's thought there. Santo may be able to tell you more. He's been told that the airplane he invented is an extension of the artillery. Will that interest your President?'

'It depends where his interest lies. He may be playing the diplomatic game, in which case he may try to restore the status quo.'

'What's that?'

'Stop the manufacture of aircraft!'

'Did you ever hear of a certain English King, one Canute? His lickspittles put a chair on the seashore and he was supposed to halt the incoming tide. When they saved him from drowning, they understood he had *no* power. What power has the President? Or anyone else? Santos-Dumont took his finger out of the dyke once and for all. Pandora's box is open. Have you thought of the Germans in a few years' time?'

He gnawed on the cigar, looked out of the window, and threw the butt into the wastebasket. It started a fire and he had to stamp in it, and caught his boot, and danced about, a cartoon, until he kicked it off, and then his secretary came running in and held up her hands and took the smoking tub out.

'I don't know what I'm going to say,' he said.

'Show him this,' I said, pushing the file of accounts across the desk. 'Remember, these are figures for the past three months. There are others down to the day. They aren't complete, which is why they aren't here. France is in a curious position. She had an obvious advantage. She hasn't now!'

'With your help!' he said.

'Baron, you should know that throughout, Monsieur Santos-Dumont has been completely his own master. All I have done it to complete orders commercially. Whatever was wanted, I supplied. It may occur to you that the Germans, the Russians, and others will wish to use my sources of supply until they have arranged their own. It won't take long. And then, where is France?'

'I must accept your viewpoint. Disagreeable though it is, I shall ask for an audience. A most unpleasant business. He's very much of the old guard, you know, and he favours attacking rather than retreating!'

'Let him attack *this*. There *can* be no retreat. It belongs entirely to the future. We all used to see Santo here, buzzing about like a horsefly. Thousands shouted to see him. But what a marvellous man, don't you think? Then he exchanged the balloon for an air machine. Was that easy? And all that time, he carried that enormous expense from his own pocket. All right, he won a few prizes, and what? He gave the money to the poor of Paris. Has anyone else?'

The Baron got up and pulled down his waistcoat.

'Very well,' he said. 'You make a solid case. I shall see the President. God knows what he'll say!'

'Let him know that Santos-Dumont, a magnificent Brazilian, is a champion of France. Marianne is his love. He cannot allow the Germans or any others to take advantage of all that has been done at Saint Cloud and Neuilly. It was for his love. It was for France!'

'Those are useful words,' he said, craning his neck. 'They'll appeal to him. If they'll advance the case or not, God knows. It's a matter of the national budget. That's the private affair of bankers and politicians. Always a shallow collection of bastardy!'

'Perhaps you ought to tell Santo that. He might go over to the Germans?'

'God forbid! We must keep him. I shall see the President

as soon as possible. Perhaps this evening, unofficially of course. You'll be in if I call?'

'Depend upon it!'

I went home and spread the Santo dossier over the dining table. It showed the millions he had spent, and the paltry sums of his prizes which he had always given away. The generous – even princely – heart of the man was apparent in the figures, a formidable account of pioneering, of adventure, of success, of providing jobs for so many people, of training a school of mechanics, of providing a basis for the French air arm, all out of his own pocket. What greater friend had France?

Andrea had gone home, and although I felt like going to the Folies, I had to stay in for the Baron's call, and so I had dinner on a corner of the table, and with dessert I heard the bell, and jumped.

'This is your friend,' the Baron's voice said. 'No need for names. My interview was a success. May I come round?'

'I shall be waiting for you!'

I went downstairs and told Tanzi I was expecting an important guest and to absent herself. I saw from her eyes she thought it must be a woman, and the width of her mouth made it clear, in thought of Andrea, and she disapproved. Tanzi was utterly loyal and she loved Andrea. I loved her all the more for that.

The electric car, something new in Paris, came so quietly to the door, and the Baron got out, white beard wisping in the evening wind, smiling, shaking my hand.

'It's done!' he whispered. 'Really, he was tipped over by the figures. It's a marvellous record. I'd never thought Santo'd spent so much. It helped, of course, that the figures were certified by that firm of accountants. He used to be a chief shareholder, and he therefore has instant access to information. You will not be forgotten in this. He understood that without you, France would have lost him a long time ago. Santos-Dumont stayed with us because of you. That service will not go unrewarded!'

'I'm most happy to hear it, Baron,' I said. 'But there is one matter?'

'What is it?'

'None of that equipment should be moved. Wherever it

170

is, it remains – especially if it is paid for – a part of France. It is the property of the French air arm. The other side, pouring gold into his pocket, may think they also bought everything he has. I shall be here to prevent it!'

He stood.

'Excellent!' he said. 'That hadn't occurred to me, but I see exactly what you mean. It's a most important matter. I must see what can be done to make it impossible.'

'That in itself can be the very devil of a job,' I said. 'Every little part of those machines was tooled by hand in his own workshops. You can't buy them. But you *can* copy them if you have the master. You follow me?'

'Perfectly. By retaining the master, you are years ahead of your rival?'

'Exactly. What's required is a ban on all Santos-Dumont's machinery or any of the mechanistic parts he had made – always without a patent – to the dismay of so many of us. It should never be moved from France. It is all French property. He meant it to be so. Why should it be taken away?'

'I agree. I shall see to it. What do you advise?'

'Let the Army take over as soon as he returns from Cologne. It's a two-seater aircraft. It's enormous. It holds God-knows-how-many gallons of petrol. He intends to fly to Nice, so far as I know.'

'From here?'

'He's done it elsewhere. I've got the figures!'

'Damn it!' the Baron said. 'I can hardly believe it. A few metres a little time ago, and now hundreds of what –? Kilometres? Great God, where are we going?'

'Into the future, obviously. And because of him, France has always been in the forefront. Why should she be left behind?'

The baronial fingers took a cigar and carefully lit it with a cedar chip from the candle.

'I agree,' he said, quietly. 'We must treat this with more than usual care. In fact, we must devote a great deal more than routine care. We must be quite certain that we are doing all we may to promote the strength of the French air arm. That can't be done by giving things away, can it?'

'I should hardly have thought so!'

'Then I shall see a few friends and promulgate a law,' he said, scratching the back of his neck. 'The Santo-Dumont company as it stands must become national property. Is that the idea?'

'Exactly that and nothing else will do. Otherwise France will lose everything that's been done. Under, of course, French skies. Wouldn't that be the essence of stupidity?'

'Exactly my idea. I'm sure that the President will agree with me that it shall never happen. One last question. I ask in considerable trepidation, but I must be quite sure. In the event that the Santos-Dumont company, or whatever it is, should be taken, let's say, in trust, for the air arm, or the country – I'm still uncertain of the terms – do you stand to make any money?'

'Not one *sou*!'

'Very good. I'm satisfied. You realize that this is no ordinary business?'

'Of course. If it were, then obviously I would have bought the company!'

'But you couldn't have bought Santos-Dumont?'

'That is exactly why. He is not the man to be bought. Either he gives or he does not. That is *your* problem!'

'You think he won't?'

'I'm sure he won't. Or I'd have bought him out long ago. He's an idealist. It's difficult to explain. Flying, to him, is a sacred mission. He wants to put mankind in the air to surmount all barriers, all frontiers, all the idiots issuing passports, all the other idiots stamping them. He wants one world, where all people are one. Where everybody can say "I can go anywhere," and nobody will disagree!'

'Another tulip, and I shall go. It's a most excellent wine. I wish all meetings were as fruitful!'

But after he had gone I began to think how the devil I could presume to arrange the future of so great a man as Santos-Dumont. Who was I to begin with? A mere entrepreneur interfering with a genius. Pretending to help? For the sake of France? He might not see my reasoning in that light. He might see it in terms of trade. I had heavy trade with Germany and increasingly with Russia. How could I deny it? I had no intention, but the figures were there, and so were the bank drafts. At base, Santos-Dumont was my patron. It was simply not to be denied.

What could I do to serve him? As my friend.

As someone who through him had become a multi-millionaire.

I had too many tulips and went to bed drunk.

But still in the morning the question burned.

What was I to do? How was I to protect him?

In a curious way I felt like an older brother. I have no idea why, except, of course, I felt an enormous affection for him. I believe Santo inspired that feeling in everyone he met. I had a lasting memory of the exquisitely beautiful Gioia bending down to breathe fragrance and whisper 'My *little* man!' and his eyes staring up at her and saying all a man may say without a word.

They were such a lovely pair, she the tall *exquise*, and he the not even teat-high partner.

'He has to stand tip-toe to get his milk!' one wag said. 'I wish to God I could!'

But I hesitate to think he ever did. No man was ever purer in thought than Santo, at least from my experience. He was never one to join in any bar jokes. He always left and it began to be known that if you wanted to keep him in company, then language had to be watched. Anything to do with the denigration of women he abhorred. He became known among some as the Jesuit, which in fact did him no harm. Frère Chevrillon was almost ecstatic.

'Any father in the village would give him any or all of his daughters!' he said. 'But he never looks to any of them. He could take any of his sewing women. After all, they are girls in fullest bloom. They would love to become the love of so great a man they all adore. But? Absolutely nothing, and they don't understand it. After all, I receive confessions!'

Chapter 34

Santo came to talk to me on the late evening he arrived, and I was amazed at the size of the aircraft, larger than the earlier model I had seen, with two engines in tandem and larger petrol tanks. The two seats in front had belts but even so the idea of flying in it frightened the very devil out of me, though Gioia said she had loved every moment and only wanted to fly for the rest of her life. Andrea, look-like a lily gainst an orchid, and nothing to her disadvantage, said she wanted to fly as well, but there were impediments, first of all, marriage.

'Won't stop me,' Gioia said. 'I'll have my own aircraft and I'll go when and how I please. Any objections?'

'None,' Santo said. 'When you know what you're doing. You have still a great deal to learn, you know that?'

'I piloted for a couple of hours today,' she said. 'I took off and brought her down. You told me it was a superb performance. Did you or didn't you?'

'Yes, I did,' he said. 'Nobody could have made a better job of it. But there are still the details. You still cannot turn correctly. You haven't proper control of the stick. In a high wind you'd be in danger. You need much more practice with the flaps. Still, we'll go into that next week. Bob-a-dee, may I ask a great favour?'

'Anything and immediately!'

'Gioia dreams of going down to your farm. So do I. May we? For a week or so?'

'Of course. At any time. Everything will be ready. I have a telephone there now. D'you need the number?'

Santo raised his hands.

'I've had enough of them,' he said, as savage as I ever heard him. '*No* telephones, and *no*body knows where we are. Agreed?'

'Completely. Go when you please and let me know when you've gone. I've got a new boat there. I'm told the lake's full of excellent fish. Let me know how you find it. Are you taking new rods?'

'He's certainly taking one for me,' Gioia said. 'I want to learn more of what this nonsense is about fishing. Is it something of a magic?'

'Well, no,' I said. 'Fishing is a rather lovely way of spending time. What else do you do with time? Until you die? You sit in a boat and you pit wits against a fish? Could anything be more absurd? Yourself, a human being, against a fish? But then you see you must have some lovely link with fish. That idea, that cannot be pulled down? That has to be fished? That must be fished for? Against the intelligence of the fish? Has it intelligence? On the evidence, it has. You can't hook it when you want. People have to go into business to design and manufacture lures and flies. Hands, brains in motion, to hook a fish? That so often gets away? Only the seabirds, and notably the heron, can take what they like from the water. Man is a joke. He sits there dangling his balls and the fish laugh at him.'

'Odd way of looking at it,' Santo said. 'But then there are other occupations where one dangles one's balls. For example, flying!'

'I haven't got any balls,' Gioia said. 'What are balls?'

Santo looked at me. We looked as men look when there is really no reply. Only a clearing of the throat and a shift of movement. And in that moment I knew that Santo and his lovely Gioia were not lovers. I was simply, but simply, surprised.

'In any industry, they're called governors,' I said. 'They swing from here to there. They control the speed of the entire apparatus. In fact, nothing happens without them. They are extremely useful. You agree, Santo?'

'Without reservation,' he said, and nodded. 'Balls are all-important. In anything else besides industry. I don't know where Gioia would wear them?'

'Around my neck?' she said, with squeezed eyes sideways, almost smiling at Santo, which brought deep suspicion that she knew more than she wanted to tell. 'Cartier might make them for me?'

'I'll see what they can do,' Santo said, at the ceiling. 'May I have one of your very good Havanas?'

I held out the humidor.

'When do you go back to Germany?' I asked.

'At some time next week direct from your farm,' he said. 'Without pleasure. From peace into disaccord. I've gone too far to withdraw. Or I most certainly would!'

'Why?'

Santo sighed hard and long, and Gioia put out that hand of long fingers to cover his, and fold them.

'Ah, Bob-a-dee!' he said. 'God damn it, I know that my

idea is going to be misused. Other minds have taken it. Any other mind distorts. They have distorted my idea. They think of it as a weapon of war. Instead of a long-winged bird reaching across the world, they make it a predator, a killer. I feel I was born as a monster. I have brought a blight across mankind. It was never my thought. I simply saw the crossing of frontiers and the ease of lovely skies. It's too late to fight. Too many others have the idea. Too many of my mechanics have been taken away. What can I do?'

Gioia put her arms around him and cuddled his head and I was sure she loved him, and he settled there, under her corsage, and who would not?

'For the love of God,' I said. 'You're in a business, and people get work. They get pay. There are jobs. They need them. What's wrong with the whole concept?'

'Nothing wrong. Simply misused. The people in uniform took hold of it. They are the power. We are not. Do you argue?'

'I'm not competent,' I said. 'To me it's a new form of business, and it helps hundreds of people. What's wrong with that?'

'You heard that moron say it. An extension of the artillery. That was never my idea. It disgusts me. And there's nothing I can do. I expect I shall be accused of being a mass murderer. Think of that!'

'*I* think you worry far too much, don't *you* think?' Gioia said, as he sat up, and her tone seemed wifely, light and yet with a certain strength. 'You have little enough to complain about after all. Your contracts make you wealthy. If you'd taken out patents you'd be a multi-millionaire and wealthier by the day. What I don't like is to see others making money out of *you*. You're not a businessman, all very well and good. But it was your own money and ideas and *you* should have the benefit. I'm furious that anyone else should take a crumb away from you!'

'There're other things to be furious about,' he said, a little wearily. 'I'd like a cognac, if I may. Pick things up. Well, then. The farm tomorrow morning?'

'Settled,' I said. 'The trap will meet the train.'

Santo drank as a cavalier, head back, and down, patted his chest, and held out a hand to Gioia.

'Thursday week,' he said. 'The night we dine with the Baron at the Château. I shall ask you to take Gioia because I'll be flying the first Demoiselle possibly for the last time. She's going into the museum, with all the tools that made her, and she'll be followed by the others and a library of all the prints, etcetera, framed around the walls. I shall give it to Paris!'

'They'll charge admission and again you'll lose money!' Gioia said. 'Who could be such an idiot?'

Santo bowed to her.

'Me!' he said, and took her hand. 'I don't need it. I have cattle and coffee growing, and wheat and sugar where I was born. That's the heart of my life. The industrialist, the clerk, the banker, has no appeal. They live well, off other people. Very well. So do I. I shall leave a memorial here to the French, always my friends, and particularly here in Paris. I don't wish to live on admission tickets!'

'True!' Gioia said, tying her scarf. 'You live on millions in contracts and then curse your luck? I hope your cattle look at you cross-eyed!'

'So long as you don't!' Santo said, and took her hand. 'Bob-a-dee, next Thursday?'

We went down with them to the door and said our good nights, and watched them enter the door guarded by Tanzi, and go in. I wanted to put my arm about Andrea's waist, but she took skirts in hand and ran up the stairs, and by the time I got there, I faced a wildcat.

'Why did you let them have the farm?' she whispered. '*I* wanted to go there. *I* wanted to fish. *I* wanted to go in the boat. *I* wanted to count the linen. *I* wanted to talk to the staff. *I* wanted to do so many things. How long will it take that house to settle down after they've gone away? I love Gioia, but she upsets people. She doesn't notice them. She never gives them a nice word or a wave. She's herself and completely selfish!'

'You're not?'

'Of course I am. If I'm going to marry you, it'll be *my* house and I want to know exactly how things are. *That's* what I'd intended. We can't get married next week!'

'For God's sake why not?'

'Because I want my house in order before we get back. I

refuse to return to confusion. I *will* have my house in order so that you realize I am there. Or what sort of a wife shall I be?'

'The best?'

'Then let *me* take charge. You have nothing to do with the house. In fact, the farm is badly run down. You haven't given it enough attention. I spent some time on a farm. I kept the books. Except for the agent's accounts, you have none. Do you know which stallion serves your mares? How many colts, foals, names, bloodlines? Where they went? How many were sold without your knowledge? That agent is a drunkard and a thief. Everybody knows it except you. They are ticks feeding off a bull. Now let them try feeding off me!'

'Bulls, of course, have their partners?'

She turned and looked at me almost with bared teeth.

'They'll find out what sort of a *cow* I am!' she said. 'But you'll never be cheated again!'

I knew I had a wife at long last, someone I could come home to and know that all was well.

I was at rest, content, whatever the word is, and no man happier.

Chapter 35

About an hour before the Baron's dinner was to begin we got to the Château, and I garaged the car, and the girls went to the cloakroom to be rid of the dust. The white roads of France powdered under the wheels of the motorist, and the hedges and the fields for a distance were white and the farmers complained. We had to wear dustcoats and the women wore veils, and in any event, breathing was a problem, but in the exhilaration of speed, nobody cursed about dust. We were the creatures of the future. The motor was a sign of progress, and that was all.

I went out to join them in the resplendent marquee with an enormous silver buffet, out on the lawn that except for the flowers looked like a billiard table. Nothing more gentle ever came under foot. I began to realize the scope of the truly wealthy. Guests were gathering and there were, I thought, more than a hundred already accepting glasses from waiters in medieval dress, and picking niblets from the buffet. I found the girls near an enormous Lalique bowl of caviar with dishes of chopped egg, onions, and racks of thin toast, and waiters served the famous champagne, in my case with a dash of Angostura and a kiss of cognac.

'You have to be different,' Andrea said.

'That's because I am myself. Let anyone else do as he pleases!'

While I was saying it we heard the distant pop-pop-pop of Demoiselle, and she came over the low hill, a lovely white bird with a black body, and Santo in front, an arm-chaired beak, waving to us, turning her, until her wheels touched the grass, and the pop-pop stopped.

The crowd cheered and moved forward, but the Baron went in front and turned, holding out his arms, and the evening breeze played in the long white beard. Santo got out of Demoiselle, took off the heavy coat and cap, folded them, and stuffed them under the seat. He took a box slung from one of the ribs and opened it to take out a top hat, giving it a rub with his sleeve, and put it on, and came towards us in evening dress as if he had just walked across the Champs.

The noise almost made the Baron's words little but a movement of the mouth, but his meaning came through, that Santo should be allowed to enter the marquee and enjoy the usual toast of triumph for a conqueror.

With all that, of course, nobody heard a word, but they all raised their glasses on the motion of the Baron's hand and his gesture towards Santo. Gioia stood beside him and put an arm about his shoulders, but she was almost taller than his top hat, and she bent towards him, down, where his nose came immediately over the rim of her corsage, and he breathed in, and his mouth widened and he stared up at her, if I know anything, a man enchanted, forever grateful, and speechless because a woman's fragrance cannot be bottled, though in her warmth it may be alchemized or magicked into passion, and that is dangerous ground. It can lead astray. I felt that Santo was being led, and when I saw Gioia talking to the Baron, I wondered again. She could influence, and obviously. But influence what? A deal between the Baron and his banking and merchant friends? Given the softness of heart and the complete aversion of Santo from the scene of commerce, what might Gioia be discussing? She had nothing to do with the business of Santo as far as I knew. But she had been with him for most of the German and Polish flights and therefore knew far more than could be told in diaries and flight reports. I wanted to know what she could possibly have to say to the Baron in private conversation. This was nosey-parker at its worst, but after all, there is that curious sense called instinct, and I have my share. Andrea and Santo were talking near the buffet, and it seemed that he liked caviar with onion and chopped egg with a squeeze of lemon juice as much as I did, though I had to restrain myself to leave splendid room for dinner. The kitchen at the Château was famous and twelve courses was the least to expect, and I proposed to tighten my trousers in the pleasantest way.

She did, finally, leave the Baron, and I met her.

'Permit a friendly snout,' I said. 'What were you and the Baron talking about? Omelettes and their perfect mix?'

She laughed, but beautifully.

I saw why Santo would want to put his nose down into that corsage. Not a proper thought for a man intent on marrying another woman, but then, men have those thoughts.

'A secret between us,' she said, the conspirator. 'We shall promote a company to put on the market all Santo's patents, if it's not too late. I shall give him the company's charter and sixty per cent of its shares as a Christmas present. I am tired of seeing him robbed. It won't happen any more if I can help it. *Damn* them!'

'You have the right ally. But why didn't you come to me?'

She looked at me, and not the friendliest look.

'I thought you were one of them!' she said.

'Never. I have never made one penny out of any of Santo's production. I simply sold him the material he asked for. Beyond that, nothing!'

'Then forgive me. I believe you. But at least we'll prevent the others. I want to see Santo make a fortune on the industrial side. He's spent a fortune on the other. I simply want to see his face when I give him the papers!'

A great silver bell rang from the swinging arm of a footman on the steps, and people paired to go into the Château's foyer, a crimson damask chamber of portraits and sculpture, and on, through the cloakrooms to the antechamber to be served a fillip of champagne.

Coming towards me, I was surprised to see, was the Baron.

'A word with you,' he said. 'You know Santo probably better than anyone else. What – do you suppose – would he think of a company set up unknown to him to protect his interests?'

'If I know him, he will fly without a Demoiselle! He'll be furious. He's done everything altruistically. For the sake of the entire human race. A strange man? Strange ideas? Of course. Look what he's done. On his own. At his own expense. He's won prizes? And what? He gave them to the poor of Paris. Then how do you think he will like a company formed to make money for shareholders and himself?'

The eyes I looked into held all the glint of an eagle's and I forgot for not one moment the nature of the man I spoke to.

'Then you have no wish to join us?' the Baron said.

'None, absolutely,' I said. 'What would Santo think of me if he saw my name in a list of shareholders? Behind his back? Against his will? What sort of a friend am I?'

He nodded and I heard the rustle of the beard against the silk of the waistcoat.

'I understand,' he said. 'But you see I'm entirely in accord with Gioia. She believes that Santo is being cheated. So do I. Therefore, with a few friends, we shall form a company in his name, and give the rights to him whenever she thinks. Perhaps as a Christmas present from her. What do we lose? He gains. That's what matters, isn't it?'

I shook my head.

'He won't like it,' I said. 'He's the human bird. Flying where he likes. Untrammelled. He wants nothing to do with merchants or money. He does what *he* wants. *He* pays for it. He has no desire to be patronized by anyone. He has a truly fierce Brazilian pride. He is himself. He will remain so. What sort of friend would I be if I tried to deceive him?

181

Between us is the trust of brothers. Should I destroy it for the sake of extra money? Can you hear him spit? This is the difference between the Brazilian and the European or any other. The Brazilian has his own way to be, and of course, there is no other way. For him, or for anybody else!'

'Strange business,' the Baron said, through the cigar. 'Very strange indeed. I have a tremendous feeling for Santo. But I can't say I altogether understand his point of view?'

'Very simple,' I said. 'He simply says "Leave me alone and I will do as I want, and I will give everything back to you, but without charge. I shall be a dragonfly to land here and there, but so lightly you will never know, and I will fly off. I don't need your help. Simply leave me alone." Is it too much to ask?'

'A strange man,' the Baron said.

'A Brazilian,' I said. 'Anything wrong?'

'To the contrary. He teaches us!'

'What?'

'How to be a man. Alone. With an idea. And a persistent will to carry it foward to success. Without help. Without troubling anybody. I have almost a reverence for this – what? – puck of the skies. Where else do we find him? Those who try to follow? Very well. Of course, men try to copy. They might even overtake. But the master must always supervene. As Santo has done. As everybody knows. His latest plane – this last aircraft – is far and away in front. The pride of his career. Far beyond the reach of his rivals. After all, he has his own workshop, and his workmen. He trained them. We in France can only be grateful he chose to live and work with us. Where will you be this weekend?'

'I'm taking Andrea to Nice. It's a favourite of ours.'

'Oh. Not to the farm?'

'I promised not to tell. Santo's going there with Gioia. Mum's the word!'

'Naturally. And by the way, do you know a certain Madame Dufresne? She's applied for a post as secretary. She said you'd employed her?'

'That is correct. She disappeared in an odd way. I would advise you not to employ her. She's efficient, first class in every way. But!'

'That settles it. Let's go to the bar!'

The second bell chimed, and we took partners and trooped into dinner, to a table that must have held two hundred guests with the Baroness at the south and the Baron north, and certainly, under the chandeliers, I had never seen a spectacle more beautiful, whether of women in jewels or men in uniforms and medals, though I was glad to see that the Baron and a few of his friends were dressed – with me – in black, together, of course, with Santo.

We were in excellent company.

After dinner, and the appearance of Arab coffee-makers, and the attendant paraphernalia, we all went out on the steps to see Santo walk out to Demoiselle, put his top hat in its nest, take the heavy coat from under the seat, put on cap and goggles, wave to us, start the engine and pop-pop across the grass, and up, as a bird, over the hill.

It all looked so simple.

Chapter 36

Mayor Jacques Craillot met us at Nice with the pony cart and a pair of cobs, nothing smarter or shinier on the road, and we trotted to his village in perfect weather along a lane in marvel of wildflowers. We stopped at the café in the Square, and took a table in sunshine to eat crusty bread not long from the oven, and the local smoked ham, creamy cheese, wonderful butter, the crispest lettuce and reddest, sweetest tomatoes and a bottle of the Mayor's own wine, naturally, because he owned the café. He had a place outside with cattle, sheep, and goats, and a vineyard making his own wines and cognac, and he had the cognac of his grandfather's time in his cellar. We promised we would visit him, because his son was at University, and except for an infant daughter, he was lonely.

He was a dear man, in his frock and plaited straw hat, and the high collar and black silk scarf of years ago, and the shrewd eyes and lined face of the fieldsman. He was a curious mixture of town and country, in some ways a yokel, but in others smart enough to have bought land and fishing boats and almost all of the village, in fact a millionaire although perhaps he would not have said so. He and those like him were the backbone of France, and I had the greatest respect.

He took us to what we began calling Our Steps, leading down from the Square to a small beach, all ours, with a blue boat drawn up on rollers, and we took our shoes off to walk through the hot white sand to a long, low cottage in stone with whitewashed endwalls, white window frames, and a plum-red door, low and broad, with a huge copper knocker in the shape of an artist's palette, and the colours were all in enamel round the edge, simply – as Andrea said – beautiful.

We went in to a long, low, raftered room, with a huge fireplace at the far end, and an enormous log against the back already fired. The walls were painted with scenes of the circus, exquisitely drawn in fragile blues and pinks, of clowns, Pierrots and Columbines, and a few nudes that reminded me of Rubens and the miracle of the female body, though, of course, Andrea turned away.

In a clop of clogs and an apron whisperous with starch Berthe came from the kitchen, slate-floored and window-sills filled with geraniums that made me feel I was blushing.

Berthe was our cook and housekeeper, a big woman rosy as apples, with the legs of Goliath, but her smile held all the perfume of France, and her shy welcome made her a sister. In moments Andrea had looked into the larder, a cool place of tiles, to find that everything – from a flitch of ham, a leg of bacon, the biggest brown eggs I ever saw, joints of meat, to vegetables and fruits – was there in profusion. And what to say?

The Mayor excused himself, saying that we should be left to warm ourselves and touch the walls and tread the floors and make our nid our own. The boat was always ready to put to sea for fish, and Berthe's father would sail us. The Mayor went, and Berthe came out in her cloak and said she would come back to cook dinner, but Andrea said that she would cook, and Berthe bent a knee and went. I read the papers, and in proper time, Andrea brought out an unbelievable boiled haunch of bacon with steamed cabbage and potatoes, a marvel of simplicity and taste that I, used to restaurants and rubbish, instantly knew to be true food, with of course, her own mustard sauce.

The days passed in the blue boat with Blic at the tiller, a retired fisher captain knowing the sea lanes as we knew the paths up the cliff, and we brought up lobster pots and crab baskets, and we fished in rich waters and never came home without a dangle of kitchen's marvels for us to eat and for Berthe to take home to her family, although she always saw to it that we had a marvellous fish in aspic for lunch, but I doubt we ever knew what they were. That Thursday morning Andrea caught the biggest fish I ever saw, and Blic had to help her pull it aboard, wider than the stretch of my arms, fatter than the stretch of my hands, and Blic nodded his grey beard and said that, for a girl, she was more than a champion. We went back and winched the boat up on the rollers, and the fire Blic had lit on the stones became white hot. He scaled, and cut off the fins, tail, and head, opened that enormous fish, and took out the spine and all the other stuff, and our cats made a meal. He cut three steaks from the centre, and the tail end went home with Berthe, and the top went up to Mayor Craillot. They were baked on hot stone, with olive oil and dashes of wine, with all the herbs. I never tasted anything to compare. But I never found out the name of the fish. Perhaps that sort of food is told only in fairy stories. Better it is.

But the days pass and thoughts go to the work, and mine went constantly to Santo. I knew he was in Germany or Poland, and perhaps in Russia, but I was his source of supply and I had always supervised his requirements rigorously and in person. That responsibility began to worry and I told Andrea on the night we came back from our extraordinary dinner with Mayor Craillot – of a shoulder of pork, smothered with clay and baked in a brick oven fired with bracken, a mash of carrots, white turnips, parsnips, and potatoes, and hearts of artichoke in a vinaigrette and honey sauce, and after that, a cherry pie, more than three fingers thick, with a flake pastry that could blow away, and coffee, with, naturally, his grandfather's cognac, deserving of every word of praise – that we must consider leaving.

Our time had come to think of business, commerce, the nonsense of modern life.

I went down Our Steps in front of Andrea to give her a shoulder to lean on and her voice came to me with the sea breeze, asking why I could not sell the business and live between the farm and this beach, and enjoy all the following years without one moment of worry. After all, I had far more than Mayor Craillot, though he enjoyed a greatly richer life, and I listened, yes, because she was right. I pretended to throw it off, but she persisted, pointing out that with very few improvements, the cottage could become a small but beautiful mansion, and all it required was a garden planted up the cliff and a man to tend it. The more I thought about it, the better the prospect seemed to become. A life between here and the farm and the apartment in Paris appeared to me a small vision of an earthly paradise, and better still, I could well afford it. I could live very well on the farm. It always returned an excellent profit. We could live here on investments alone, without turning a finger. The more I thought about it the better it seemed, and to cap it, I had no desire to go back to the office and look at any more paper. But I had to think of Santo, and that settled it. I had to make my peace with him, and see to it that he was properly supplied however long it took.

Andrea nodded, shrugged, and agreed, with her back to me, when you know perfectly well that she disagrees but has no good reason for denial, none, at any rate, she can think of for the moment.

We had one more party with Mayor Craillot and all the village people at his sixteenth-century farm, a glory of stone, raftered, panelled, and hung with pictures by the same artist as down below in our place and many more, older, bought on the advice of the artist – the Spaniard called Picasso, some Dutch, French, German, and Italian – even to my eye, a marvellous collection. Our *paella* was cooked in a copper pan about six foot across, filled with olive oil and wine, and piled with all the sea riches, from the smallest shrimp to giant lobster, and every sort of fish, and quarterings of duck, chicken, and turkey, and then, the smaller birds, and the larger, up to the cock pheasant and the goose. You took your horn mug and dipped into the broth, and twisted a piece of bread from the oven, and you began to savour the riches of the earth.

I was taught a lesson. This was how I wanted to live, and it was my absolute intention. Andrea put her arms about me, and kissed me a fishy kiss because she was eating a lobster, and I went off to find Mayor Craillot, and there he was at the fire, prodding the cookery of the *paella* with a big wooden paddle, and handfuls of herbs, and splendid pourings of his own olive oil. I told him I wanted to buy the cottage and the surrounding land, and he bowed, and stirred, and said he would answer me in the morning.

The morning answer came in an envelope brought by one of the village boys. With squirarchial courtesy, Mayor Craillot wrote his price – about a third of what I expected – and I showed it to Andrea, and we went up to the village to the bank. I signed the order, and we went to the attorney, and waited in the café. Within the hour, signed, sealed with red sealing wax, the cottage was ours. We danced down Our Steps, and through the sand to Our Cottage, and we touched the walls and the doors, and we sang though I really don't know what, but in that condition it is possible to sing nonsense and not know it.

Blic found a gardener, Ulric, a strange name, but his father had been headmaster at the local school, and he came down, a giant, with five children, and he wanted farmyard manure, and sacks of forest leaves, and I waved a hand and his smile shone. All the rest of that day men came down our steps with sacks, and all the next, and in just those two days, the back of the house, and all the surround was piled with earth and manure, and dug in, and then the plants came down, great heaps of them, and Ulric put them in new ground, and we had some argument about the winter tide and I decided on a five-foot stone wall, and a garden outside the front door for all the bulbs and spring plants. Andrea was enchanted, and so was I. Never in my life had I had the will to form a garden. Ulric had worked at a nearby château, always a junior, for the past twenty years, and this was his chance to show what *he* wanted to do. I gave him a free hand. In those days we had left, the wall was built, the garden was laid out, and the difference was strange, not to say extraordinary. Master craftsmen make an entirely new appearance, nothing to compare with your mundane imagination or what you might have thought.

I was delighted, and we left at five o'clock on that morning, in dawn's blue and nippy air, perfectly happy, with a swallow of Mayor Craillot's cognac now and again to carry us to the railway station, and the warm restaurant car to Paris.

Tanzi had a message from Santo that he and Gioia would be back on Saturday, and inviting us to dinner that night at Fouquet's, always the best choice because it was just across the street, and to come in for a drink at nine o'clock. I called the warehouse and found everything in excellent order, and the office in Paris ran on oiled wheels. I found it strange that I could go away for almost a month, and everything went as well without me as with me. Not the happiest conclusion, I thought, but then practice makes perfect, and the company had practiced perfection since the time of my Grandad, God bless his memory.

I went out to the warehouse, and Andrea went shopping and Tanzi told me that no woman seemed happier, or had become more beautiful. It simply showed, she said, what could happen when a woman fell in love. She bloomed as a flower. She even walked differently, as she moved to her lover in bed.

Chapter 37

After an excellent dinner at Fouquet's, Santo said he had an early appointment with General Ferber, and Andrea had to go home to her parents, and so instead of going to the Folies, I took Andrea home, not far away, and Santo invited me to call in for a drink on the way back.

Immediately I noticed the huge photograph of Gioia in a gold frame on his desk, with all the vases of blossom in the room, but only white roses beside her.

He told me he was worried about the aircraft industry.

He looked at the ceiling and blew out his breath.

'It goes beyond fever, to hysteria,' he said. 'They all want more. Bigger, quicker, and to carry men. It's all military. Germany, Russia. Here in this country, they're stealing my best men for ten times what I pay them. I don't know till they've gone. They're ashamed to come and tell me about it openly. They go!'

'Can't you put your men under contract?'

'If a man's made up his mind to go, what's the use of a contract?'

'You could sue?'

'In which court? Here? In Germany? Russia? Under which law? How many years of litigation? No. I'm steadily losing control. Perhaps I should have taken out patents, as my beautiful Gioia still insists. But I wanted to present to all men a new system which would free them of frontiers. Make them part of each other, even of each other's families. I can fly from here to there. Nobody can stop me. Nobody tries. I have spent nights in mansions and in peasant's huts. They were marvellous nights. I have flown all over Europe. For me, it is one country. With a wonderful good-hearted people. As I know. The others, like General Ferber, I detest. I've met so many of them. Different uniforms. All the same. I wish I could send them all to hell!'

'Dear Santo, you climb a mountain in snow-fog without a peak you can see. What's the use of that? Why don't you make a proper business deal? I can take care of it for you, in any country. I have the advantage of more than a hundred years' experience. I know the patent lawyers, those close to the Ministers. Let me take charge of this business. You are in complete charge of the technical and engineering side. Let me manage the business side. Make Gioia happy!'

He nodded.

'I never thought it would be as difficult as this,' he said, but so hang-headed dejectedly. 'Flying was a new idea. Then it became engineering. And business. And armaments. What did I do? Create a monster?'

I had to sit back.

From the screech in his voice and fists drumming on the desk and the spittle foaming he was near to a crisis. He was not the Santo I knew, the cool, the brave.

I had to think, sit back, use time.

Chapter 38

It took the patience of Andrea and nearly six weeks of solid work by patent lawyers, accountants, and my own law firm to bring Santo Enterprises into even the most fragmental form and there were large gaps, especially in France, Great Britain, and Germany. General Ferber stamped in and out of my office, demanding this and that, which of course he never got, though I realized his plight. He had to go back and talk to a Minister, and the Minister had to talk to the President, and he had to talk to the Cabinet, and they had to decide, and the business passed to the politicians, and so the endless nonsense went on. Everybody suffered except Santo and, I shall say it, myself. Everybody had used Santo, had made money out of him by using his work, that now had to be paid for, and now we were turning the screws and a lot of people were howling.

I leaned back and laughed with Gioia. She read each letter of complaint with the laughter reserved for comedians and clenched her small, beautiful glossy fists and told me to murder them, and of course, I did.

Andrea did as much work as anybody, and two girls helped her, each with a typewriter, wonderful time-savers. All our correspondence had been done by hand and gelatined to take a copy ever since I could remember, but the new page of fresh print was a revelation, although to the clerks it meant and end of their jobs. That was not my intention. I still loved penmanship, and I told Ridat that their places were safe as long as they lived, but the younger staff would take lessons in the use of typewriters until they were all proficient, and the outer offices rattled day-long, a good sound that helped letters out two and three days ahead of the old time, and that startled General Ferber.

'It could take me a couple of years to get them voted in the Budget,' he said. 'That's the state of our efficiency!'

'Not a bit,' I said. 'I can supply them on my credit note. Can't I?'

'If everything were so simple, yes. Two dozen to start. I hear you've promoted a company to commercialize Santo's business interests. Will that prove deleterious to us?'

'Certainly not,' I said. 'Supplies go on as before but *not* as gifts. I have a back-payments account which will have to be settled at the end of the financial year, and current supplies will be paid for monthly. So far, you've been getting gifts!'

He stretched his legs.

'Why has he suddenly become a merchant?'

'He hasn't. I prodded him into it. Why let other people use his patents for their own profit?'

'He hasn't any patents!'

'I've got half a dozen patent lawyers in my Paris offices working on it. So far, I'm well-pleased. We have a solid case. We shall sue wherever we must!'

'Fighting words?' he said, getting up. 'So long as we don't suffer, that's all. I could put you out of business, you know that?'

I stared him in the eyes.

'The aerial part of my business is extremely small,' I said. 'Don't confuse my business with that of Santo. The two are entirely different. And if ever you threaten me again, you can get your own supplier. I won't deal with you or your department. Is that clear?'

'I simply wanted to make things plain,' he said.

'I've made them plainer. Is there anything else?'

'Yes. Details of Santo's latest aircraft.'

'Get them from him. I supply material, not facts. He's the man to ask. Good morning!'

From his glare I believe that had he not been in civilian clothes he might have had me put against a wall and shot. But he went, and the door closed quietly, and I thought I knew why. Any trouble with me, and he would be held responsible, whether to his Minister or the President, and he also knew in which circles I moved. It was dangerous ground, more especially at a time when he knew that France had to make an effort to fend off the German and Russian threat. With that weight of responsibility, poor lad, I felt sorry for him.

I telephoned Santo and told him, and he laughed.

'Don't worry about him,' he said. 'He's been a plague to

me since I got back. He wants to see the latest Demoiselle and I refused because I have several more adjustments before I am ready. I had my girls sew a big canvas shirt over her!'

'Is that what all those rolls of canvas were for?'

'Of course. It's a splendid fit. This afternoon, we're having a party for the children. It's their Confirmation Day. Why not bring your own people over? And, of course, Frère Chevrillon. I'll send over the charabanc.'

'And I'll use cars and transport wagons for those left over. Lovely idea. Why not more time to prepare?'

'We didn't know till this morning. Gioia's in the village now, ordering the food. Those children eat like starving elephants!'

'I'll bring a few pastries over.'

'Excellent. They'll gobble the lot, be certain!'

Andrea and the girls in the office went to warn the priest and the pastrycook, and to buy what was thought necessary in the way of wine. We had a splendid local vintage, and we thought a couple of dozen cases would do for the grown-ups' party to come later that night, with a case of cognac, and a mixed case of Chartreuse, Bénédictine, and Cordial Médoc for the girls. They had to go home in a good mood, naturally.

It was a lovely day almost in midsummer, and the flowers were out, and we had the village band in one of the big wagons, and they played and the children sang, and Frère Chevrillon conducted all the way to the hangar, and the people along the way came out to shout, and many a one climbed up to have a fork in the feast. Initiative is always part of enjoyment.

We got there to the cheers of Santo's people, with their banners and two bands, and we made an enormous crowd, with marquees already up, and the tables being laid, and vases filled, and the wine casks were broached, and coffee urns poured for the children, and people started dancing.

'A lovely beginning,' Santo said. 'Gioia is simply ecstatic. She's wanted to do this all the time, but I've always said work comes first. But now there's an excuse. The children. I think to see the innocent confirmed into the rites is a most proper custom. We create Christians. There is no more important duty. Therefore, let us make it a really beautiful day. Let those young minds remember the coloured lights, and the bunting and the music, and the feast, of course, for the rest of their long lives, please God!'

The parents and most of the monks and nuns went up to the main office for a tulip of champagne, and then went down to take their part in the children's games, and their reliefs came up, and Santo talked to Frère Chevrillon about his idea for an infant school where mothers could take their children while they went to work in the hangar.

I noted that as an idea for my own place.

Andrea took my arm and pressed close, and is there anything more beautiful?

'Isn't this a marvellous idea?' she said. 'Listen to those children. When do *we* do this? We'll do it better, I promise you!'

'Whenever you wish,' I said. 'Choose the date!'

'I shall, and you won't be disappointed!' she said. 'What about the date your great-grandfather founded this company? We could have everything ready without a rush. You agree?'

'Perfectly. I'd never have thought of it. I think it would give *him* great pleasure, too. He reconstructed the church, down there. I wonder if old Chev has any trouble finding funds for repairs? Ask him, and we'll pay what's needed. It'll employ local men. They're all craftsmen. Keep them busy. That's what matters!'

'I'll find him and bring him up!' she carolled. 'Let him hear for himself. What a glorious day!'

She kissed me, and almost flew, and her grey voile skirts resolved the beauty of her body, and Santo came over to put a hand on my shoulder.

'I'm having trouble with Ferber,' he said, under the clinking of glasses being gathered by the waitresses. 'He wants the newest Demoiselle I've covered up downstairs. Nobody's going to so much as see it until I'm entirely satisfied that it's the best I can do. At the moment it's easy to pilot, well, let's say in mild winds. But in the average day, she's like a bedevilled bull. One has to push and pull. I'm learning to live with it. But that's not enough. I have a new engine in the prime stage which will give me at least three times the power. That's where the problem is. That, and the ailerons. It's a matter of design. But the dear General wants everything *now*. I've told him he'll kill his cadets. He doesn't care. But I *do*. Every death in a machine of mine is on my conscience. There have been many. Do you think I sleep more comfortably?'

'Let him bear the responsibility!'

'He's a General,' Santo said, opening his hands. 'What the devil does he care if young men die? That's what they're there for, isn't it?'

Frère Chevrillon and another local priest, Père Tuvant, came in and the office staff and waitresses going out stood aside for them to join us at the table. There were cheers and howls of laughter from below while Santo poured the tulips, and we raised a toast.

'That's the clowns,' Père Tuvant said, and smacked his lips. 'Not often I have a wine like *that*. Children love clowns. I believe we all do. God be praised that at precious little least there's still something to laugh *at*!'

Laughter outside had quietened, and more cheers began.

Père Tuvant raised a finger.

'The cycle act!' he said. 'The father carries his daughter on his shoulders riding a single wheel. Imagine!'

Louder cheers, and an engine began a loud drone, and I thought a mechanic might be tinkering, but I turned to see Santo staring down at the inkstand in wide, narrow-eyed horror, and he seemed for one moment to be stone but then he kicked aside the chair and ran to the door, flinging it to strike the wall and screamed to the women on the stairs to get out of the way, and the priests followed, and I, last.

What I thought in those moments I shall never be sure, but I got outside in time to see that enormous aircraft flying over the trees, with two hats in front, one Andrea's and the other, with ostrich plumes, Gioia's, and she seemed to be wrestling, and then, over the elms, the aircraft tipped to the left, and Gioia seemed almost to stand in an effort to correct the course, yet the aircraft went down steeply. The screams of the crowd running towards the elms covered all other sound, but that first high flash of orange flame and the ruffle of black smoke blowing away silenced them. The crackle of trees burning seemed a benison, but the flames

194

went higher and smoke flew blacker, and the wind took it away in long furls.

The two priests hurried towards the copse, kicking dust, holding up their *soutanes*. Santo knelt at the corner of the hangar, leaning against the wall, fists to temples, eyes shut.

He knew.

I went to him and pulled him up, but he threw me off, and I saw the stone-mask Brazilian face once again, and the tears ran and his collar was wet, and he stared, and I knew the meaning of basilisk.

'Leave me,' he said, with startling calm. 'I have a great deal to do. You understand?'

'What?'

'Never mind. Leave me. Take these people away. Send those priests away. You, please, go away. *Please!*'

I looked at him, and I knew it was useless.

His grief somehow reduced or dredged mine, or at any rate, numbed. In his tears I felt cleansed, if that's the word. I went upstairs and got two cognacs, and came down and offered him one but he dashed it out of my hand, and looked me cold in the eye.

'*Leave* me!' he whispered, but savagely. 'I know my responsibility to you. Don't remind me. I *know*. Please? *Go!*'

The crowds were coming back with the priests in front, and the village fire pump galloped over the field, but what can men do with buckets, and water more than several hundred yards away? It was lethal comedy.

I waved Frère Chevrillon and Père Tuvant away from Santo.

Both turned to meet me, and Santo leaned against the wall, bumping himself off to go into the hangar, and I watched him holding on to the stair rail to go up, a black silhouette of tragedy.

'There's nothing left,' Frère Chevrillon said, out of breath. 'Some white-hot metal. Nothing else. An incineration, but complete. Incineration. You understand? There is nothing. But *nothing*, hmh? Not even the ashes. It is blown away. We looked. We searched. Everything has been blown away. In this wind, what could survive?'

'Get everybody home,' I said. 'Divide what they want

between them. Everybody out of this place of Golgotha. You may do me a service?'

Frère Chevrillon held up his hands.

'Anything!' he said.

I wrote Andrea's address on a card.

'This is the address of her parents,' I said. 'Go to them and explain what horror was here. They'll believe *you*. What would they think of me?'

'You didn't know them?'

'I never had the opportunity of meeting them. Let it be said, to my shame. Will you go?'

'Immediately,' Frère Chevrillon said. 'Tonight I shall stay with my colleague. Tomorrow we shall have a Mass at sometime in the afternoon, depending on the wish of the parents to attend.'

'Please use my car.'

'We shall go to their parish priest, first. He will come with us, and we have our own transport. We —'

A terrible sound of animal cries, howls, came from above in the hangar.

Frère Chevrillon looked at me.

'Santo?' he whispered.

I nodded.

'Time for us to go,' I said. 'He knows he was responsible. He left the aircraft filled with petrol. Without it, no chance of incineration. You realize that?'

Frère Chevrillon looked down, and nodded.

'Let us see the parents,' he said, looking up at the awful sounds of a man *in extremis*. 'We owe it to them. To him. No?'

'I agree,' I said, still listening, and cringing. 'I hope you'll let me know the time of the Mass. I'd like to be there. The repairs to your parish church will be a memorial to this day's destruction. Start work immediately. Present your accounts monthly. Perhaps I should go up there?'

I pointed upstairs.

'I counsel not,' Père Tuvant said. 'Every man has his own cell. Let him shut the door and be with himself. What you hear is the voice of a soul in the anteroom to Hell. He divests himself of grief. Leave him!'

They walked across to the road, and I looked up at those

awful sounds from two lit windows in the hangar, and irresolutely turned down for Chabannet and the car. He had been so patient in his cap, twisted a little by long use. I told him the garage, and we went off through still-smoky smells, and a low glow of burning leaf. I put my hat over my eyes and thought of Andrea and mouldered, because what else is there to do?

I stopped him at the corner of the Matignon with a sudden idea, and walked, as I had so often done with her, holding hands, stopping at a café to to sit down and talk, drink, and go on to another café. That night, I walked everywhere and sat down wherever I remembered sitting together, and each time I saw her lovely face and felt my arm about her loveliness, and at last I was drunk, and I had sense enough to call a taxi and I could just remember the address.

Tanzi met me at the door, shawl in tight clutch – why do drunkards forget so much and retain the little things? – and I blundered in.

'This letter was delivered to you,' she said. 'It's from Santo. He was here. God knows what happened upstairs!'

I went up to my place. All in order. I went up the backstair, holding on to the rail, up to the roof, and everything in bloom, and across, and down the stairway to Gioia's apartment where I had seen her as I saw her now, in the holy light of candles, a woman, an Eve, glorious in beauty.

But the place had been wrecked. Everything was smashed. Mirrors in shards, where she had seen herself as I had seen her. Vases, tables, the bed, all cut, smashed as though some madman had been at work, and flowers had been torn and thrown about as if in some funerary ceremony.

Downstairs the same. Santo's desk was cut to pieces, his chair was chopped in shreds of leather and mahogany on the floor, and the gold frame and photograph were gone. The rest was utter destruction, even to the small cabinet, that I know was where he kept her smallest message, almost always on little bouquets of flowers, generally lilies-of-the-valley, his favourites, with violets.

'Say nothing of this,' I told Tanzi. 'Get Montret in here tomorrow and clear everything. If they can repair, very well. But nothing in words. You understand?'

She bobbed and held the shawl tighter.

'Call the garage,' I said. 'I want to go to the hangar. Did you see him?'

She nodded.

'He was completely quiet. In control. He gave me a thousand francs. Sir, should I keep it or give it back?'

'Keep it!' I said. 'And when the newspapermen and the photographers come in the morning, and you say nothing, I will give you another thousand francs. Understood?'

She bobbed again.

'Nothing will pass my lips except coffee!' she said. 'But what happened to –' her voice trailed, and I crumpled, and held her bones.

'They both died,' I said. 'They died. In a hell before Hell. Can Hell have any sting for them?'

She fell against me, and I put her in her chair.

'Call the garage,' I said. 'I want a car for the hangar. I have a feeling about what's going on there. I hope to God he's sane!'

I went upstairs to my own peaceful place, and I wished I could stay there and go to bed, but I was more than worried about Santo, because of the damage in those apartments that only a lunatic could have caused, and I wondered what might be going on at the hangar.

The car came and I told him I wanted to arrive quietly, at a little distance. When I awoke I was about two hundred yards away, and I got out, not very wide awake, and stared at flame everywhere. A line of barrels were on fire, the main hangar burned, and the workshops with the balloons in the roof were almost burned to the ground. While I watched, Santo came out with an armful of blue rolls, and paper, and plunged them into a barrel. I threw my coat in the car, and ran to him.

'What the hell are you doing?' I shouted.

'I'm getting rid of a part of my life I loved!' he said. 'Nothing else will matter. I have finished. *Finished*!'

His arms were burned, his face was burned, his hair was almost burned off, his clothes hung in burny rags. His eyes tried to see me through burned eyelashes, and the blistered face wept tears.

'Go away,' he said. 'Please go away. I have cut myself off. I have comp*lete*ly destroyed everything. I *hate* it. I have

198

my love. My work was for nothing except to destroy my love. For nothing else? Of course. Not even ashes? Then? Everything else will be ashes. Nothing will be left. Not even *ashes*!'

The early morning winds blew strong and made that curious sound as though a fine knife cut in taut canvas, a high whistle and a low moan, rising again, falling, rising.

He pushed the last armful of paper into the barrel, utterly ignoring the flame that burned.

'Go!' he said, across the flame. 'We have common horror. We shall live with it. I was to blame. I was your enemy. I took your love. Now I destroy what was *my* love. Go, dear friend, Bob-a-dee. She said it sounded like a bird. With a sweet song. Try to remember me as your brother. Not your destroyer. *I* am the horrible destroyer. Please *leave* me. *Via!*'

In that burn-scarred face I saw the Brazilian stone-mask. I knew there was nothing to say, or do.

I trudged to the road, seeing my shadow black in front from the flame, breathing the smoke from the barrels and the burned-out hangars. A few villagers ran up and stood at the roadside, and more were running.

'Get back to your beds!' I screamed at them. 'It has nothing to do with you!'

I got in the car and Chabannet turned, and I saw Santo come out with another armful of paper and cram it into the flame, and brush his arms, and drag himself into the doorway.

Chabannet asked me where to go, but I heard him through a fog of drunken grief, and I said the Champs, anywhere, and naturally he stopped nearest his garage, and I got out and begun walking. I went into every café still open, and certainly there were many, and came back to something like my usual self, despite a headache, not far from my Paris office, so that I knew where I was. I made a move to get up, but in the dawn sky I seemed to see Andrea, and I knew what I had lost. I fell back in the chair and swept the glass and all the saucers off the table and put my head in my arms and cried as an infant.

The waiter put his arm about my shoulders.

'Come on, old lad,' he whispered. 'What's wrong?'

'I lost my love,' I whispered. 'The most beautiful of them all!'

'I know the feeling,' he said, close to me. 'I lost my wife. You wake up in the morning, and there's an empty bed. You go to bed, and there's nobody. Dear brother in pain, I know how you feel. You have no account to pay!'

'Please call a fiacre to take me to the rue Washington,' I said. 'But listen. We working men do not exist on charity. We pay our way, in love or out of love. Here!'

I gave him a note, and he looked at it, and up, with his arms out.

'An angel appears!' he said.

'Her name was Andrea!' I said.

He whistled towards the rank, and a dear old horse lifted hairy fores to come alongside.

'Good luck, sir!' the waiter called. 'We all need it. But most of us don't get it!'

I used my keys and stumbled up the stairs, but taking off my overcoat I felt the crackle of the letter Tanzi had given me, and I took the paperknife and slit the edge.

Brother Bob-a-dee, Santo had written in a strange straggle, *here is a blank cheque to pay for any damage I did to your property. I had known such happiness. Complete. Such a woman exists only once in an era. I filled poor Demoiselle with enough to fly without a stop to the German border and over. It would have been a record to set the Tricolour flying for the next twenty years. But the Lord God tells us that pride goes before a fall. I did not allow for a woman's excited wish. She had been first to pilot a dirigible. There is no doubt about it. She had piloted Demoiselle beside me, and how proud I was to see her handling the controls. She did pilot for many hours. But she knew little about cross-winds, the most treacherous. She had not the arm-muscle to counter-act. My brave, my beautiful, Gioia is ash. I shall burn everything else to ash. An embrace, in shame. Santo.*

I remembered my feeling, sprawled over that café table. Possibly most memories pass, all the stupidities done and said and so often regretted. Those are the emptiest moments, filled with the mental dandelions that infest, and what can you *do*? For Christ's sweet sake what *can* you do? The indulgence of getting drunk brings torpor, but in wakening the day is greyer, and a hammer thuds.

Other thuds and the door swung, and General Ferber in uniform stood looking at me, still in my street clothes, legs out, trying to think through the hammer.

'Where is Santo?' he whispered, and his face was pinched, sallow, nothing of its usual health. 'Did you know that his place is burnt out? Everything. Ah, for God's sake. Did he go mad?'

'I don't know,' I said, trying to get up.

'But you were there?'

'There was nothing I could do!'

'You allowed him to destroy his work?'

'It was *his* work. What had I to do?'

'But have you no sense of responsibility?'

'All his business had passed from my keeping to yours. I had no right to interfere!'

He punched a fist into a palm.

'The drawings are gone,' he said. 'The models. All the detail. The motors. What in the name of God am I to say to the Minister?'

'That he did as he pleased with his own property?'

'It was the property of France!'

'You should have taken care of it!'

He walked over to the window. Bells chimed for seven o'clock.

'I'm told that two women died,' he said, without turning about. 'How?'

'Ask the witnesses. Who were the women?'

'I'm here to ask *you* that question, and why the fire was permitted to happen?'

'I have my business. He had his!'

'The hangars are burned out,' he said, counting on his fingers. 'There isn't a single piece of paper left. The barrels are full of ash. The petrol store is gone. The toolshop. The engine shed. The engines are molten deadweights. The machine shop. He left nothing. Why?'

I heard the bread van's horse in the street, and the paper-boy throwing his bundle to the newsagent opposite.

Everything was going on as before.

Lucien put the tray on the table, turned the cups, and

looked at the General.

'Not for me!' he said. 'I'm waiting for an answer!'

'I don't know,' I said. 'Who knows what's in a man's mind? Why did he destroy the work of wonderful years? He had millions to gain. But he never *cared* for millions. He cared only for the air and his Demoiselle. What else?'

'You will attend the enquiry,' he said. 'You will be notified!'

'*If* you can find me,' I said. 'I have nothing to tell any damned enquiry. I shall sell this business and retire. You and your aircraft may go to hell!'

'I've lost a friend,' he said, and turned for the door. 'But so have you!'

I did not attend the enquiry. I sold my business and began to live between the farm and the sea cottage, wondering why it had taken me so long to find out the pleasure of time without paper, charters, manifests, piles of mail, typewriters and telephones.

I was free but I never saw Santo again.

I heard of him, to my everlasting regret, while I was on honeymoon with the daughter of Mayor Craillot in Yokohama. Copies of months-old newspapers came aboard and we settled on them as chickens to corn.

London newspapers reported a revolution in Brazil, and I might have skimmed them all, except that I caught Santo's name, and I folded the paper to read. Army aircraft had bombed the rebels in São Paulo near to Santo's house.

Along the banquet table I saw once again that black polished head tip up at the ceiling, and the blinding stare, and the savage nod to Gioia while the General droned on.

Aircraft were nothing more than a further extension of artillery, simple and useful, certainly, but little more.

Andrea followed Gioia and I went out in a sudden muted gabble of shocked muttering. The guest of the evening had left without any word.

I knew why.

La Demoiselle, dream of his life, used for bombing?

Taking lives, destroying?

And now, in his own country?

I could only imagine those last, tragic, tortured moments. He hanged himself with his necktie.

202

But I shall always see him leaping over that wicker basket in the flop-brimmed panama clipped to a lapel, and the trouser turned up almost to the calf, and polished patent leather boots with tan uppers, and an orchid in his button-hole, shouting 'Let her go!' and sailing up, over the Champs, riding his beautifully silent mare, and the crowds standing still and quiet, to look up and wonder, at a hero.

He lived for an ideal, a glory, without any selfish thought, and he was never less than a hero, and my *bem Brasiliero* brother of the stone mask and the brilliant smile of whitest teeth.

God bless him every moment, and God love his magnificent memory.

Santo, I lift this tulip to *you*. Yes, dear lad, my brother.

R.L.I.

FALSE FLAGS
by Noel Hynd

'. . . some sort of false flag job. It means someone is made to look like he's working for one country when actually he's in the employ of another.'

Bill Mason, ex-CIA, survivor of a Chinese prison, contemplating an empty future . . .

Robert Lassiter, the man who taught Mason everything he knows, the man who now urgently needs his help . . .

Six silicon chips, tiny micro-circuits that could mean everything or nothing, found in a London flat. They are the triggers in a devil's game of life and death and betrayal . . .

NEW ENGLISH LIBRARY

THE SANDLER INQUIRY
by Noel Hynd

Thomas Daniels sits in the charred ruins of his law office, pondering the riddle of the late Arthur Sandler. The answer could unlock an inheritance conservatively valued at fifty million dollars. To find it, Daniels must probe the labyrinths of the Intelligence community on behalf of his client, who purports to be Sandler's daughter.

Her father, she alleges, murdered her mother and twice tried to eliminate her. *Why* is not at all clear, except that it had something to do with the key espionage network Sandler operated.

But who did financier Arthur Sandler work for during the war? The Americans? The Nazis? The Russians? Or all three? The trail has had thirty years to grow cold. Now, suddenly, it is a blazing hot fuse, as past treacheries come alive and the shards of Sandler's unfinished business fall horrifyingly into place.

NEW ENGLISH LIBRARY

HOW GREEN WAS MY VALLEY

by Richard Llewellyn

In the beginning were the green mountains and the fertile valleys and the people were happy.

Then below the meadows they discovered coal. And the men of the fields were transformed into people who laboured in darkness. People who fought, loved, drank and sang in the shadows of the great collieries. People who lived with danger and disaster – who had forgotten how green their valley had been.

'Vivid, eloquent, poetical, glowing with an inner flame of emotion . . . To write from the heart, to measure experience in love and sorrow, to bear witness to nobility or the idealism of men – this is not the sort of thing a serious novelist tries to do nowadays. It is what Mr Llewellyn does, however. His story makes a direct and powerfully sustained appeal to our emotions . . . deeply and continuously moving.' – *The Times Literary Supplement*

'A work of fiction which enlarges for us the whole bounds of experience . . . I say with all my heart: read it. It is a most royal and magnificent novel.' – *Yorkshire Post*

NEW ENGLISH LIBRARY

Book Tokens

**Give them
the pleasure of choosing**

Book Tokens can be bought
and exchanged at most
bookshops in Great Britain
and Ireland.

NEL BESTSELLERS

T045 528	THE STAND	*Stephen King*	£1.75
T046 133	HOW GREEN WAS MY VALLEY	*Richard Llewellyn*	£1.00
T039 560	I BOUGHT A MOUNTAIN	*Thomas Firbank*	95p
T033 988	IN THE TEETH OF THE EVIDENCE	*Dorothy L. Sayers*	90p
T038 149	THE CARPETBAGGERS	*Harold Robbins*	£1.50
T041 719	HOW TO LIVE WITH A NEUROTIC DOG	*Stephen Baker*	75p
T040 925	THE PRIZE	*Irving Wallace*	£1.65
T034 755	THE CITADEL	*A. J. Cronin*	£1.10
T042 189	STRANGER IN A STRANGE LAND	*Robert Heinlein*	£1.25
T037 053	79 PARK AVENUE	*Harold Robbins*	£1.25
T042 308	DUNE	*Frank Herbert*	£1.50
T045 137	THE MOON IS A HARSH MISTRESS	*Robert Heinlein*	£1.25
T040 933	THE SEVEN MINUTES	*Irving Wallace*	£1.50
T038 130	THE INHERITORS	*Harold Robbins*	£1.25
T035 689	RICH MAN, POOR MAN	*Irwin Shaw*	£1.50
T043 991	EDGE 34: A RIDE IN THE SUN	*George G. Gilman*	75p
T037 541	DEVIL'S GUARD	*Robert Elford*	£1.25
T042 774	THE RATS	*James Herbert*	80p
T042 340	CARRIE	*Stephen King*	80p
T042 782	THE FOG	*James Herbert*	90p
T033 740	THE MIXED BLESSING	*Helen Van Slyke*	£1.25
T038 629	THIN AIR	*Simpson & Burger*	95p
T038 602	THE APOCALYPSE	*Jeffrey Konvitz*	95p
T046 850	WEB OF EVERYWHERE	*John Brunner*	85p

NEL P.O. BOX 11, FALMOUTH TR10 9EN, CORNWALL

Postage charge:

U.K. Customers. Please allow 30p for the first book plus 15p per copy for each additional book ordered to a maximum charge of £1.29 to cover the cost of postage and packing, in addition to cover price.

B.F.P.O. & Eire. Please allow 30p for the first book plus 15p per copy for the next 8 books, thereafter 6p per book, in addition to cover price.

Overseas Customers. Please allow 50p for the first book plus 15p per copy for each additional book, in addition to cover price.

Please send cheque or postal order (no currency).

Name ....

Address ....

....

....

.... keep prices steady, it is sometimes necessary .... tice. New English Library reserve the right to .... new retail prices which may differ from those .... where. (3)